An Enthusiastic Welcome For The XYY Man!

"A really good story. Best of all for me, was the central character Spider. He was alive; I knew him and what's more I cared about him . . . first class!

Victoria Holt

"A well constructed and brilliantly sustained thriller!"

Ngaio Marsh

"Fresh in conception and lively in execution!"

The New York Times

THE XYY MAN

KENNETH ROYCE

AVON
PUBLISHERS OF BARD, CAMELOT, DISCUS, EQUINOX AND FLARE BOOKS

AVON BOOKS
A division of
The Hearst Corporation
959 Eighth Avenue
New York, New York 10019

First Avon Printing, February, 1973

AVON TRADEMARK REG. U.S. PAT. OFF. AND
FOREIGN COUNTRIES, REGISTERED TRADEMARK—
MARCA REGISTRADA, HECHO EN CHICAGO, U.S.A.

Printed in the U.S.A.

For Andy,
Hoping That You Are Still Out

1

When I stepped into the street and the Scrubs gate closed behind me, my first inclination was to run back to hide behind its shelter. As I had been waiting five precious years for this one moment and had verged on gate fever these last few days it was a curious reaction to say the least. Yet although fleeting, the feeling was strong enough for me to hesitate and look back at the small gate set in the larger one.

Behind those gates and others like them I suppose I had received some form of protection; three meals and a bed; no financial worries. Provided one kept clear of the strong arm boys, out of the hands of the tobacco barons and did not cross too many screws it was just about endurable but only with the knowledge of a not too distant release. The 'Moor' was the worst; if ever I had to return there I'd 'top' myself.

I walked slowly with the bundle under my arm that everyone would recognize as soon as I turned the corner. This had not been my first stretch yet I had not felt like this before. I was very much aware that I was on my own and afraid of the inexplicable. If I didn't keep clean it would be a ten-year stretch next time. I was afraid of myself, knowing that at the age of thirty-four this was my last chance. And something else nagged at me, the more worrying because I could not pin it down.

The Governor's last little lecture had been odd, almost pitying. I had the strange feeling that in some way I was up on show, an object of curiosity, and if the last five years had not blunted some of my crude perception I would have taken heed of that feeling right then. I don't know what I would have done about it but at least I would have been forewarned and on eventually meeting Fairfax would have been a little less gullible.

The good feeling of freedom did not kill my fears but it sat on them as I got farther from the gate. I'd done two years in Dartmoor before working my ticket to Grendon Psychiatric Prison. They are not nutters there, but the hopefuls, blokes they think they can do something about. I found it helpful and, by filching a confidential report, found out a little about myself without being much wiser.

The two sex chromosomes that make up each male cell in the body are tagged X and Y. At Grendon a number of men have an extra Y chromosome. The XYY man; that's me. They are all more than six feet tall and predisposed to crimes against property rather than violence. That's me, too. Clever these doctors; but had they effected a cure? When I faced the answer to that one I wanted to turn back again. I hoped I would not let them down, but had no confidence.

The last six months of my sentence had been spent at the Scrubs Hostel. You sleep in and work outside preparatory to the return to normal life—if life had ever been normal for me.

As I walked slowly away from these grim walls, my fear grew. The squalid surrounds did nothing for my morale and seemed part of the prison environs. It was late September and warm, but cloud patches plugged the sun. I had no real plans and the nerves in my stomach played spiders on my spleen. I was out—and desperately wanted to stay out, but my great dread was whether I could.

I hoped no pious so-and-so would tell me that hard work is the miracle cure. My record would show that I could work my guts out. But after a time the job would bore me, I'd want something new, another interest, and that is no way to progress.

It was going to be tough. You see, I'm a 'creeper', a cat burglar. Coppers and screws have always been surprised by this because of my height and weight. Just the same, shinning a drainpipe close to a wall has never been a problem to me.

A creeper is a loner. With one exception I'd never worked with anyone else. I've run away rather than strike someone. So during the long years in prison I was faced with a recurring problem. What would I now do if I was faced with the alternative of a ten-year stretch or of striking someone down. The answer scared me.

This was only part of my fear. There was something

beyond my knowledge that nagged at me. Years ago I had experienced a similar feeling. I had entered a house by an unlatched window on the ground floor. There was a big hall with a semi-circular staircase. As I mounted the first stair, I had the most squeezy sensation of something wrong. By the time I was half way up it had grown to such intensity that I stopped, wet with sweat, and the hairs standing out on the back of my neck. I tried to go on but could not. It was my first sensation of real terror.

I was doing something I had repeatedly done yet I could not continue. Finally my 'bottle'* went, and I fled. What I now felt was the warning I had experienced on the first stair. Not sufficient to allay me, yet disturbing. I wondered what I was walking into.

The sun came out and put colour into the grey tiles and dirty bricks. I stepped out briskly and decided to make straight for Maggie's place, a nice pad in a modern block; she'd be mad at me for not telling her exactly when I was being released but I didn't want her in the shadow of these walls.

Working outside had staved off some of the surprises. Mini skirts I was already used to, but when I caught a bus up to Notting Hill they seemed to get shorter as the shops multiplied.

As I watched I vividly recalled the deep hunger I had suffered in isolation for just this. Don't lose it now, I kept repeating to myself. Don't ever give it up again, for a stark cell and a daily half-hour slog in an exercise yard.

My mind drifted to Maggie. I shall never understand why she tolerates me for she must know that I'm no damned good for her. From my viewpoint she is missing her chances and it chokes me to see such a lovely girl go to waste. During the periods I've been outside, I've done everything to try to dissuade her for her own sake. I've been as unfaithful as hell and she knows it yet she's always been there. She spoke a couple of languages fluently and worked for the United Nations in London. With her intelligence and background you'd think that she would have worked it out but I suppose like all women she is illogical. She knew I would never marry her because I could not reduce her to my level but it made no difference.

Maggie had taught me a lot; little things like cleaning my nails and sounding the 'ng's' on the end of words. She

*Nerve.

9

had encouraged me to read while 'inside' and I did a lot, particularly when I finally became librarian at Grendon. She deserved better things but right now I was glad that she hadn't taken them.

I slipped in quietly, unheard by Maggie. There was a white blouse on the ironing board. She was carefully smoothing it over. As she bent her jet hair hung forward framing a face that should have been recorded on canvas over and over again. Five years is a long time; I thought she would hear my heavier breathing. Her mouth was unfashionably small, firm yet sensitive lips; her brows carefully pencilled in because of their contrasting lightness. As she stood I could not see her eyes—she wore large framed glasses—but I knew them to be blue green capable of almost chameleon changes dependent on mood. Maggie had always looked after her skin and from where I stood it was as clear and as petal soft as I always remembered. It was an essentially feminine yet firm face, now with a new mature loveliness that made me want to weep at my own stupidity and whisper truths that I knew I could not.

She wore a light woollen sleeveless pullover, tight over her small breasts, and the ironing board obscured her good legs. It was almost too much for me, but I managed to remain close to the door.

"Hello, love. When did you dye your hair?"

She almost dropped the iron. She stood staring weakly, her breathing heavy. She lowered the iron but I could see she was still dazed.

"It's a wig. It's all the rage. How did you get in?" It was doubtful if she knew what she had asked. She slowly removed the wig revealing her own close cropped auburn hair. I held up a piece of stiff mica.

"I told you to change that lock years ago."

Her lips twitched and I thought she was about to cry. Instead she said angrily, "Take that grin off your face. You might at least have given me time to put on my make-up."

"You look all right to me," I said, still grinning.

"Oh Will! Oh God!"

She came to me, whipping off her glasses. Holding her was one of the great moments of my life. It was wonderful; better than the thousand times I had conjured this scene in a cell. She was warm and soft and firm at the same time and we were welded, unmoving, just desperately clutching each other. After a while she began to cry and

I curbed frustration and stroked her hair and arm, wanting to prolong the emotional taste of so wonderful a moment. The tears went and passion returned like an unquenchable blaze, consuming and hungry, eager to spread and devour and gain enormous strength before being reduced to an ember.

A long, long time later Maggie gazed up at me from the cradle of my arm, one hand softly touching my chest, and asked,

"How is it your body is so brown?"

I gave her a tender squeeze. "Been working outside, love. I can see you've been sunbathing. Glad you kept something on." She looked down at her body and I found no difficulty in following her gaze.

"Bikinis were smaller this year."

"So I see."

She leaned over me, lowered her body on mine, and kissed me lightly. "Are you hungry?"

I grinned. "Not any more."

"Oh." She nudged me hard in the ribs and swung her legs over the side of the bed.

I ran my fingers up her spine and across her back. "It's funny," I said, sitting up on one elbow. "When you're inside there's a lot of talk about the first thing you're going to do when you get out. Oddly enough women come second to an enormous meal of everything you like best. I was wrong, wasn't I?"

Maggie kept her back to me as she dressed but I could see her quiet expression in the dressing table mirror. "Is that all I am to you? A woman?"

I started to get up. "No. You're something very, very special. A nut for sticking it out, but special. Too special to waste your time on me."

She turned to face me, zipping her skirt. "Let's not go through that again. Not today."

She came to me and we held each other for several minutes. Eventually I said softly, "We'll be back on the bed if we're not careful."

"I know." Maggie leaned back so that she could look up at me. Her long, strong fingers were digging into my arms. "Will, promise me you'll stay out this time."

I tried to promise her, God knows I wanted to badly enough, but the words would not come. My lips were moving and I saw her expression change, concern and fear hardening eyes meant to be soft, yet something was

11

stopping me. Finally I burst out, "Look Maggie, Dartmoor frightened the pants off me. It's a vile, putrid place, and I've no intention of ever going back."

"That's not a promise."

"Perhaps I'm afraid of myself."

"You have only one real weakness which you can conquer. I'll help you. I know you to be honest in every way, bar one. If you promise I *know* you'll keep it. Please, Willie."

"I promise," I said, but it had been forced out. I had not the faith in it that Maggie seemed to have. I had said it to please her, not because I believed it. She gave me a peck and seemed satisfied but I felt wretched and wished I really knew why.

"You can move your things in here," Maggie said as we entered the tiny kitchen.

I put an arm round her shoulders. "You know I won't do that, not yet. I'll fix myself up with a room near by."

Maggie didn't like it because she knew my motive—it cropped up before. I had always insisted on retaining my independence mainly because I did not want to bind her to a villain. She got on with the cooking instead of arguing but was perturbed.

"Look, I want to phone Dick and Walt, may I use your phone?"

She stopped swishing the butter around in the pan and belatedly slipped on an apron. "You *must* ring Dick, but why Walt?"

"He owes me money." I could see trouble looming already. She removed the pan from the hot plate and faced me.

"That sort of money you can do without."

"Look, Walt's as straight as a die now. He promised me this ages ago. This isn't bent money."

"You mean he wants to pay you for keeping him out of prison?"

"If you like. I've earned it." I saw this as injustice and that always made me hot under the collar.

"You've earned nothing of it, Willie. You went to prison for a crime. You were punished. Don't expect to be paid because you covered someone who should have been punished with you."

I stomped into the bedroom and grabbed the phone. Dick is my kid brother and is as honest as I am bent. We're different sides of the fence; he's in the Metropolitan

12

Police. We have always had a great affection for one another, something a lot of people could not understand, and he knew for certain that I would never operate in his manor. He was at home and we had a good laugh and waffle and arranged to meet. In spite of Maggie's entreaties I rang Walt Sandford and fixed a meeting for the next day.

I stayed that night and was restless. After so long I could not get used to Maggie beside me without making love to her but during periods of exhaustion I found the bed too soft. We talked a lot too, lying naked under the sheet and trying to sort out things between us. I'd be happy to drift on like this but that was a prelude to drifting back and I knew that Maggie wouldn't let me.

I took her breakfast to bed next morning and made her sit up and eat as she was. For a villain I suppose I've got some old-fashioned ideas. I've never sworn in front of a woman nor used smut. That's the way it is. With the 'boys' I'll dredge the bottom of the verbal barrel and feel right about it.

Maggie said, "You have not lost your charm or your wide blue-eyed innocence which you can divert elsewhere while I get up. Damn you, Willie, I've never seen anyone look less like a villain than you do, so you've got a good start."

I left fairly early and went down to Winchester to see Walt Sandford. He'd lost some of his ginger hair and was plumper but his greeting was the same; a huge smile, no airs and a warm double handshake that went on for ever. Yet he had difficulty in meeting my gaze.

He opened a solid-looking safe which I eyed professionally and threw across a couple of bundles of wrapped notes.

"There's a grand there, Spider. It'll see you right for a bit." No haggling, no magnanimity. I should explain that because I'm a creeper all the boys call me Spider; Maggie is the only one who won't use it because of its associations.

I spread the money about me. "So it's not hot?"

"You know better. Was it bad inside?"

"It scared me, Walt."

"Enough?" He watched me shakily, almost pleadingly.

"Yep. Enough. I couldn't go back."

He seemed relieved, remembering his own fear.

We shook hands warmly as if for the last time and it

turned out to be. I was sad and a little emotional. We had been good friends but I think the fact that I had gone up on my own played on his conscience; it didn't worry me.

I went back to London thinking that somehow Walt had lost some of his integrity and wondering how that could be now that he was no longer bent.

From the station I had the strong sensation of being followed. It may have been due to carrying so much money. But I didn't like it for I couldn't pin anyone. But who would want to tail me?

I met Dick in the Duke of Wellington in Wardour Street, well away from his divisional boundaries. We greeted each other like a couple of kids; it had been a long time for I'd refused to let him visit me inside. He told me he'd now been in the force for three years and enjoyed the work, hoping later to get into the C.I.D. I eyed him over a pint of beer which I eked out for I don't drink much. He was now twenty-six and had filled out. They tell me we both have the same easy-going grin so I suppose I was seeing a little of myself—as I gazed back at him. Like me he was blue-eyed, with a slightly snub nose, good teeth, and firm of face and jaw, although his hair was darker than mine, almost black. If I looked like my kid brother then I was more than satisfied and people liked him.

"I hear Alf Bulman's with you," I said.

"He's a good sergeant, Spider. I know you don't like him but he is."

"Do you know why I don't like him?"

"I've heard rumours."

I banged my glass. "If you ever get a promotion the same way I'll wring your neck."

Dick laughed. "Watch it, I've been studying karate. Do you really believe it?"

"Look, I met a bent copper on the Moor who had served with Bulman. Bulman used to come to an arrangement with vagrants and tramps. He would get them to confess to a small breaking and entering job; they would spend the worst of winter in 'nick', free food and lodging, and it was another arrest on his record sheet."

"I don't think he'd be like that now." And then more carefully Dick added, "It was a mistake to tell him that you knew."

I almost drained my drink. "I can't stand bent coppers. Don't you go bent, by God."

"I only have to look at you to remind me not to."

I stared dazedly at him and I could see that he wanted to bite his tongue out, but it hit me hard under the belt. Who was I to moralise. "Sorry kid," I said quietly.

"I didn't mean it that way."

"Good," I was grinning again. "I'll buy you the other half."

On the way back to Maggie's place I was sure that I was being watched but I played it cooler than I felt for I couldn't understand it.

Passion wasn't wearing thin with either of us and it was some time before I realised that she was hiding something from me. We sat on the sofa, the lights out, the gloom relieved by filtering street lamps and passing cars. A single kilowatt electric fire glowed like a red hot poker, its exaggerated image showing dust on the reflector.

But Maggie's acute honesty betrayed her. She was no politician and truth was her only weapon even when she realised it should not be used. She was distracted. "Out with it," I prompted. She almost jumped.

"Am I so transparent?"

"Only to a villain like me. I've mixed with some of the best liars in the world. You're uneasy. I can feel it under my fingers."

"A man called Roberts phoned."

I looked down at her. "Well, what's wrong with that?"

"Please, Willie. Keep away from the boys."

"You don't play about with people like Knocker Roberts. He belongs to the Reisens and those boys play it very rough. They still paid their staff who were inside—and without much trouble."

"Isn't that a good enough reason for keeping clear?"

I didn't tell her that through Roberts I had been offered a job in their strong arm mob while I was on the Moor. They have long memories and recruit carefully. And the money is in the mobs.

Maggie slipped from my arms and knelt between my knees. Her soft hands took hold of my coarsened ones and she was breathtakingly lovely in half shadow. Her eyes lost their colour in the deepening gloom but light patches caught the whites of them so that they looked bigger and phosphorescent. I'd always loved the timbre of her voice but now it was at its best, cool and pleading.

"Willie, I love you with everything that is in me. I won't preach because I know that you hate it and I understand that. I'm not pious but we both know that this is your last chance. Give up these people—all of them. Give yourself a real chance."

I was about to answer but she gently covered my mouth with her hand. "I know your feeling for me is not as deep as mine. I've always accepted it and I'm not complaining. I'm pleading for *you*, Willie, not for what I want from you."

It had been a moving appeal that made me feel all kinds of a bastard. Just the same I had to say it. "Maggie, in my book there's no one like you or ever likely to be and you know it. You know why I won't be tied down. But you must understand that these people are my friends. They may be villains but we've suffered together and I could no more ignore them than I could turn my back on Dick. You're judging me guilty already for doing nothing more than passing the time of day. It will be all right, but you must give it time. Sooner or later they'll get the message and it will be *they* who will lose interest in *me*."

The next morning I made arrangements to take over a bedsitter, with a miniature kitchen that you could miss if you turned round too quickly. It was shabbily furnished, but light with a high Victorian ceiling. Maggie liked it because she was nuts on antiques and it was near the Portobello Road.

That afternoon I bought a four-year old second-hand 3.4 Jaguar that made a hole in my thousand pounds but refused to accept delivery until they had fitted a burglar alarm. As I left the garage there was a short, middle-aged, trilby-hatted gent looking at the used cars on the forecourt. He appeared completely innocuous until his gaze accidently caught mine. He revealed nothing but averted his gaze too awkwardly as if he had been caught out. For some reason he roused latent fears in me. It was silly. Yet it worried me. I was certain that he knew me, although his face was new to me, the kind unnoticed in a crowd.

2

By the end of the week I had found a job as a car sales-man. The basic would prevent me starving and the com-mission was not too bad. I couldn't see my future in it but it was a start.

Maggie was delighted. I didn't tell her that the garage which had employed me serviced a lot of the boys and was up to its neck in hire purchase fiddles. She thought I had only to be open about my past for employers to fall over themselves offering me jobs.

In a short time memory of cells and quarries and slop-ping out began to fade. I began to believe that I was out for keeps, that it could work, although I was uneasy about the feeling of being under surveillance.

Occasionally one of the boys would give me a ring via Maggie; I had yet to get a phone, but it was only for old times' sake and she began to accept it. Then Sergeant Bulman called on me at my bedsitter. Judging by the speed he rapped the door after I'd got in after work, he must have been waiting for me.

He stood in the doorway, sharp-eyed, black hair short and traditionally combed with a nice white parting cor-rectly at one side. His nose and mouth were good and straight, and I suppose in a coarse sort of way he was good looking. He had strong brows and a nice set of teeth if he ever got round to smiling. Just over medium height, he looked up, hands in the pockets of an old raincoat over a neat blue suit. He could have been an insurance man but to me he smelled copper and that meant trouble.

"Hello, Scott. Can I have a word with you?"

"*Mr.* Scott to you, Sergeant. I'm no longer a name and number. Yes, you can have a word."

His quick gaze darted over my shoulder. "Can I come in?"

"A word can be said from where you're standing."

His mouth tightened and he was needled. The strange thing is that I've nothing against the police. Screws are different but the police have always been reasonable with me, even helpful on occasion, except Bulman. There was a thing between us. He managed a lop-sided grin. "It might be embarrassing saying it here."

"For you or for me?"

Glancing behind him up the stairs, he said with relish, "For you. *Mr.* Scott." His eyes were mocking.

My stomach began to flutter and I knew that I was glaring at him. I have a conscience, you see. There are still some old jobs that have not yet been pinned on me and there is always an outside chance that they might.

"Come in," I said begrudgingly. I made certain that he didn't nick my favourite chair. At first I thought that he was not going to sit at all but when he saw me ostensibly relaxed he carefully sat opposite, keeping his coat on. When he began to pull out his cigarettes I said, "I'd rather you didn't. I'm allergic to them. Something I developed on the Moor."

Wearing a quiet smile he slipped them back into his pocket without appearing put out and I knew then that the bastard was playing with me. He could hardly wait to get it out but was delaying it in order to savour every syllable and watch me cringe. Inside I was fluttering like a moth, but he wasn't going to know.

"Where were you last night between eleven and two in the morning?" He sat enjoying himself, his gaze sweeping the room including under the bed and I guessed it was about a job. Well, my conscience was clear, but I was still uneasy.

"What, no caution?"

Benign Bulman wore a smile I would have liked to wipe off. There are some people who provoke my latent violent tendencies.

"This is a friendly chat, Spider. There's no need for a caution."

"But you will still get up in the box and swear that you gave me one."

He spread his hands, still grinning. "If you think that then you've had your caution. You don't think much of me, do you?"

"I don't like the way you became a sergeant."

18

His face hardened, his gaze diamond sharp. "Do you always listen to bent coppers in nick?"

"Why not? I listen to them out of it."

Bulman lost colour and his hands bunched. I was being a fool needling him but my feeling was deep, springing from a world and codes that I'd lived with for too long. I suddenly realised that my directness wouldn't do my brother much good.

Bulman won the little battle with himself, and anyway I'm bigger than he is, and he relaxed again, but there was a craftiness in his gaze I didn't like. "Do you know Nightingale Terrace?" he asked.

He knew that I did. I nodded.

"Coltmore House?"

My stomach muscles started an involuntary isometric exercise. I let them relax slowly before answering. Coltmore House was a drum I had cased many years ago. It was a wealthy home in a rich Georgian area fringing Holland Park.

"Not particularly."

"But you know it?"

"I know the area. I don't know the names of the houses."

He changed his tack. "You know that every nick keeps a book of addresses of empty houses—you know, people on holiday and so on; who has the key and all that?"

I had the glimmering of where this was leading. I nodded again slowly, my wits sharpened by caution.

"Well, Coltmore House," said Bulman with relish, "is listed in our book as being at present vacant, owner out of the country."

"Has it been screwed?"

"I wonder why you said that, Spider?"

"Because it's bloody obvious from the game you're playing. And I don't like your aspersions against my brother."

"Come on, Spider. They told me you're the non-violent type. That's a nasty temper you've got. What have I said against your brother?"

I stood up angrily, falling straight into his trap. But I couldn't help myself; it was Dick I was worried about, not myself. "Listen, Bulman, try to pin a screwing job on me if you like, it's right up your alley, but if you try to pin my brother I'll do life for you."

He was now openly mocking me; he'd got me on the run and held all the cards. "I haven't mentioned your brother."

"No? Then why mention the vacant premises book? The implication is that he supplied me with the information. Well, Bulman, even a thick-headed bent copper like you should know that I wouldn't foul my brother's nest."

Bulman rose to face me, his expression vicious. "You can always change your habits. But you can't change your style. This job has your handwriting all over it. Where were you last night?"

"With Maggie Parsons."

"Convenient. What time?"

"Ask her the times."

"I will. I'm asking you now."

I turned towards the windows, fuming and dismayed. "From about eight through till two or three."

"Busy."

I swung round while he openly taunted me to land one on him. With difficulty I said, "My record of non-violence refers only to my customers. It does not extend to scum like you. And when you speak of Maggie Parsons swill your mouth out first with Dettol."

Bulman was shaken at that, but he wasn't going to forget. "You're taking too many chances, *Mr.* Scott."

"You try to involve my brother again and you'll find out just how many I'm willing to take. And understand this, Bulman, I didn't do that job although you'd love to hang it on me. Don't try it on with me again."

Near the door Bulman faced me. He'd won a good round even if I had come back strongly before the bell; the points were clearly his and I was still rattled. "The hallmarks are still yours, chummy. Don't wander too far, will you?"

After he had gone I sat down broodingly. I thought I knew who had done the job. In prison it's not unusual to exchange useful information. If a man has cased a place and is imprisoned before he can screw it he might well pass it on to someone else. I had cased this one before Dick had joined the police and had passed it on to a screwman called Ossie Jenkins. It had been a good tip, but it looked as if Ossie had got round to it at the wrong time.

If Bulman *really* wanted to nail me, he'd manage it, over the course of time. But what sickened me to my stomach was his oblique accusation of Dick. Now that really worried me because it showed too clearly his prepared line of action. I had the uncontrollable and inexplicable feeling of being pushed in a direction I had no wish to go.

I went downstairs to my car and found that a window had been forced and a small transistor radio had been nicked. It didn't amount to much but I saw it as a sign and cursed the finely tuned burglar alarm that had failed to work. Which only shows that you can't trust anyone these days.

As always Maggie pulled me from the doldrums. She said, stretching her long legs over mine, "Why don't you go and see the Police Superintendent?"

"What for?"

"Oh, Willie. Tell him you're being victimised and why."

It's strange but I don't think I could grass even on Bulman. There were plenty of bent coppers who needed reporting but they were protected by codes they themselves despised; that and the fact that reporting them often detrimentally involved one of the boys. So I laughed at her naïvety. Here it was again; tell the truth and all will be well. But her innocence touched me.

A few days later Bulman called with a detective constable, whom he didn't trouble to introduce, and his behaviour was much more correct. Again there was no caution; so I knew that he was groping. He wanted more details of the time I spent with Maggie and where, but this was a case of following Maggie's code—if we both told the truth it would cross check. You have to be an ex-con to know the effect of police questioning, the more so if you're now straight.

His visit was followed closely by two of the Reisens boys. They were both mobsters and they wanted me as a driver but I scared them off by telling them with bitter truth that the police were watching me. You can see why it's so easy for good intentioned villains to go back to crime; the pressures are on from both sides of the law if they think you are worth it.

I started to ease off my visits to Maggie because I knew that she was worried but that she did not really know the form. I knew what I was up against and if it was useful to lie then I lied because I have proved that the truth can land me right in it. I tried to get her to visit her parents in Yorkshire for a spell. I believe they have

21

a good home up there, but there was her job and she was independent minded and knew what I was up to. She was worried that I might go off at a tangent.

Early in October Bulman came for me at the garage just before closing time. More than anything else it was this that really griped me. He couldn't wait another half hour until I was home. He had to make a splash of it in front of my employer and some of the mechanics.

It was a warm autumn day. I was standing outside the showroom, ready to drive some of the display cars back under cover for the night. The sun was down but it was still light. Workers were beginning to go home and the pavement was quite crowded in front of our forecourt. I was slipping some of the price cards into the cars when I saw the blue light flashing along the road.

Traffic was fairly heavy and the black police A60 was held up once or twice—I thought it strange that the flasher was being used, yet not the siren to clear the way. Because of this I didn't connect it with me at first, not until I saw the amber eye of the left trafficator pulse on and the car swing into the kerb. I saw Bulman next to the driver and my stomach turned. The bastard took his time getting out and left the flasher going so that people stopped and stared, hoping for a bit of excitement.

"Mr. Scott?" As if he didn't know. "Would you be good enough to accompany me to the station? There are one or two questions we would like to ask you." He kept his voice fairly low but some of the gapers heard it just the same and I could see them nudging one another.

I kept it dignified, wiping my hands on a handkerchief because I didn't know what to do with them apart from making them meet round Bulman's neck. But two could play this game.

"Who are you? May I see your identity card?"

The pretence was crazy but he had to fumble for his wallet to produce it. I took my time, giving the swelling crowd good value.

"A detective sergeant, I see." They'd love that. "And why do you want to see me?"

But Bulman had to win in the end and he looked as if he knew it. "Just a few questions—" he almost choked on "sir", and couldn't get it out. "We think you can help us with our enquiries."

I looked over his shoulder. "Do you *have* to keep your flasher going—Sergeant?"

I scored one. He looked a bit silly then called out to his driver to switch it off. While I still had a small advantage I said, "It's inconvenient now. I still have work to do. If you think it really necessary I'll come down later."

Then my boss put his big foot in it. His voice came from over my left shoulder and it did not sound too pleased. "It's all right, Spider, you go off. We'll clear up."

I did not turn round; there was no need. Bulman gave the boss a polite smile of appreciation and nodded in a friendly way, then stood aside for me to precede him to the car. It was all wrapped up. The audience went silent as I stepped forward, craning their necks to see what sort of a thug I was.

Once in the car we both reverted to type. After a quick exchange that startled the driver, we lapsed into a silence of mutual hatred. Bulman refused to give information until we were at the nick.

What happened next was all too familiar. They parked me in an interrogation room, bare table and chairs, and left me there for over an hour. I would have demanded to see my solicitor if I'd had one.

Finally Bulman came in carrying a cup of tea, for him not for me, accompanied by the detective constable he had brought round the other night. The D.C. sat at the end of the table with a notebook while Bulman sat opposite stirring his tea. To impress the D.C. of his impartiality after the fracas in the car, Bulman offered me a cigarette, knowing that I don't smoke, so I took it without thanks and slipped it in my breast pocket. I thought he was going to hit me and suddenly I felt better.

"Where were you last night?" he asked brusquely, his harsh eyes biting at me.

"Oh no. Not that again."

"Just answer the questions, we'll do the funnies."

"I was out."

"We know you were. Anywhere near South View Gardens?"

"Where are they?" This could go on all night.

"Let's cut it short, Scott." He had to have something on me to have dropped the 'Mr.'. "You were seen near number 37 South View Gardens at one a.m. this morning. The house was entered from a first floor bedroom window at the side of the house."

"I was nowhere near the place, as you well know."

"You were seen there."

23

"Then I insist on an I.D. parade right now."

"You can insist on nothing." I noticed that he didn't take me up on it.

"If you weren't there, Scott, it should be easy enough to prove. It was only last night."

I could not prove it. In a fit of remorse I had left Maggie alone last night. To the best of my knowledge she had gone out with a girl friend. I was glad that she was not implicated in this one. In fact I had gone out on my own. As corny as it sounds, I had walked for quite a time and then gone to bed.

"At the time you're talking about I was in bed."

"Prove it."

"You prove I wasn't."

He sat back sipping his tea, playing with me, enjoying it, trying to scourge his own conscience.

It went on for two hours without getting anywhere. He tried the double act with him shouting and the D.C. quietening him down and then trying the smooth technique, but they were not a good team and anyway I'd seen it all before. In the end they reluctantly let me go. I demanded a police car to run me back and that choked Bulman but he managed to dig up a driver.

By the time I was home it was too late to contact Maggie which was too bad in the event. Some of the boys might still be up though and the quickest way off this hook was to establish an alibi. See what I mean about truth? I would have to supply a good lie to satisfy Bulman. Digging up a pocketful of change I located the nearest phone booth and did the rounds of the boys, keeping away from the Reisens mob.

Finally Balls Up Balfour came to my rescue. Tug Wilson had been released that day and Balls Up and one or two of the boys had a private party to celebrate. I was given the details, times and so on, and Balls Up promised to contact the others. I knew that he would, I had no doubt of that, but he had not achieved his name for nothing. A short untidy master forger with a soft heart who was constantly broke because he was an inveterate gambler usually finishing up at the losing end of the gaming mobs, he lived over his dilapidated printing business in near squalor. Short of cash he would invariably find himself forging something for the wrong people and as a consequence nick was his second home. A master crafts-

24

man who balled things up by a weakness and inability to judge people.

The following morning I rang the nick and left a message that I would call on them at lunch time. In fairness to Bulman, he made a point of being there.

"Look," I said sheepishly, "I've been thinking things over. I didn't want to drag in the boys and I still don't like it. The fact is I was at a party with Balls Up and a couple of the lads because Tug Wilson came out that day."

"I heard he was out." Bulman was sitting opposite me again looking very satisfied. "Didn't know Tug was a friend of yours."

"I know what it's like to come out. We just gave him a good time, that's all."

"Well, let's get it all down." He pulled a notebook across. "Stag, was it?" He asked without looking up.

"Yes."

"No women at all?"

"There wouldn't be at that sort of party."

"That's what I thought. Only Maggie Parsons told me that you spent the night with her."

The coldness started in my chest. In a second I was stiff with it. I stared helplessly as Bulman began to laugh quietly, the sincerest act I had seen him make. In breaking her own golden rule Maggie had as good as locked me in and thrown away the key.

3

I was like a man without legs, not knowing which way to manoeuvre in case I fell right in it. Desperately I said, "You know Maggie was trying to protect me. I wasn't with her."

"Of course she was trying to protect you." Bulman was leaning back, his smile fixed.

"Well then——"

"Well that's it. She was trying to protect you the first time too, wasn't she?"

"No. That was the truth."

"Come on, Scott, do better than that. I *know* that you weren't with her last night because she was out with another girl. They got back about midnight. So she lied for you. So far as I'm concerned she's always been lying for you."

What could I say? It would make no difference now. Bulman raised his pen. "Well let's get on with it. Those other names."

I gave them to him, then he sat back tapping the pencil on the table and musing over the names as if they were very special emblems.

"You know, you're not doing so well." Bulman could afford to be relaxed, he was laughing up his sleeve. "First your girl friend lies for you, and now you present me with names of four villains who are not exactly pillars of truth. I wouldn't fancy my chances if they depended on the evidence of this bunch in a court of law."

It was not possible to retract; on top of Maggie's lapse it would fix me for good. As it was he still had to pin it on me.

"You know," he said conversationally, "it's funny that this drum in South View Gardens is also listed in our vacant premises book. It's beginning to stink a bit."

So he was still after Dick. I was feeling so morose that I began not to care. Except about Dick and I was really scared for him. Still, I tried.

"You know damn fine how it works. All any villain has to do to locate empty premises is to follow the copper on the beat and see which houses he inspects in detail. You know it but you don't want to believe it."

Finally he had to let me go because he lacked real evidence and he had to check on Balls Up's alibi.

This time I elected a long walk before going to Maggie's. What worried me most was Dick. If they seriously began to suspect him then he was as good as out of the force and I would never forgive myself.

She met me at the door like an excited schoolgirl who'd just nicked teacher's apple. Her auburn hair spread copper tints under the light and her eyes, green tonight to match her blouse, were alive. "I've been looking all over for you," she gasped anxiously.

Putting my arm round her we entered the room. "I knew, love. You've been looking in the wrong places."

"Oh, Willie, I had to see you before that beast of a policeman did."

"You didn't make it, Mag. I've just left Bulman."

She looked so crestfallen that I gave her a big squeeze. "Don't worry. I'd give anything for a good strong cup of tea." While she went to make one I spread myself on the settee, feeling bushed. Maggie called from the kitchen."

"Did he tell you I said I spent the night with you?"

"He told me."

Maggie appeared in the kitchen doorway. "I'm making you a sandwich too. Willie, what's wrong?"

"He told me *after* I had already told him that I'd been out with the boys."

"Oh God, no." Her hand went to her mouth and she lost colour. Getting up, I held her close, rocking her slightly, holding the back of her head in my hand so that her face was against my chest.

"It's all right, Maggie. It's all right."

"I've landed you right in it." Her muffled voice reached me like a disembodied wail.

"No you haven't. I admire you for it." Her head jerked back.

There was a rapping on the door, and there was Dick, pale-faced, and beneath his light overcoat I could see his uniform trousers and regulation boots. By the look of him

27

he had just come off duty. I just stood there dumbly at first, it had to be bad news. Maggie called from behind me. "Come in, Dick, for goodness sake. I'll get another cup." She darted into the kitchen and I closed the door. "What's the trouble? Sit down."

He undid his coat and fell into an armchair. His hair was ruffled as if the wind had caught it and he gazed dazedly at the electric fire. "The Governor's had me in. He's been asking some very pointed questions about the vacant premises book. He thinks that someone is giving out information."

"Because of two lousy jobs?" I poured out scorn. "You know I've been in again, don't you?"

"I know. That's what it's all about."

I didn't like the way Dick looked; it was an expression of hopelessness as if this was all inevitable. I had never felt so wretched. "I didn't do them, Dick."

He gazed over at me and gave a feeble grin. "I know you wouldn't operate in the manor."

"I've got news for you kid. I haven't operated *anywhere* since I've been out. I don't intend to either. This is Bulman's little caper. He's so drenched in his own guilt it's warped his judgement."

"He wouldn't much like the idea of me knowing either."

Maggie came in with the other cup and passed it to Dick. She had heard us and now sat down beside us.

"I'm sorry, Dick," I groaned. "Does the super suspect you?"

"He bloody well suspects someone."

"But our connection adds up to the obvious?"

"Wouldn't you think so in his shoes?"

Sinking back on the couch I could feel all my nerve ends jangling. "I'll go and see him tomorrow."

"Who, the governor? What good will it do?"

"I'm going to tell him that I'm being victimised."

Draining his tea Dick rose and carefully put the cup and saucer on the white pine mantelpiece.

"Look," I said, "I know what it means to you and you're going right to the top. All the way. Commissioner."

He grinned. "Commander would do."

"Right. Commander. Even if it means I have to remain straight for the rest of my life. And I can't be fairer than that." We all laughed a bit but after Dick had gone I was in the depths of despair for him. Even Maggie's magic did not work. I rang the nick to discover what time the

Chief Superintendent would be in then left a hopeful message that he might deign to see me at ten. Maggie agreed to ring up my boss and straighten it out with him, because by now he must have been doing a good deal of speculation.

Chief Superintendent 'Mike' Cummings was grey-haired and ruddy faced with eyes that twinkled when in the mood. He is what I call straight as it is meant by a villain. I trusted him and expected a fair deal. He could not be touched with money.

I sat in his modern glass-panelled office, with its metal desk and chairs, feeling a fool. Now it seemed a sneaky, childish thing to do, yet it could affect my whole life. He sat there, half smiling, probably amused by my discomfort, and waited for me to start. I had difficulty so he encouraged me with, "Come on, Spider. Out with it. It can't be a confession or you wouldn't have asked to see me."

"I don't know how to put it, sir." I was playing it humbly. "You see, it affects my brother."

His gaze hardened, his smile became more fixed. I'd sent up the warning light and he was suddenly all policeman.

"Look," I burst out. "I didn't do those jobs Bulman is chasing me for. He knows I wouldn't ruin my brother's chances. Dick loves the force and one day he'll be sitting where you're sitting."

"Well, I hope they give him a warmer office. Go on."

"Well, that's it. Dick's under suspicion of passing information to me and it's bloody ridiculous."

"Who said he's under suspicion."

"You've interviewed him for a start."

"Amongst others."

"No one has passed information to me and if they had I wouldn't touch it in this manor. I'm being victimised by Bulman."

"Why would he do that?" Mike Cummings was no fool, but his easy manner was deceptive.

"I can't grass, even on a copper. But there is something he hates my guts for."

"Even if he does, Spider, he's got to hang a case on you that will stick, and to my satisfaction."

"Meanwhile he can make life almost impossible for me. I could easily lose my job the way he's chasing me."

"Well, I wouldn't want that to happen. But listen to me." Mike Cummings pushed his chair back so that he was watching me squarely across the desk. The smile had gone but his tone was still friendly.

"You've been to prison on three separate occasions and on probation before that. You're a villain and we both know it. You're in no position to demand special privileges. If you're going straight then you'll get every help from us but it's early days yet; don't blame *us* if we still see you as a possibility.

"I think I know what's between you and Sergeant Bulman but he would have got his promotion anyway. If a job is done and it bears your hallmark then we'll follow it up whether it's Bulman or any other C.I.D. officer. If there is real victimisation then I'll jump on it but apart from a mutual dislike between you two, I haven't seen much signs of it. The jobs have been done—in your style. What should we do? Say to ourselves 'Spider wouldn't have done them because of his brother'?

"It can be argued that a crafty villain would want us to think just that. Now listen, Spider. You decided to go into crime. Don't start crying because things get rough. You threw the first punch, and the second and the third. You'll remain suspect all the time there is suspicion. Remove that suspicion and we'll get off your back."

He sat back, his face a little redder than before, eyeing me cagily.

"Bulman didn't have to pick me up at my job just before closing time."

"And you didn't have to supply a very shaky alibi from some very shady characters with a lie thrown in from your girlfriend."

I stood up wearily. He was right, of course. I had only myself to blame; it was part of the cost of being stupid.

"Thank you for seeing me, sir," I said morosely.

Mike Cummings was too experienced to be beguiled but not too hard to feel sympathy. "You've nothing to fear if you didn't do it, Spider."

I left him, sorry that I had called. I stood outside the station feeling a fool. But for my brother I would not have considered pleading my case with a police officer. As I saw it I had lowered myself to no avail and could only hope that the boys did not get to hear of it.

I walked towards my car wondering if Balls Up Balfour and the others had yet been interviewed. Somehow it no longer mattered. I must be patient, ride it out and hope time would solve the matter. That's what reason dictated.

But there was no reasoning about the churning in my guts that I had suffered on and off since coming out.

So the only warning I had was animal instinct. But that's like a doctor, telling you you're ill but that he hasn't a clue what it is. It achieves nothing except a step or two towards the box. As I drew away I noticed a grey van pull out after me. When I reached the garage it continued on.

At the garage I got some strange looks. Out of courtesy I went to see the boss in his little office next to the spares stores. Never the gay type, he looked none too happy now; his black moustache drooped in mourning.

"Did Maggie phone?" I asked him. He nodded, looking up with the liveliness of a bloodhound. "Well, I'm sorry I'm late, but I had to settle this once and for all."

"And did you?" He had a grinding voice like an ungreased axle.

"No, not really. But don't worry about it. I've done nothing wrong." For a while he searched my face with his sombre, not unfriendly eyes. "I may as well come straight out with it," he managed at last. "I'll have to get rid of you, Spider. It's all bad for business."

I stared at him numbly but not entirely surprised. "But I tell you I've done nothing."

"It's not the point, son. Look, I don't want to sack you . . . you're good at your job, but the business can't stand police enquiries. The boys who use us won't like it and I just don't want the police around here. Look at last night, I ask you; like a bloody film set."

"They won't be coming again."

"You don't know that and I can't afford to take the risk."

I had a certain sympathy for him. He was really worried about his hire purchase fiddles. I nodded slowly in acquiescence. He could see that I was hit badly so he stood up awkwardly. "Your notice would normally come on Friday so you've got an extra couple of days. Take what time you need off to scout around. I'm sorry, son. Maybe later if it all clears up . . ."

"Yeah." He wasn't a bad bloke and it wasn't his fault. "Thanks anyway." I did not want to make it worse for him so I left then to stand on the forecourt for several minutes. What now?

Later I told Maggie that I had jacked it in but she knew better. She also knew that I was perfectly capable of knocking up a steady five to ten thousand a year tax free without too much effort and it was this possibility that really frightened her. It frightened me too.

This was a testing period for me for I realised just how easy it would be to go back to old habits. The excitement beckoned me but I had the sense to look beyond it to the squalor and heartbreak of prison. So I reassured Maggie as best I could and went job hunting.

About this time, more from anger than anything, I decided to find out if my certainty of being watched was just the jitters or fact. I did not warrant police surveillance and I could see no reason why one of the big crime syndicates should tail me. So I was both perplexed and worried.

One night I decided to find out definitely. There are plenty of back streets in the Notting Hill area and in some of the old squares the houses are what I call back to front. That is to say that the respectable looking side of the buildings faced inward towards the grass rectangle in the square; what should have been the back doors faced on to the streets and with them the usual array of drain pipes.

I deliberately stayed late at Maggie's and left after 1 a.m. I kept to streets that were particularly badly lit. It was eerie listening to my own footsteps on practically empty streets and it is strange how late at night Old London creeps from its shell. There was a mixture of Victorian and Edwardian around here and the two periods emerged in shadowy form as if aware of their ultimate demise even in mordant bricks and mortar.

It had rained earlier and the skies were still swollen with black tumbling clouds that cut off the moon like heavy drapes over a lighted window. This was how I wanted it for good night sight was part of my equipment. I did not hurry. Nor did I stop or hesitate. I listened carefully but could hear only the rustle of wind as it swept autumn leaves from the gutter. I tuned in and satisfied myself that someone was about, unheard, unseen. Whoever it was may have had nothing to do with me but someone was there.

Keeping on I chose my route carefully. The fact that I could hear nothing did not mislead me; in my profession it had been essential to move completely noiselessly even in leather shoes.

I kept my own footsteps at a steady pace, not too light,

not too heavy, just sufficiently audible. Then turning into one of the small squares I decided to make my move.

I was at its narrow end. There were only two street lamps but plenty of shadows. The decaying houses reached up, pillared porticos, ethereal columns of moulded concrete. There were two lighted windows with drawn curtains, and behind one of them came the faint sound of argument.

What pleased me most was that I was as relaxed as I used to be and somehow this was important to me. Keeping close to the terraced buildings I reached the corner, turned it, kept walking at the same steady pace but now my gaze was rapidly taking in the scene. This longer stretch of the square was also empty. There were a few more lights on but nothing worried me. I ran forward.

Gazing briefly up the stack I intended to climb I gave it a solid tug. It didn't budge and I started up, feet getting a purchase on the rough bricks on either side and my hands gripping the stack firmly. It had been a long time and yet it seemed only yesterday. I had no trouble although my breathing might have been a shade heavier than it used to be. I kept going without looking down until I reached a junction of pipes, got myself a good foothold in the angle of the two pipes, held tightly with my hands and then half turned so that I could see along the square.

Just above me to the left a light came on in a small window. There was a rough shadow on the frosted glass but I kept my gaze on the street. I was not in the most comfortable position but I could hold it for a few minutes; about twelve to fifteen feet in deep shadow above the pavement my O.P. was good.

I listened. A variety of noises reached me. Above me the water cistern started filling and the light went out. The street lamps threw bleak pools of light at their own feet as if afraid to emerge into the darkness. All told there was the sort of quietness you would expect at this time of night in an unfashionable square. And I felt good. The old tingle was back in my fingertips.

I thought he would never come but did not doubt he was there. When he did he was so good that I nearly missed him. He must have turned the corner while my gaze had been distracted by a lighted window. Even now I couldn't hear him and saw him only because the streets were wet and I caught a brief reflection. He hugged those shadows like a cat and it was difficult to judge his size because I couldn't get a really close view.

He had evidently been keeping a fair distance behind me yet he made no effort to hurry now that he could no longer hear me. I waited, ready to jump and give him the shock of his life. He still had a little way to come and I positioned myself for the leap.

In the distance two drunks began to argue then a window flew up and someone shouted at them. Above the medley of sound came another. Footsteps. The unmistakable crunch of a regulation tread in duplicate. Bloody coppers. I swore to myself. It was difficult, because of echoes, to judge exactly where they were. The sound seemed to be approaching from the opposite end of the square.

I began to sweat. They would never believe my story if they found me up here. "A man was following me, officer, so I climbed a drainpipe to surprise him." Christ, I could hardly believe it myself. Suddenly everything changed. The double tread was nearing the square and my man was only a few feet away. I dare not jump now in case he yelled and I certainly couldn't thump him with the law round the corner. As if to deride me further, he crossed the road just before he reached me.

He came into full view then; almost a runt of a man. I would never know him again because his dark coat collar was turned up and he kept his head down as if following footprints. I caught a glimpse of light on a dark head but he seemed almost shapeless; small, nondescript, hands in pockets and utterly silent. I had to let him go because the police rounded the corner at that moment.

Angrily I clung to my perch because I dare not come down until they were out of sight. I first prayed they would not see me. From the other side of the road there was more chance that they would than passing directly underneath me. Shining their lamps in a couple of doorways did nothing for my nerves and my perch was becoming difficult to maintain.

When they finally disappeared round the corner I shinned down that pipe like a monkey as relieved as I'll ever be. I padded quietly after the little chap but I wasn't hopeful.

The next morning I knew the tail was off. My third eye in the back of my head had stopped operating. I wondered why. Had he seen me? There was no profit in this sort of speculation so I resigned myself to being released from observation but it still puzzled me.

I didn't tell Maggie any of this, in fact I was telling her increasingly less. About my recurrent depressions for instance over not finding work and the way my bank balance was dwindling. Of course I could sell the car and I would but this was no real solution. Quite simply the number of employers willing to take on an ex-con were strictly limited. The few ideas I had needed capital backing and the only money I could raise would be bent from the boys; that I could do without, I had to. Another thing that worried me was the kick I had got going up the drainpipe. I could not pretend that I had not enjoyed it.

One night I said to Maggie, "I'll have to get out of London, sweetheart. Go to the provinces or somewhere, anywhere there's work."

I remember her looking at me with something like reproach and saying softly, "There *are* jobs you could have had, Willie." It was a sore point between us. Maggie wanted me to take anything at all as long as it kept me straight.

She did not like the idea of my leaving London because we would lose touch; nor, for that matter, did I.

So I was drifting. Then Bulman called on me again, had me down at the station, tried to break down what I had already told him and endeavoured to bluff me over Balls Up's alibi and prove that I was where I wasn't. I could see that he was just itching for the next job to come up especially if it was a house in the vacant premises book. He jibed me about having no job yet managing to run a Jag, but I let it go.

I had never felt lower. Dick called to tell me that he had been passed over for a C.I.D. course when initially he had been half promised it and the pattern was all too clear.

One morning early I had just left a most depressing interview for a job. It was pouring with rain and I was in the vicinity of the Strand. Even the pigeons had taken to the window ledges for shelter, and the recently cleaned Nelson's Column was steaming with wet patches. I was thoroughly soaked and depressed more than usual. Just then I could see no end to it.

I turned into Lyons near South Africa House for a cup of tea. Even with my early warning system it was impossible to know just what I was walking into. For that was the real start of all that followed. Had I known I

35

would not have entered. I would have hoofed it down the Strand and broken records all the way.

I went downstairs to the self service. The rain had pulled in a lot of people but there were still plenty of empty tables; it was a little early for shoppers. I found a table opposite the double staircase and in the least crowded part of the restaurant. I turned so that I could sit with my back against the wall and disconsolately stirred my tea.

After a while I heard a chair being pulled out, vaguely saw movement on the edge of my vision. Then a cultured voice said politely, "Hello, Spider. Another bad day?"

4

I looked up slowly, scowling. He was as out of place as
champagne in a beer glass. As soon as I saw him I knew
the face—vaguely, but I'd seen it somewhere. His hair was
thinning, brushed back and had once been black, like his
thick, finely arched brows. Sixtyish, there was no sign of
age in his clear eyes, an honest grey that met my gaze and
held it; they were good eyes, perceptive and, I suspected,
could be ruthless or humorous. At the moment they were
non-committal. His face was narrow and lined, long chin
and thin, uncompromising lips. A dark overcoat was sufficiently open to reveal a Savile Row suit, white shirt and
a club tie. As I took all this in he was placing his bowler
hat carefully on the seat beside him and hanging his umbrella over the chair back.

"Who are you?" I demanded brusquely. I was in no
mood for this. The chap looked as if he was something in
the city and the city gents don't accost my type with a
straight motive in Lyons tea shops. I was suddenly suspicious for the wrong reason.

"Does it really matter?" he replied gently, amusement
touching his eyes.

My mood was black and belligerent. If someone wanted
to talk to me then he could identify himself. "It matters
to me." He smiled, practised and charming. I briefly wondered if he was a con man. The 'Brigadier' used to dress
like this before he exchanged it for government issue.

"Spider, I can assure you that it doesn't matter at all.
I'll give you something to call me by if you insist." He was
pushing his cup of tea away as if he had never intended
to drink it. I noticed his fine hands; they had never quar-
ried.

But I had enough on my plate without mystery men. If
he had some sort of proposition I did not doubt that I

would come out the wrong end of it. A smooth bastard this one; yes, just like the 'Brigadier' who was a great entertainer on form. "Look," I suggested bluntly, "why sit here? There are plenty of empty tables, why not take one and stretch yourself."

He gazed at me, taking me in, and I wasn't interested in his analysis. His eyes had hardened a little as if he was puzzled. If he was out of place he was most certainly at ease. Without fuss he quietly retrieved his bowler, put it on to meet the faint pink lines where it had previously rested, and took hold of his umbrella. The nylon was not as wet as I thought it might have been. He rose.

"I've clearly called at a bad moment," he said pleasantly. "Forgive me for having mis-timed it. I'll see you during the week; one evening at your place." He raised his bowler and was gone, leaving his tea untouched. He went up the stairs like a guards colonel in mufti. I like to see a man carry himself well.

Having half finished my tea I could see what an idiot I had been. It costs nothing to listen. Raincoat flapping, I darted for the stairs and went up them three at a time, past the bread counter and out into the pouring rain. There was no sign of him and I cursed myself. The pavement was quite crowded but almost everyone was hiding under an umbrella.

When I nipped downstairs to finish my tea it had gone along with his. I bought another and sat brooding again. Now where had I seen that face? Inside? I would have remembered. Meanwhile my stomach was doing its high wire act, red lights flashing like a petrol gauge warning; unmistakable and persistent. For the rest of that day I was preoccupied with the 'city gent'. Sooner or later I would place him.

At Maggie's that night I sat with my arm round her and we were comfortable on the couch, but there was tension between us due to the way things were. She was beginning to be afraid that it would not last, that once again she would be back on the heap. Because I did not want her hurt it made me miserable for I was never a great one for hiding my feelings. Suddenly I told her all about the city gent.

"But you would know a con man."

I laughed. "Even a con man doesn't know a con man; they con themselves more than their victims. But I don't think he is. Yet I know the face."

We sat talking about it not really getting anywhere, when Maggie suggested, "Why don't you contact the newspaper reporter you used to know. The one who showed interest after your trial."

"Oh, wait a minute. Ray . . . ?"

"Lynch, I think it was."

"That's him. What could he do?"

"Newspaper offices have photographic files. He could arrange for you to see them."

"There must be thousands of prints, Maggie. And anyway it's a helluva long time ago, he wouldn't remember."

"Oh, don't you believe it. Those chaps need all the contacts they can get."

"I'll bear it in mind. When his Lordship calls I want a stake out, the number of his car."

"I'll do it for you. I don't mind waiting outside for two nights if it helps you. I'm perfectly capable of remembering a license number. Don't use the boys."

It wasn't such a bad idea. "All right." I came round to stand over her. "Whatever you do, remember the three S's.'"

"S's?"

"Shape, shadow and shine. Keep away from skylines and straight building lines. Merge. Keep in shadow but ensure that you are not throwing one. And don't wear anything that shines." She nodded and mumbled a repetition.

"There's one more thing," I said.

"Yes?"

"I like that perfume you're wearing." I'd said it for her sake. And I made love to her for the same reason, but how can you relax when you're filled with gnawing doubts and obscure fancies?

His Lordship, as I'd named him, called the next evening. There was no prior warning, just a soft knock on my door and there he was, rolled umbrella, bowler hat, immaculate overcoat and all. Doffing his hat he gave a slight bow. "Good evening, Spider. I said I would call, you remember."

I let him in. He stood there, too polite to gaze round my shabby room but I was left with the impression that he could still give me a fair inventory of its contents just the same. This time I liked him on sight, without necessarily trusting him. Helping him off with his coat I laid it on the bed with his hat, annoyed myself by playing the

39

gentleman and letting him have my armchair. He had that effect on me.

"I'm delighted your mood has improved, Spider. I really do apologise for yesterday."

"Can I get you a drink?" I asked without moving. You can go too far with this hospitality stuff. He laughed and it was a good, genuine sound that brought out my own smile. "I know you don't drink, or hardly. And I must say I approve of your discouragement. I'll join you in abstinence."

Pulling forward an old kitchen chair I straddled it, arms along its back. "You *know* I had another bad day yesterday; you *know* where I live; you *know* I don't drink much. What else do you know?"

"Oh, practically everything. Look here, do you mind if I smoke a cigar? If it annoys you I won't."

I gave him the O.K. and hooked out a tin ashtray. He got it going and I wafted away the clouds of smoke but even I could tell that the cigar was rich and pleasant. When he dropped the match into the tray there was a faint tinkle that made me realise how quiet it had become between us. He had used the time spent in getting his cigar going to give me more than the odd shrewd stare and I reflected that he spent every second in some form of observation. I was now comfortable in his presence as a person but I was highly suspicious of his purpose. I waited for him to get down to it.

"I have a proposition for you. One I fancy will appeal to your sense of adventure."

"In or outside the law?"

"I'll answer that later. Let me explain . . ."

"You've already answered it," I said rising. My neck was prickling in too familiar a way.

"Now don't be a chump. Sit down and listen."

"I'm not breaking the law. Not any more."

"Well, I'm relieved to hear you say it so convincingly. Nevertheless I think you should hear me out. It could solve your problems with Maggie and your brother's with Sergeant Bulman."

I sat down slowly. "This is too one-sided. You know too much about me and I know nothing at all about you. Let's even it up a little."

He surveyed his cigar, rolling it slowly. "Well I don't intend to tell you much about myself. Look here, I don't want to stand on ceremony, call me Fairfax."

40

He took a good long pull at his cigar "Y'know, I haven't pulled your name from a hat. I, and others, have spent a considerable amount of time in researching your background, character and so on. There was a short list but it's to your credit that you are our choice."

The old flannel, flattery first, I thought. I wasn't that soft.

"We know about your mother and father, how they constantly fought, how your father died and your mother just disappeared. We believe that this is at least part cause of your—er—criminal tendencies."

I had heard all this rubbish before. "And what about my brother? How do they account for him?"

"He is younger, missed much of what you experienced. He may have been shocked into honesty by your own dubious activities. But don't interrupt. This is all necessary, I assure you."

I was hooked so I leaned forward over the chair back and let him get on with it.

"We think you are basically honest with this particular flaw. We know that you are loyal, for instance, and that is terribly important to us. Your word's your bond, an old-fashioned trait that many so-called honest people would envy."

"Never mind the diplomas. Let's get at it."

He smiled again. "And your directness has not gone unnoticed."

"So I'm a good lad. What is it you want me to do to change all that?"

"Tolerance is not your greatest forte. You are quick to boil against any form of injustice, no matter how trivial. Those are your weaknesses. I want you to recover something that has been stolen from us."

"Who's 'us'?"

"I could have arrived wearing a little Union Jack in my bowler."

I laughed. "You remind me of the 'Brigadier'."

"Oh?"

"One of the best con men in the business. Once you know a con man you simply don't believe a word he says."

"But I've made no claims, Spider. The information I have on you no confidence trickster could acquire."

"So we come back to it. Who or what are you?"

"Y'know, I do wish you would stop interrupting. We'd get there much sooner. I want you to break into a house
41

and recover something of immense importance to this country. It has no commercial value but it is extremely important to us all."

He must have known that my old-fashioned loyalties also stretched to a bit of flag waving for the home base. I had enjoyed my spell in the infantry; it had been the only period when I had remained out of trouble.

"But it will still be a felony."

He nodded gravely.

"I can't understand you," I said. "You can't seriously expect that I would stick my neck out for a job like this."

"I certainly would not expect you to stick it out for nothing. But you have not properly considered it. Think. Bulman has an obsession about you. You are out of work and must be considering moving right away to obtain better luck. If you do you'll be deserting the one person in the world who is of any value to you—Maggie Parsons—a charming girl. Your brother will be free of the hazards of having you around if you move but you'll largely lose touch with him. Bulman will pass the word on wherever you go because he is that sort of person. Like you, he has a flaw."

Well, he was right about one thing. He did know all about me.

"What are you offering that's different?"

"I can stop police persecution. I *know* that you did not do those jobs because I was having you watched. I can see that an injustice is put right over your brother's C.I.D. course. It might mean moving him to another division but he will have the opportunity he so badly wants."

"And how will I know that these things will be done? Presumably the job is soon. I won't know if Bulman will pop up again for a month or so and my brother's affairs could take as long."

"Within three days of your agreeing to help us, Bulman will call on you to officially announce that he knows you are innocent. Within another few days your brother will undoubtedly inform you that he has been fully promised a C.I.D. course. From that point he is on his own—he can only pass on merit."

I had to admit something else about this character. A lot *was* self explanatory. And he was infinitely better than the 'Brigadier'. I began to warm towards him and then suddenly realised that I was going mad. I had been so pleased to hear that he could fix Bulman and Dick that I had allowed myself to be carried away. What the hell was going on? "What's involved?" I asked. I was beginning to realise that anyone willing to pull these sort of strings had a dicey job up his sleeve.

"Well, Spider, it's in your line, I can assure you. Basically I want you to burgle a house, remove from its safe a green metal deed box and hand it over to someone who will be waiting outside. The job is then done. There is no more."

"The safe will be open of course?"

"You'll have to blow it."

"I'm not a peterman. I've never blown a safe in my life."

By now he had a good long ash on his cigar which he carefully removed by rolling it on the tin tray. He was eyeing me very shrewdly all the time, as if weighing my every word, every reaction. Although he was relaxed, through those eyes of his I could see that he was completely and utterly alert to the slightest nuance of tone or gesture. Because of this I became immensely wary myself. His trained intelligence was on a higher plane than mine but I had the basics, the practical experience of an animal on the run.

"That is true," he admitted at last. "It is equally true that you were taught safe-breaking by the finest peterman in the country—Larry Soames."

"Oh, come off it," I said scornfully.

"Taught in the welding shop at Dartmoor," he went on, undaunted. Then he smiled briefly. "You never dealt with the tobacco barons on the Moor, did you, Spider? Too damned awkward and independent. But Larry Soames could never get sufficient tobacco so you saw to it that he had yours. And in return he taught you safe-breaking."

"It's hardly practical experience."

"We can give you that. We can even supply you with an identical safe to the one you have to blow to practise on."

It all sounded nice and pat but I was crazy even to consider it. As much as I loved my brother was I willing to face a ten-year stretch for him? At the end of it I would still be out of a job.

He anticipated me, or rather, I suspected later, at each sign of reluctance he timed another inducement. "You will be paid for the job, of course."

"How much?"

43

"Enough to set you up in business. I believe you are interested in diving work—enough for that."

"How much?"

"Fifteen thousand pounds in a Swiss bank account."

The shock passed through me as if the chair was electrified—momentarily welding me to it.

"Fifteen thousand? What is it I'm nicking?"

"I could tell you anything. But I won't. It really does not matter and has no intrinsic value."

"You are not giving away fifteen thousand. What are the risks and what happens to me if I'm caught?"

He shrugged eloquently; he had me on the end of a line and was playing it as he saw it. "I can give you no protection. If you're caught, then I'm afraid that's it. Your brother still carries on and you have one thousand pounds when you come out. The fifteen is for success."

I considered a ten stretch on the Moor for they wouldn't be mug enough to send me back to Grendon. I knew that I couldn't face it. I'd go mad back there and fit for nothing but crime when I came out; which meant that most of my remaining life would be spent behind bars. No. On the other hand my problems would be over if I succeeded. There were one or two exciting schemes that I could then finance. Maggie would be happy. Dick would be on the way up. Even so—the Moor again if I failed. I would be writing off my life—it would become a living death. Even Maggie wouldn't wait that long.

"That's only one hundred a year for every year I'm sentenced. How could I know that the money would be there anyway."

"You must not forget remission, Spider."

"Your records must show that I'm not good at obtaining remission. I'm like a sparrow in a cage; I kick up a bit of a shindy."

"Look here, don't you think you're taking all too pessimistic a view? You're good at it. Why on earth should you not get away with it?"

I was about to answer when he threw out yet another of his timely inducements. "Of course, any cash that you find in the safe you can please yourself about. I'm in no position to pass judgement. I want only the deed box."

I should have let it drop right then. All the warnings were at full blast but there was something pushing me on. Even so I wasn't stupid enough to agree. I said, "Let me get it straight. If I do this job Bulman's put back in his

44

hole, Dick gets his chance and if I deliver the box I get fifteen grand. If I'm nicked on the job and fail to deliver I'm sent up with only one lousy thousand when I come out."

"That's a fair summary but for two points. On your word of acceptance Bulman will toe the line and your brother will get his opportunity. So you see, Spider, the trust is twofold. If you agree and then break your word you have gained something, have you not? I am entirely reliant on you honouring the agreement once entered into. You must also accept that I will pay the money."

"It's the one thousand I don't like."

He shrugged unrelentingly. "This is too important to pay for failure. I am interested only in success. I am here because you are the man most likely to succeed. I am prepared to put complete trust in you."

The inference being that I should be prepared to do the same in him. I gazed at him thoughtfully while he stared musingly back. His brain was ticking in a well-oiled, well-trained rhythm and I could see that he had himself well under control even though it was clearly all-important to him. Just how important I had yet to discover. My own thought processes were like an engine falling apart: bits were flying all over the place. However, I did have protective devices that recognised my own confusion and prevented me from making a decision at that time. I could see that there was little more to learn from him; the issue was clear apart from location.

"Where's the job to be done?" I asked, almost off-handedly.

"Do you know Portland Place?"

I stiffened. A wealthy area near the B.B.C. Too open for my liking. I nodded without enthusiasm.

"It's the Chinese Legation."

5

For a full two minutes I was unable to speak. The whole crazy proposition fell about my ears. He not only wanted me to screw a place but to invade foreign territory as well. If I was caught inside the Chinese Legation I imagined that a ten-year stretch would seem like a very desirable convalescence by comparison. They would never let me out until they had soaked, beaten or brainwashed the last scrap of information I had to offer. And then they would not let me go because they would not have admitted my presence in the first place.

My God, he was crafty, this Fairfax. He had fed me a bit at a time, led me on and saved the worst until the end. Had he mentioned the place at first I would not have listened to the rest. "Has it ever been tried before?"

"Not here."

"Where then?"

"Rangoon."

"What happened?"

"Two of our local boys went over the wall of the Chinese Embassy."

"Did they get out?"

"They were never seen again."

For the next five minutes I told him what sort of a bastard I thought he was. I was angry at the way he had done it and livid at the ridiculousness of the suggestion. What made it worse was the way he sat there while I harangued him. His cigar was poised and his gaze steady through the spiralling smoke; his legs were crossed, his immaculate creases somehow symbolising his relaxed yet disciplined attitude. My quick impression was of my volume of disjointed words, curses and vehemence striking him at some central point in his forehead, pouring into it and being computerised and reduced to brief terms of sense. Certainly he did not move or show a single sign of distress. When finally I ran out of invective he gave a short nod of approval.

"You know you almost managed that without repeating yourself. Do you feel better?"

"Get out," I snarled.

He rose, unhurriedly, walked to the bed to retrieve his coat. While putting it on he said, "Remember this number: 930-0932. When you ring insist on speaking to me and ask for Fairfax. That is all you need remember." He repeated the number again twice, then added, "I expect to have your answer during the next two days."

As if I hadn't given him my answer. He had led me up the garden path, given me false hope, and now it was worse than before as he had known that it would be.

He picked up his bowler and his beautifully furled umbrella and went to the door. For a short time he stood watching me as if trying to make up his mind but without change of expression. Then he offered his brief little smile and said, "I can let myself out."

And so he bloody well could, the smooth bastard. I was still seething so much that I was afraid to make any kind of move. So I watched him open the door, give an exaggerated wave of his hat, a final reminder to ring him within forty-eight hours, and then go.

Sinking into my own chair I could feel his warmth and I could have wept. The Chinese Legation, a friendly little mob who had attacked our own police with an axe and pick-axe handles. That's what they had done *outside;* I wondered what form it would take inside.

My mood of fury made me forget that I was expecting Maggie so that when she came in she took me by surprise. I just held her until I simmered down and sank myself into her presence. We must have stood like that for some minutes, neither of us stirring. Poor Maggie. I stole a glance at her face and knew that it was she who would bear the brunt of the suffering whatever I did.

Slowly we sat down, anxiety clouding her features now that we had broken. She realised that something was terribly wrong but gave me time to collect my wits. What should I tell her?

"It's all right," I said at last. "I can't tell you what he wanted because there is some secrecy attached to it. He is *not* a villain so don't worry about it."

"But what upset you so much?"

47

"He said something which I took as a personal insult. You know me. Anyway it's over."

She was by no means satisfied but she knew me well enough to know that she would get nowhere by pushing it at this time. Instead, she gave me a piece of paper.

"What's this?"

"I was your stake out, remember? He did not come by car but by taxi. The same taxi picked him up afterwards. I don't know how he signalled it but it came round the corner just as he left the building."

I turned in surprise. "You've been out there all that time? No wonder you're cold." Leaning forward I switched on another bar of the fire. "Stay there. I'll get some coffee."

I was glad to get into that corner called a kitchen to turn my face and my thoughts away from her so that she would see nothing of my desperation. Fairfax had gone but his offer remained; that crazy, suicidal, utterly ludicrous offer that promised escape or eternal damnation. He had well known that my tirade would be followed by speculation. It was mad, there was no doubt of it, but it offered advantages that would not come again. Just how good was I after such a long lay-off? Fairfax did not seem worried by it. I had certainly gone up the drainpipe easily enough but that was second nature. What had happened in the world of alarms since I went inside? Advice on many of the gadgets had been passed on to me by new arrivals as the years went by. But what of those I had not heard about? The more I thought it out the more I turned away from the idea in spite of its attraction. Perhaps time had robbed me of my 'bottle'.

Even after Maggie had gone I could not stop speculating. I tossed and turned in bed, glad that she did not see me like this, so that eventually I merely lay on my back and gazed up at the darkened ceiling. The whole thing was so calculated; perhaps that was its strength. I wondered what it was that he wanted me to nick. For such a harebrained scheme it had to be something very important. I did not know then just how much I was underestimating its value.

Assuming that Fairfax represented some form of British security, and the odds were heavily in favour, it seemed to me a desperate step indeed to break into a foreign legation in London. His face still played on my memory and I would have to do something about it. Once I had decided that to case the place would at least get things in perspective I managed a little sleep.

I left about mid-morning. I approached Portland Place from the Oxford Street end, scanning carefully. There were no uniformed police there and I don't know how the place rated with D.I.5. It was always possible that the smooth Fairfax had placed someone to see if I would do just this.

Portland Place is a wide street, pseudo-Georgian and bright. Although terraced the buildings varied in height and so offered individuality. A great air of respectability encompassed the place and I noticed other embassies.

There are two lanes of metered car parking in the middle of the street and I got my first real appraisal of the Chinese Legation from the island separating the lanes. A pale porticoed building, the first thing I noted was that it stood on a corner and was lower in height than its immediate neighbour. It was a good, solid, quite attractive building with huge, lace-curtained ground floor windows. I found the corner site attractive for many reasons. My first impression was good but it was not to last long.

Crossing the road I came nearer to the building, seeing the sign on the closed double doors in Chinese and English. Slipping into Weymouth Street I had my first misgivings. I had stopped just below the intersection traffic and appeared uncertain of direction. There were railings set in concrete outside the building and below them a basement. The basement windows themselves were solidly barred outside so entry that way was out of the question. There were two wooden doors, one swinging open in the gully of the basement and leading under the footpath that might be entrances to coal holes.

Casually I crossed the road to get a more complete view of this side of the building. My heart sank. I did not need binoculars to detect some of the burglar alarms; they had been painted over with the same cream colour as the window frames but to a trained eye like mine that was no camouflage. Alarms have never worried me much; they slow down an operation and thereby add to danger, but they can be tackled. What really upset me, though, was the way the windows were barred. From the first floor upwards internally across each window were huge grids, the kind seen on elevators. One set of windows was wooden shuttered and the wood wasn't three ply. And these were just the visible signs. I wondered about infra-

49

red alarms. The more I looked the more the place appeared a fortress.

One of my earlier ambitions was to beat the infra-red system at Buckingham Palace just for the hell of it. I know I can get in because I've worked it out. To beat the system over the walls would not be too difficult. But then I knew something of the system. Here at the Legation it was different. The signs did not read 'try it', but 'God help you if you do'. It is the only place in London that I have seen so visibly barred and unfriendly. Its chill warning reached out to me. The place was no part of its surrounds. It demanded isolation and left you in no doubt. There was no sign of life but I could not help speculating as to whether I was being watched.

The building adjoining the Legation in Weymouth Street was much lower, flat-roofed and would present no problem. Incredibly a fire escape reached up from the flat roof to the top of the Legation. It was so easy an access that it *had* to be wired. Of more interest to me were two solid looking drain pipes which looked as if they would take my weight. But this was merely professional appraisal. As I crossed back to the main road and the traffic island I was completely despondent.

The front of the building was as utterly formidable as the side but I gave it a good casing just the same without finding anything to lift my depression. There was only one place left. Casually, miserably, I sauntered along the line of proud buildings to the other intersection, turned left down it, and first left again into Devonshire Mews. At the far end of the cul-de-sac was the rear of the Legation. To my left huddled a delightful row of mews cottages that only London can provide with such colourful charm. I could have reached the roof of any one of them without difficulty. On my right was a row of heavy-doored garages through the cracks of which I detected the odd gleaming Rolls Royce.

Outside one of the cottages a green-uniformed chauffeur was cleaning an olive-green Rolls which looked as if it had just been cleaned but maybe he was polishing the polish. I realised that my thoughts were becoming flippant, that I had given up serious consideration of the job. The chauffeur looked up at me as I approached as if I didn't belong. He was right.

"Is there a way out down there?" I asked him, nodding towards the Legation.

"It's a cul-de-sac." He did not rate me worth stopping polishing for, but he was giving too good a look for comfort. I ambled past him, the regular tripper. "Nice, isn't it?" He didn't reply. Access to the Legation roof would have been easy from the rear. But culs-de-sac are a burglar's nightmare; a trap. I would consider going in by one if circumstances were right, but never coming out. As escape routes they were treacherous.

And yet as I made my appraisal under the unfriendly eye of the chauffeur I was strangely reluctant to move. Even as I made up my mind to tell Fairfax what he could do with his fifteen thousand I was assailed by my old malady. My finger-tips began to tingle. My blood began to race and I was fast becoming irrational. Suddenly I *wanted* to break in. It was all so bloody impossible that I *had* to break in. My mind was filled with the old urge I hoped I had left behind in prison. But now it was here and I was excited and afraid at the same time. Blast the damned feeling.

Yet it was no use telling myself that. My eyes were taking on new coverage, my mind registering a different complexity to the problems. The answers were the same but the approach was different. The place was impregnable; had been made so with cold, unfriendly calculation. If I got in and they caught me then I wouldn't get out again, certainly not alive. I knew that I was not over-dramatising, that I would merely be another case. These things happened in embassies all over the world where there was political contempt and pathological hatred of one system for another. The only difference would be that I would have entered forcibly yet freely and thus be unique. But nobody except Fairfax and the Chinese would know it.

My sudden difference in attitude found remedy. Yet a moment ago analysis had reached a conclusion of gloom and finality; now it merely provided a starting point. So the place was hopeless—right, what to do about it?

I gave the chauffeur one of my cheeky grins as I turned to leave. "Thank you, my man," I said as I passed him and for a moment I thought he was going to kick the Rolls as I am too big.

I felt better already. As I walked north towards the General Post Office Tower, rising like a dirty bandaged finger high above London, I was fully aware of my cursed elation. It was childish to want to break in because the

51

Chinese clearly considered it impossible, but there it was. This was why I had seen the inside of prison walls for too long. But on a job like this I could not afford to be careless, not for a split second. There was one thing I had overlooked in the event, I could have well used a magnitude of clairvoyance.

Paying my four bob I joined the queue for the fast lift to the observation platform. Once up there, London was murky through the glass. The old town spread below in a series of grey lamps and familiar landmarks; St. Paul's, Houses of Parliament, Big Ben looking like a father figure. What I wanted was much nearer to hand. I suppose I walked about three-quarters of the way round the circular floor before I stopped. Near to the glass I spotted Portland Place, a steady stream of traffic going along it, in slow motion from this height. Reaching for the nearest telescope I dropped in my sixpence and focused down.

The roof of the Chinese Legation drew up under my eyes as if I was hovering just above it. There was an upright projection with a green wooden door on the flat roof. It was so simple that I ignored it; they weren't going to bar and wire up their windows to leave such an easy access. To the left, facing the side street, was a long sloping projection with small windows, like a built-on attic. The rooms were obviously low roofed and would be used either as store rooms or for the lowest comradely hierarchy of the all-men-are-equal-except-the-top-ones movement.

I gave the long raised attic structure my full attention. Its roof was covered in lead. Carefully I examined the rest of the roof, then possible escape channels along other roofs. Finally I swung back to the lead-roofed attic again. We were in business. I held on until the shutter clicked off.

By the time I had completed the tedious queuing for the descent my mind was working constructively, like the creeper I am, and I suppose will always be. I despised myself for my turn of thought but the fantastic sense of challenge engulfed the feeling as it had always done. I had a brief, deeply painful regret for Maggie, but it was gone before I could dwell on it. What a place to break into, I reflected. Get in there and you can get in anywhere. Getting out again was something different so I chose not to dwell on it.

I walked from the G.P.O. Tower to Frith Street in Soho, and that's a good long walk. But I wanted time to think and I wanted to see if Fairfax had put someone on my tail.

Soho had changed enormously during my years inside. Basically its function was the same as before and it was still the biggest chunk of concentrated continental Europe inside England. And there were still some friendly faces who recognised me. But a good deal of its character had gone. The 'Brasses'* had been replaced by strip clubs which as I saw it was a sort of free advert for the former. As I heard it, the girls were doing better than ever and the cops had more difficulty in picking them up.

The smell of fresh fruit, spices, salami and roasting coffee was as good as ever as I went searching. I found it sandwiched between a strip club, or as they say, the old man's rest home, and one of those newsagents' shops with the suggestive ads painted in bold ink on postcards. It was appropriate. On the brown-painted door between the others was a shabby notice pronouncing that the 'Gainboy Studio' was on the first floor up the stairs; in brackets underneath 'Neil R. Palmer'. He was my man.

Pushing open the door I went up the narrow, uncarpeted wooden stairs. It was musty and the walls were Victorian off-white which had yellowed with age. The stairs weren't all that strong and the landing creaked even under my practised tread. The sign on the door was brighter, freshly painted, but no different in content from the one downstairs. Opening the door I faced a solid, oriental screen round which I peeped. I was in the right place all right.

The room was large. In odd corners had been pushed pieces of scenery and backcloth, old ropes, nets, curtains and unlit floodlights. There was, nevertheless, a high density of arc lamps concentrating on a nude, heavy-breasted woman in a pose which worried me more than it did her. I decided to stay behind the screen for a bit.

A small, mincing figure of a man in blue dungarees and a white roll-neck sweater moved among the lamps like a female sparrow, quick, eager and expert. His canvas shoes made no sound on the boards and his blond, straggling hair was like a loose *toupee* of straw. There was a camera mounted on a tripod but he wasn't yet ready to use it. He spent some time on the lamps, casting shadows, multiplying breasts, arms, legs, until he had the effect he wanted.

* Prostitutes.

The girl was straddling a dummy capstan against a backcloth of harbour and wheeling seagulls. She watched the man dispassionately and did not flinch when he handled her body, easing it this way and that, moving legs and arms and angling her trunk. She well knew that she had nothing to fear and her coarse, pretty face registered a faint contempt that her voluptuous body had no effect on him.

He patted her deftly. "You'll have to diet, darling. You're getting too heavy on top. I'll bring the lights down a bit." And he minced away as I came round the screen.

"Bluie!"

He wheeled round holding himself in a woman's pose, his pale eyes lighting up with joy, his soft lips puckering into a pouting smile.

"Spider! Come in, dear, let's have a look at you, you gorgeous beast."

Thinking he might throw his arms round me I backed off, eventually offering a hand on the end of a long arm. Bluie Palmer was small, almost petite, his face pale and sensitive. I knew that his eyes could harden like old ivory; his hands were delicate and he used them expressively with speech, his long fingers performing a language of their own.

"Oh, it's nice to see you, dear. When did you get out?"

"I've been out a few months."

"And you didn't come to see me? Really, that's not very nice, is it?"

I winked at the nude blonde who had not bothered to move and who eyed us dispassionately. She must have caught something in my eye that she had missed in Bluie's because she suddenly appeared uncertain. When next I glanced at her she was donning an old dressing gown and watching me cagily.

"I want your help, Bluie. I want to borrow one of your cameras."

"They're valuable, dearie. Take me out to dinner and we'll talk about it."

"I want it now and you know damn fine that I'm not like that."

"Really? Anyone would think that it's not legal. What do you want to take?"

"A building. Look, I'll need it for a couple of hours at most."

"I'll do it for you, duckie. We can go together."

54

"Does Blondie know what you were in for?" I nodded towards the model who showed interest.

"Spider, you wouldn't."

"I would if it saves time."

Bluie had got his name for producing 'blue' pictures. He had been convicted for showing and selling pornographic films. He was a brilliant photographer but had used the sex outlet to supply the money for his real photography, much of which was not commercial, and for his boy friends. For some time he explained the intricacies of a telephoto lens as long as an arm. He didn't like the idea of my having it but it was clear that this blonde did not know about some of the other models and he had a fear of her discovering, particularly as his more dubious money-making projects did not reflect his own needs. He had always been afraid of women laughing at him.

Within two hours I was back in his studio and he was developing the close-ups that I had taken. The blonde was now dressed in high heels and a mini and was on the verge of departing. She looked as if she was going back to her beat, but maybe I'm unkind.

From the studio I rang the *Daily Mail* and asked for Ray Lynch. It took some time to discover that he had left them and had moved over to the *Express*. But I did track him down and was lucky to find him in. Arranging to meet him at the Enquiry desk in half an hour, I told Bluie I would be back for the prints later on and asked him to bill me although I knew that he wouldn't; he may be queer but there was a lot of good in Bluie Palmer.

The black glass of the *Express* building had not changed and Fleet Street seemed much the same. The foyer was fairly crowded and at first I did not recognise Ray Lynch amongst the other faces. He recognised me though and came across, hand outstretched.

"Hello, Spider. Keeping your nose clean, boyo?"

"Just about. Thanks for seeing me. I hope I don't waste your time."

He smiled. "We're a blunt breed: I'll soon tell you." He had changed for the worse. Bloated, dissipated almost, his increased weight strained an untidy Harris tweed jacket and the too tight slacks. The dark hair had thinned and needed combing. His face was flabby and a whiff of spirit on his breath supplied part reason. His nose and lips were firm and his bleary eyes still restless but he was a shadow

55

of the smart, good-looking, news-hunting reporter that I remembered.

His questing gaze was roaming over me as if I carried a news item somewhere about me. His speech had developed a staccato way of punctuating as if he edited his words as he uttered them. He could not yet be forty but looked more.

"How are things with you?" I asked as we moved to one side.

He shrugged a little dejectedly and his eyes shuttered out something too quickly for me to catch. "Still reporting. They promised me a by-line, but it hasn't happened yet."

"That's writing under your own name?"

"That's arriving, Spider." He grimaced. "What can I do for you, boyo?"

"I wondered if I could look through some of your press photographs. I'm trying to put a name to a face."

Ray Lynch grinned and whatever was bugging him disappeared.

"Got thousands of them. What sort of face?"

"A well-known one. Top social, top civil servant. Someone like that."

"You've got a job on. That all you got?"

"That's all. I'll have to wade through."

He laughed. "How many days have you got? Is it important?"

"Could be."

"I'll take you along. There are six hundred odd M.P.s alone."

"I don't think he's an M.P. But you're getting warm. He'll be backroom of some sort."

"And the best of luck, boyo. I'll take you and leave you. If you find what you want get through to the reporters' room—I'll come if I'm still here."

Ray was right. I almost gave it up. But after a bit you develop a knack and the boredom sets in so you automatically scud through, resisting temptation to examine the more interesting ones. The system of filing was such that it aided my cause and it took me only three hours to find what I wanted; it might have been as many days.

It was a mixed group at Ascot, morning suits and toppers for the men, expensive dresses and hats for the ladies. I knew now why Fairfax's face was familiar. This sort of photo would appear in the social columns and society magazines and most burglars read mags like the *Tatler;* how else can we select our victims?

All the names were there, Lady this and Lord that. But no one interested me except Fairfax, as debonair as ever, binocular case slung round his neck, amusement in his eyes, straight-backed and looking the world in the eye as if he owned it. Sir Stuart Halliman, Bt. I made a note of the name, thanked the keeper of photographs and went back to the foyer where I asked for Ray Lynch. He had been sent out on a job so I said I would call back tomorrow or ring.

Dick was doing a ten to six night duty so from a call box I gave him a ring at his drum. I gave him the cab number that Maggie had got for me and asked him if he could trace it. This is easy for a copper and the answers come up pretty quick.

I evaded meeting Maggie that evening. I felt a heel and she suspected something but I knew that I would give myself away if I saw her. My nerve ends were tingling and I was full of strange fears and inexplicable little warnings. But I was excited too. I pored over the blow-ups of the prints Bluie Palmer had developed for me, using a magnifying glass.

The next morning Dick popped in before catching up on his sleep. There was no such registration under the Hackney Cabs. Maggie must have messed it up—unless
. . .

I went out early to the nearest call box and rang the *Express* for Ray Lynch, to find that he was not yet on duty. I told the operator that I was his younger brother and had just flown in from India after several years and could I have his home number.

I caught him at home just as he was leaving. I said in the phone, "Ray, I found the mug shot that I wanted. You had left. What do you know of Sir Stuart Halliman?"

There was a silence, then I could hear his very faint breathing. Very softly, he said, "Say that again, boyo."

I repeated it and I could almost hear his struggling thoughts.

"Look here, I must meet you. Can you get down to the *Express* now?"

"I can, but who is he?"

"I'll tell you then."

"Look, there's no story to it. I'll meet you but tell me now."

"He's head of Defense Intelligence 5. The number one man appointed a year ago."

The number one man of D.I.5. Dazedly I put down the phone even though I could hear Ray calling out.

6

Not a minion, not even the number two or three man. The number one man, the head, the fellow who controlled all the other fellows and was probably answerable only to the Prime Minister. A man with immense power; who could have someone tucked away without too much trouble; who could put pressure on the Foreign Office to have foreign dignitaries deported. What then was such a man doing with me? Why was he handling me personally? If the job was big enough for him to handle himself then it was important enough to scare me silly. Men like Sir Stuart Halliman don't personally deal with the Spider Scotts of the world; not unless they were playing it so close to the cuff that they could not delegate—dare not. And if that were the case Spider might become expendable.

I kept my promise to Ray Lynch and met him at the *Express*. He thought he was on the scent, of course, and he would have been had I been co-operative. But I could not afford to be. Because he had helped me and because I foresaw that I might need him again I fobbed him off with a story that one of the boys had considered screwing Sir Stuart's drum and I had said I would find out who he was for him. Obviously the drum would be left alone with the amount of wiring it was likely to have. It was a lousy story and Ray didn't believe it, but that was as far as he got. His eagerness was hard to believe, his whole face had come alive as if reborn. When I finally shook him off I went out into Fleet Street, walked slowly into the Strand then up to the big Post Office at the foot of St. Martin's Lane.

From a post office call box I rang 930-0932 and asked for Fairfax. A girl told me to hold on and some time later Fairfax's voice came on. I said, "This is Spider. I want to talk to you."

"Where are you?"

I told him and he said, "Wait outside. I'll pick you up in five minutes." He rang off before I could say anything more.

I stood outside Europe's largest post office and watched the traffic snarling up round Trafalgar Square and the people popping in and out of the Press Exchange next door. An armoured van drew up outside the Westminster Bank and I idly wondered if the boys had it earmarked. Sight of it made me think that I would have been safer taking up the Reisens offer to join the mobs. The traffic came flooding down from Charing Cross Road and a solitary taxi slipped the stream to pull up on the double yellow lines opposite me. I noted the number was the one Maggie had given me. The passenger window came down and there was 'His Lordship' deigning to look my way.

It was murky and drizzle had set in. I took my time to reach the cab just to show my independence. Fairfax knew better and watched me with a smile as he opened the door for me. He sat there in his dark overcoat, the inevitable bowler and gloved hands resting on the handle of his still furled umbrella. "Wretched weather," he observed and as I'm not good at small talk I let it pass.

The cab moved off and I noted that the glass screen behind the driver's head was dark so that it was difficult to get an impression of the driver himself.

"You were quick," I said. "You couldn't have had far to come."

Fairfax inclined his head. He turned to survey me. "Well?"

"Fifteen thousand is not enough. And one thousand for failure is crazy. I may never come out of that place."

"In which case neither sum will be of much use to you."

"I want it to go to Maggie. But I want more and I need to know more." I decided to keep to myself the fact that I knew his identity—at least for the moment.

Fairfax gazed straight ahead as if he wore a steel corset. "I cannot give you more, Spider. Nor would I if I could. The terms are fair."

"Supposing I'm caught? I could tell the judge and jury the whole story in court."

He sighed. Then turned to face me quizzically. "It had occurred to me," he observed drily. "But I wonder what judge and jury would make of it. Sounds a bit far fetched, don't you think? And with your record: I wonder, too, whether you would survive the eternal laughter in prison?"

I had wondered the same. I knew that if it came to a public showdown between the two of us I wouldn't be the winner and losing would not help my sentence. No one would believe me and this wily bird could probably prove that he was in Bermuda the whole time. Still it was a try.

He patted my arm briefly. "Anyway, Spider, you are not that sort of creature. We selected you very carefully, y'know. Grassing is not your forte."

I still haggled over terms but he was quietly adamant. To make anything of it I had to succeed and his offer was designed for success.

"You realise the job is impossible?" I tried again.

"Extremely difficult," he conceded, "but we have inside information that will aid you. Alarms and so forth, type of safe and its location."

I looked at him in astonishment. "You're asking me to rely on someone else's casing? I've got to follow my nose."

"Then follow it. We merely provide signposts. It's up to you whether or not you heed them."

"What's in the box I'm to nick? I have a right to know."

"Your only right, Spider, is an expectancy of fifteen thousand pounds if you succeed. In fact it contains documents stolen from and vital to this country. It would be futile to describe them."

I hadn't gained an inch. He was resolute in his own quiet way. He had my measure, I had to admit. "What exactly do I do?" I looked across him to notice that we were somewhere in Holborn and had stopped by traffic lights.

"First you go to a place in Brixton to take a look at the type of safe. Incidentally as a bonus there will be an open dated single ticket to Zurich in your name. All quite straightforward."

"Oh, dead easy, the police will be after me even if I succeed."

"I can assure you that they will not. Your danger is *in* the Legation."

We rode for a while in silence and I gave him credit for leaving me to my thoughts. Then I said, "I shall need some gear."

"Of course. Get what you need."

Another silence, then he turned full face and I saw the steel beneath the plastic. "I take it that you have agreed to accept?"

I hesitated, briefly thinking of Maggie, Dick, myself.

"There's not much else to do. I accept but I won't move until the first part of the bargain is complete."

He nodded and I think he was relieved. "Understandable," he said. "But once you are satisfied then we must move very fast indeed." And for the first time I thought I detected a subjugated desperation.

He dropped me near to my pad and I went home to mull it all over. Ray Lynch was waiting outside my door. I was surprised and disturbed because I had not given him my address and did not want reporters on my tail. There was not a hope in hell of him getting anything from me. I noticed that his jacket and hair were damp and that he carried no umbrella. Could he be that hard up for a story?

"Look, Ray," I said as I opened the door, "I'm grateful for your help but it was a false alarm. These things happen."

He came in with me, those eager brown eyes of his working overtime, sweeping over my room and finishing up by gazing at me like a faithful dog. "Give me the names of the boys who intended screwing this drum. I can get a story out of it without mentioning them, boyo."

"Then you don't need their names. Lay off, Ray. You're making something of nothing." I gave him a drink then told him I was moving from this district, going north job hunting. He seemed disappointed, and by the time he left his face had a pinched look of resignation and his eyes had slowed down considerably. For some reason I felt sorry for him and wondered what had happened to make him change so much.

Sergeant Alf Bulman called that evening just as I was about to leave. He stood in the doorway, refusing to come in and his words nearly strangled him. Seldom have I seen a man make such an effort. He had come to explain that I was off the hook, that he had been wrong, that he hoped that there would be no hard feelings. When he had left I did not know whether to laugh or cry but enjoyed an immense feeling of relief. Fairfax moved fast; the man had undoubted pull. It was good to have the pressure off and it was indicative that Fairfax kept his word.

I went round to Maggie's in a fairly depressed state because I was virtually saying goodbye, certainly for some time, perhaps for good. She opened the door and looked sweeter than she ever had. Candles flickered on the table

62

and I guessed that she had prepared something special. A farewell dinner?

I felt choked and suddenly could not speak. What was I doing to her? We had slipped our arms around each other and neither of us spoke. A certain shyness had crept between us as if we had only just met and I would have to court her all over again. The truth was that I wanted this moment, just the gentle warm contact of her without passion but with something far more precious and I was certain that she could sense this. I thought desperately, you bloody fool, why risk losing her? But I knew why. I knew for a certainty that the only chance of a steady life with the kind of independence so essential to me was to do what I intended to do.

We held each other as if I was already on the way back to prison.

"You're going away, aren't you?" she whispered.

"I've got to," I groaned. "I must get work. I won't be away for long."

"You won't do anything wrong?"

"You know I won't. Dammit, I don't want to go back." She did not press the point but suddenly trembled.

I said, "How did you know?" She looked up then. "Oh Willie. You're so easy to read. You've been strange for the last few days."

That night was the most wonderful yet the saddest of my life. We both wanted it to go on even when we were exhausted because we both accepted the unvoiced thoughts that this might be our last together. Daylight came on us like an assassin, silent, effective. The night had always been my friend.

The following day was dead in every conceivable way. The weather was lousy and my feelings were like the leaden clouds. I was near to reversing my decision then. There was no brightness, in outlook or mood or hope. I was pretty dead inside too.

Dick called the day after as jubilant as a puppy with a bone. He danced a jig in his policeman's boots, singing, "I've got my course, Spider. I've made it." And suddenly it was all worthwhile. Dick had got his C.I.D. course. Dick's progress was more important than my own and that was all that mattered—then. It cannot be easy to put that sort of pressure on the police; just how much power did this Fairfax wield? Where did it stop?

I rang Fairfax to tell him that the first part of the

63

bargain had been made and that I was ready to keep mine. He gave me an address in Brixton to report to that afternoon. I drove to the garage where I had so recently worked and sold my car to them after a bit of haggling. I caught a bus to Brixton. The traffic jams delayed me; the streets and pavements were thick with vehicles and people and the Christmas signs were already up. The garage was one of those old rambling affairs in one of the dingy back streets not a stone's throw from Brixton Prison. It was a reminder I could have done without.

So far as I could see there was no name to it. A dilapidated showroom and a forecourt with used cars, and they could say that again, cluttered one side of the street with a couple of petrol pumps. It was some time before I could locate anyone but eventually a greasy overalled mechanic passed by and I grabbed him and asked for Fairfax.

He showed no surprise and merely nodded. "He's in the office behind the workshops."

The workshops were on the other side of the street. I noticed that either side of it were a few drab shops and besides them what appeared to be a factory wall. The area was not ideally residential although some terraced houses started farther up.

Crossing over I went through the workshop, cars scattered everywhere, with more than a sprinkling of taxis, half a dozen mechanics working and clanking among them. There was a smell of oil and petrol and the sound of revving engines. Nobody gave me a glance although it was naïve thinking.

At the rear of the workshop a concrete apron curved either side of the doors, presumably for the cars to be run out and to circle to the street. Across the apron was a dark wooden shack like a foreman's office and I saw Fairfax through the dirty window sitting among the rough paraphernalia, appearing completely out of place.

I went in among the cans of paint and oil and the spare parts lying almost everywhere. The desk was littered with stained papers, carburetors and plugs as if it was a workbench. Fairfax still wore his bowler and carried his umbrella. He rose as I entered. "You're late."

"Traffic," I explained.

"Then you must leave earlier. This way." The bargain having been struck he was leaving me in no doubt that

64

he had taken over. I was surprised at his annoyance but as time went on I learned about his precision and just what it could mean.

I followed him straight back from the hut, left along the apron until we reached a solid concrete building that was windowless. There were double doors and beyond them by a few feet another door as if the building was insulated by thick double walls. Later I realised that it was sound-proofed.

Inside it was fairly well lit by shadeless lamps. There was no one else there. When I looked around it was as I thought a studio would be. There were cables and extinguished arc lights, what seemed to be props and the place was roughly divided into four eight foot high solid walls, none of them meeting the other so that we could wander around.

Fairfax took me into one of these areas. There was a long work bench and on it some boxes. Against the outside wall facing us was an old P. and C. safe. He nodded towards it. "Try that."

I stared incredulously. The safe was solid enough, not combination, but by no means the latest deterrent to criminals. "You must be joking," I said.

Fairfax was put out. He said stiffly. "I am assured that this is the type that you will have to open in the Legation."

"It's old fashioned. There was no need for me to come along to practise on this."

"I'm glad to hear it. But as you're here you had better get on with it. Your requirements are on the bench."

I went over to the bench rather mystified. "I should have thought they would have something more up to date with all the other precautions they take."

"Perhaps they think they are impregnable. But would it have made a difference?"

I shrugged. "I suppose not. A difference in time, that's all."

"That's probably their own reasoning. Is everything there?"

I never ceased to wonder at this man Fairfax. Everything was there in numbers including a packet of contraceptives when I only required one. "Anyone could blow it," I complained. "You don't need me for this job." All the time I was fiddling I was telling myself that Fairfax was playing it very close. Everything to do with me he was handling personally, allowing no one else near. I kept reminding myself that this man was answerable only at Prime Minister level. And here he was in this house waiting to see how well I blew a safe. It began to be unreal. I was slowly going off my head.

I took a contraceptive and gradually filled it with Polo Ajax, a plasticine type explosive, completely malleable, from a metal box which contained enough to blow the Bank of England. Going over to the safe I carefully pushed the end of the contraceptive into the keyhole, kneading the explosive so that it slipped in quite easily. When it was hanging down in the aperture through the keyhole I fixed a number six detonator to the open end and stuck it to the door with modelling clay. Then picked up the wire, fixed it to the detonator and ran it out on a drum to the bench.

"Right," I said, "we are almost ready. Are there any light points in the other sections?" I had noticed two or three with switches set above the bench.

"Naturally," replied Fairfax, a little restless by now.

"Right then, where's the carpet?" I asked with a grin. I should have known better.

Fairfax leaned on his umbrella, eyeing me bleakly. "I hope you will be more observant on the night," he replied acidly.

The carpet was rolled up under the bench. Feeling an idiot I pulled it out and draped it over the safe. It had seen better days but I could hardly expect him to produce a Persian. Clipping off a good length of wire I bared the ends, keeping them separate and rolling them tight. I tucked the box of Polo Ajax and detonators under my arm. Fairfax led the way into the next compartment and I did not waste time putting the terminals into a socket and throwing the switch.

The explosion was solid and sharp and for my liking much too loud. And it reverberated. Fairfax and I gazed at each other but it appeared, as usual, that he was letting me do the worrying. We went round the wall and the safe door was hanging partly loose with a big rent in the carpet. I had a little trouble fiddling to free the lock and then the door was open.

"Good," observed Fairfax.

"I didn't like the amount of noise. Every Chinese in the building will come running."

He aimed the point of his umbrella at the safe cavity

as if he would not deign to touch it with his fingers. "No," he said. "The room you will enter is insulated with heavy carpets, tapestry and furniture. The noise will be considerably muffled."

"They will still hear it."

"I doubt it, but in any event. I can help in the matter. We must have precise timing, Spider. Please. We will allow adequate time for you to enter, plus a safety margin of say three-quarters of an hour. During that period you must hide in the room once you have fused the safe. At an agreed time I will arrange to have a series of external explosions set off in the street. We'll provide a nice distraction for you."

I eyed the safe, then the self-assured Fairfax who was brushing his bowler carefully with his sleeve because the dust was settling on it and I said deliberately, "When do you want me to do the job, Sir Stuart?"

He didn't even blink. Finishing the brushing, he put the bowler back on his head, utterly straight, and there was the merest glint in his cool eyes when he faced me. "I'm glad to find you are not a complete idiot. It gives me a little more confidence in you."

I nearly exploded but he cut in coolly. "Perhaps knowing of me will help you to realise just how important this is."

"When do I do it?" I repeated dully.

"Tonight if possible. You're the expert. Let's have your appraisal."

Leaning against the bench, I thought quickly. I wanted it over too, but I did not intend to rush it. Fairfax stood as if he was the front man of a single file and gave nothing away. It was strange how he could convey friendliness, tetchiness, impatience, without change of expression. Something in his set features conveyed these things but I was never sure what. Perhaps an almost imperceptible manipulation of his brows.

"I would prefer to do it in daylight during a thick fog. It *is* November."

"Be realistic, man. They will be crawling all over the place."

"I know. A moonless night. It doesn't really matter except that it doesn't help if it's raining."

"Tomorrow night if it's dry?"

Suddenly it was on me. Tomorrow. Why not? It would give me one more chance to case the place. I nodded.

Fairfax sighed and stood at ease. It came as something of a surprise to me to realise just how tensed he was. He went so far as to undo the button of his overcoat but I guessed that was as far as he would go; he would never loosen his tie on the hottest day; so I loosened mine for both of us as it was getting stuffy. He took off his bowler and brushed back his grey hair with both hands.

"This is what will happen," he instructed seriously. "When you emerge with the box you will walk south down Weymouth Street for about twenty yards. You will be approached by a man in a camel coat and a homburg hat. Such a frightening combination can hardly be missed. When he raises his hat to you hand him the box. In return he will give you the number and access to your Zurich bank account, together with your air ticket. You will have to make your own air reservation but that is all. Now. Your *modus operandi*?"

I had considered it endlessly. "All you need to know is that I'll go in by the mews and out by the low building next to the Legation in Weymouth Street."

For a few minutes we discussed the time factor, then he produced a plan of the Legation and laid it on the bench. There was a good deal missing but it was adequate. Apparently there were two safes; the main, where all the diplomatic stuff was kept was on the first floor. The one I had to blow was in the hands of only one man, a Mr. Li Tshien. Reading between the lines, this character was their espionage head so I imagined that the safe contained a few items Tshien would not want even his colleagues to know about. We pored over the plan for a long time while I made mental notes because Fairfax would not let me sketch a copy.

When he had folded the plan away again Fairfax asked, "I take it that you have sufficient funds to obtain your equipment?"

I nodded. "I'll get it tomorrow morning then have another look at the Legation. You don't want any money to pass between us, do you?"

"Not even old notes, Spider. When we part this time we will not see each other again. I hope you pull it off for all our sakes. But if by chance you don't you will find it impossible to involve me."

"You said yourself I'm not the type to grass."

He looked me straight in the eye for some seconds but it was almost impossible to read the man beneath his

68

present rigidity. I had the feeling that he wanted to tell me something or express something but finally his steady gaze dropped and he said, "For all sorts of reasons people have been known to act out of character."

If there was a message there I missed it. Then he added, "I merely wanted to illustrate that if you are caught, mention of me will only make it worse for you. It's important that you understand that I would not only refute you but comfortably prove you a liar."

This made me uneasy. "You explained before," I protested. However, caught or not, you will still benefit financially."

I did not like the trend of this. "Do you expect me to be caught?"

"God forbid. I need that box badly. It is merely that in the unlikely event of failure, in the unlikely event of an attempt at grassing, I would have to be the complete hypocrite and desert a friend. I wanted you to know that it would be a hard thing for me to do but nationally necessary."

I was touched by this. "I understand," I said. He had a heart after all.

He fell behind his quick freeze mask again and said with dignity, "Good luck, Spider. I know you will succeed. And when you do remember not only the money but the fact that you will have done this old country a real good turn."

I was a little hurt that he did not shake hands with me when he wished me luck.

7

It was too late for shopping and too dark for casing, so I took out the photographs of the Legation roof and studied them again until I knew them by heart. Ahead of me was a long lonely evening. I had far too much on my mind to want to see Maggie or Dick or any friends. Somehow I did not feel right about the job. There was an unknown factor that nagged at me, something I had missed. I went over the whole series of events from the time I had first met Fairfax, and even before when his men were watching me. I came back to the present step by step in great detail.

The job was incredibly difficult but it was not only this that worried me. There was something else and it was worse because I was sure I had not overlooked anything. I glanced over my shoulder and that, I reflected, was where I should keep looking. I told myself that anticipation had made my nerves taut but I knew that it was more than that.

I should have called it off then. I should have taken full heed of the warning that bugged me and telephoned Fairfax. Knowing it I made excuses to myself for not doing it. I had my pride. Fairfax had so far proved a man of his word; then so would I. Perhaps I had simply lost my nerve while wasting in prison.

The hours dragged now. I wanted to fill in time by ringing Maggie but I dare not as I was supposed to be in Birmingham and anyway she might read the signs. I had reverted to what I was destined to be—a loner. I had never imagined that I would need people until now. Just one real friend would do. I told myself I was going soft and got the photographs out again then checked my gear.

That night I barely slept and the next day dragged. I

bought my equipment early and went to Portland Place to do a final casing. At nine I left my flat and took a walk. At ten I rang Fairfax from a call box. His unrelenting attitude was at least solid, something real. He did not greet me and we did nothing but synchronise watches. As it happened there was only half a minute between us but thirty seconds can make all the difference with a diversion from an explosion. He did not wish me luck and in fact his tone was so sharp that I realised he was very much on edge. And it made me feel better that in this I was his superior.

My own nerves were reaching the frozen stage, a detachment that could expel all ordinary sound and concentrate on the almost inaudible ones; a chair creaking, a brush of wind, friction of soft substances, faint footsteps, different types of vehicle engines outside, a photograph falling as I knocked it, and distant voices. Even with television on I could hear these things in my present state.

Still with time to fill I prepared my gear and produced a few old car ignition and skeleton keys and a crocodile clip. I laid them all on the bed: umbrella, nylon rope, cranium saw, short thin-bladed saw, a small drill, hunting knife, jemmy, keys, Polo Ajax, a couple of detonators, two contraceptives, a pencil torch, plasticine and a pair of light socks. To take too much or too little could be fatal. And clothes. Dark narrow slacks, dark jacket, chukka boots, dark socks, blue shirt and a *light* tie. The tie I would whip off while breaking in but it was handy and gave some degree of normality to my dress if I was stopped by a copper. Whoever heard of a screwman with a light tie? Finally I coated my finger-tips with nail varnish.

After midnight I left the flat. The streets had virtually emptied, but there were still people about and cruising taxis. Lining the pavement was a row of parked cars. Speed was not the attraction and I would have to find a car to match one of my old keys. It did not take long. A two-toned A55 Farina appeared in good shape.

I waited, listened and looked, found the right key then opened up and switched on. It was uncomfortable sitting behind the wheel with the ropes wrapped round me and my tools firmly fixed in my waist band but I preferred not to carry anything openly except my umbrella. Explosive and detonators were in the separate pockets of my jacket. Starting the engine I drew out of line and eased my way forward, in no hurry.

Baker Street still had life on it. Taxis were pulling up outside the tube station while passengers dashed in for the last train home. There was still a fair amount of traffic.

I was fully committed. Already I had stolen without too much thought. The jail sentence was already looming. I drove at thirty and gave all the right signals; I could do without a breathalyser test on this run. I kept off the main streets and the dark night drew in like a curtain over a window in an unlit room. In that car I formed my own prison, lights bouncing off the windscreen, the running engine heard only by me. When I reached Portland Street I drove up it north of the B.B.C. and parked in one of the quiet side streets. Not too near, not too far.

It was caution all the way. I didn't open the car door until satisfied that the street was deserted and when I climbed out did not lock it after me but closed it quietly. Now I missed the protection of the car. I started walking slowly, swinging my umbrella modestly. There was in fact a risk of rain, the skies were clouded which suited me, but I fervently hoped that the rain would hold off.

And so I stepped into Portland Place. London does nothing for me by day, its rat race of hustle was any big city anywhere. But at dead of night for me it came into its own. The broad, islanded stretch of street rolled forward into the patched gloom, its only sentinels the widely spaced street lamps. It was almost 1 a.m. and I could see nobody. That did not mean that a copper was not having a quick drag in a deep doorway so I kept my eyes skinned. I could hear hurried footsteps, a man, but could not pinpoint the location. Sound and echoes travel distances at night.

A taxi passed and I supposed it was the romantic in me that would rather have seen a hansom cab. A good deal of this was Regency London and night was the only time it could lose the years and regain the posture of a nobler age. In the early hours I loved its stealth and slack tempo.

A cat jumped through the railings and for a while it trotted alongside. The air was chilled enough for an overcoat but I would bear the cold rather than be impeded. My ears were out on stalks listening for the slightest sound.

Suddenly I knew there was a policeman near and I had to still my reflexes which demanded that I dive into the nearest basement. Homing on the warning I crossed Portland Place at an angle, my narrowed eyes scanning the intersection. There he was, standing under a portico. There was no cigarette in view but he was not taking in the scene. I kept going nice and slow, swinging my brolly a little more freely.

Coppers have a habit of stopping loners at night, particularly in London in rich residential areas. If one demanded that I turned out my pockets I was done. Clobbering him, which I was against, would not land me in the Legation, nor would running, for patrol cars would be crawling over the place in seconds. As he could still see me I turned right up the nearest side street and after a few paces, stopped.

My night London, my old noble friend, had been destroyed by the advent of the copper. In front of me, lying in the gutter under the pool of a street lamp, were two discarded disposable syringes with some bloodied toilet paper. Some junkies had taken a quick shot. It made me sick. I'd seen it before on the night streets. Doomed youth. Maybe they thought the same of my kind.

The copper's tread started on its way and it was not towards me. Giving it time, I slipped back into Portland Place, passed the Somalia Embassy, then crossed diagonally to the mid-street island. But for one or two cars the meter spaces were empty. There were very few lights on anywhere except on street lamps. I shared the empty kingdom with an equestrian gentleman of Portland stone with a flattened cocked hat who reared beside me. I could just read the inscription: Field Marshal Sir George Stuart White, V.C., G.C.B., O.M., G.C.S.I., G.C.M.G., G.C.I.E., G.C.V.O., 1835-1912. Christ! I supposed that all the 'G's' had been to remind him of his first name. It was so quiet just then that as I raised my arm I could hear my watch.

Crossing the second half of the street I faced the enemy. It stood palely in the darkness with the innocent fragility of a flower. But beneath its ethereal bloom it was solid brick and concrete and anything but innocent. Without hesitating I swung beyond it past the array of other buildings, with other secrets to hide and then turned left. At the junction of Devonshire Mews I slipped into the nearest shadow and briefly waited. Distant double footsteps echoed but they were far off—a man and a woman. Peering into the gloom of the mews I began to move down the row of cottages with the Rolls tucked away opposite them. The people were asleep but I had the feeling that the cars swivelled their headlamps on me all the way. I reached the end wall. This was what it was all about. Running my fingers lightly over the drainpipe that I had selected, I was satisfied. Glancing towards the Mews entrance I was straining my ears now. A passing copper would shine his torch down here from sheer routine.

Now I worked fast. I took out all my tools, keeping only the explosive in my pocket because I would not put it next to the detonators and placed the lot in the umbrella, tying the top with the stouter nylon. I tied the thin nylon to the other end of the thick and the loose end round my waist. I wanted freedom for climbing; it was too easy for tools to slip from the waistband. Laying the brolly flat on the cobbles I took a last look back and could see and hear nothing.

Just before I climbed a thought came up and slapped me straight between the eyes. I was just about to step on to Chinese soil. And I knew that if I got inside it would be as different as London is from Peking and far more dangerous. I gave the pipe a testing yank then I was going up it as if it was a flight of steep stairs. Only seconds later I was on the low flat roof of the dwelling in Weymouth Street. Quickly I pulled up the thin cord which produced the thicker, and so my gear.

Picking my way carefully across the roof I cagily inspected the fire escape leading to the Legation roof. There were two good drain pipes running up the wall and these I trusted. This was the most exposed part of entry, for once on the pipe I was visible to anyone passing in Weymouth Street. So I lay flat and took stock. It was half past one. A good time and on schedule. No sound. I started to climb.

There was nothing new in the feeling for me but it was always a good feeling. I was going up a wall like a fly in the deeply silent hour of a dark night and there were thousands within voice call. I was doing something against odds that society decreed wrong. I knew it was wrong, and I was elated. I felt good and powerful and the psychiatrists had missed out on me because I was enjoying every single moment, and I was reaching for the sky. Before reaching the top I heard the footsteps I knew so well as if they were following me up the wall. There was a nasty moment when I broke the skyline and tumbled over the parapet but I knew that I could not have maintained my position so far up.

I peered over the edge. There he was coming towards the Legation, long raincoat, lamp occasionlly flashing. The nylon cord was hanging down the side of the building. Should I pull it up quickly or leave it? Either way was a risk. I decided on the old-fashioned way—no movement.

It was impossible to keep him in view without showing something of my head so I drew slowly back and listened behind the low parapet. It was agonising this way and all I could do was to count the regular beat of his footsteps and wait for a break in the tread for I couldn't see even the flashing reflection of his lamp. At any moment I was expecting him to falter for the nylon, though thin, would be light against the wall. He had only to see it to speak into his radio and I might not know until the cars drew up.

I heard him turn the corner into Portland Place and wasted no more time in quickly pulling up my gear. My tension eased because once on a roof you are free from prying eyes: you can work all night long without interruption.

Moving across the raised roof of the attic I laid out my tools as a nurse would a surgeon's instruments. My enemies now were beneath me. Somewhere in this attic section, or possibly on the floor beneath, was the radio room and I imagined that it would be constantly manned. I had to be as stealthy as a cat.

I found I could work by straddling the raised long stretch of roof. The first part was difficult as I embedded my hunting knife into the thick lead. I had a little trouble slipping the blade underneath, but once I got good purchase the rest was hard physical work but straightforward. Lead cuts quite easily and I drew a line across then made two incisions back from the base line wide enough to take me. The sweat began to roll and I paused to wipe it off while I took a look round.

The sky was still thick with cloud. Across from me was the intriguing little outhouse with a door which must surely be wired. Regaining my breath I slowly rolled back the flap of lead until I could see the close boarding beneath. So far all to pattern. Drilling two holes through the wood I dropped one end of the cranium saw through one of them, then with stiff hooked wire ferreted for the dangling end until I could pull it up through the other hole. With

75

an end in each hand I simply cut through. The saw was designed to go through hard bone—it found little resistance in wood. The rest was sheer routine.

When I had a large hole in the wood I drilled through the plaster until the hole was big enough to take the furled umbrella. Stuffing the jemmy in my waistband and the detonators in my empty jacket pocket I pushed the umbrella through then shook it so that it loosely opened up in the room below; holding its handle I began to saw a fairly wide circle through the plaster with my thin-bladed saw. The plaster dropped quietly into the open umbrella and there was now a hole big enough for me. Still holding the umbrella in one hand I slid my legs through the gap and listened. Then I shone my torch down.

It *was* the storeroom all right. Dusty bundles and crammed shelves lined the walls and immediately below was a stack of neatly piled files. I jumped lightly off them to the floor. I don't think I made a sound. Dust immediately assailed me for I'm allergic to dust and fibres of almost any kind but I quietly blew my nose before a sneeze came on. There was no door but at one end of the room were some rough railings and banisters indicating stairs leading to the main body of the building. From that moment the whole action ceased to feel like a burglary to me. That old unwanted feeling came creeping up as if someone was hiding behind the cabinets in the room. Later I was to recognise it only too well but as yet I had not crossed that other dimension, now so near.

Anyway there was only one thing for me to do; I was in, get on with it, for work steadied the nerves. Picking my way through piles of papers and wrapped parcels I reached the stairhead and listened. Nothing; as though they were all silently waiting for me down there. Treading carefully I reached the bottom of the stairs, to find a locked door. I tried my skelton keys, fervently hoping that I would not have to use the jemmy.

The lock clicked as if I'd dropped the key. Waiting a little, I opened the door sufficiently to peer through. The landing was dark but at its lower edges there was a vague suspicion of light as if somewhere below a bulb was on, its fringe barely reaching this point. Reluctantly I had to use my torch. Its beam was narrowly restricted, its power weak, but it was enough. There were other doors, all closed, one with a tell tale light strip.

The radio room? Beyond it were the wooden banisters

of the main stairhead. The strip carpeting was flimsy and a little shabby up here.

I tested each foot before putting my full weight on it; I wanted no creaking boards. It's laborious work crossing a wooden floor within earshot of sleeping ears. Pausing to put an ear to the door with the light strip under it I could hear vague movement from inside. This then was the danger point now and particularly when I returned. I just prayed that no one would come out for if I was burgling a house it was a gauntlet I would hardly rise if it involved the strong possibility of trapping myself. As it was I was committed to meeting its dangers and I didn't much care for it. Passing it was like locking myself in.

Committed, I took to the edge of the stairs near the wall, again testing each step. The room with the safe was on the floor below.

Someone was patrolling somewhere beneath me. I could hear the faint cushioned tread, regular, sinister. It was probably from the main hall from where I suspected the faint fuzz of light was escaping. They must maintain a regular night guard. Did they patrol the whole building? Fairfax had not told me about the guard and I solidly and silently cursed him. Although up here the light was dim I could have well done without it, even so pale a light could throw me up as a deeper shadow.

Suddenly the fact of being surrounded by Chinese hammered me hard. I had better make a good job of getting out. I descended the stairs in slow motion fully aware of my own restained breathing and the soft rub of my trousers. But my feet made no sound at all. Any danger of a creak was stifled at the suspicion of its start; my feet were my eyes until I reached the landing, and even then I spent a full minute in dark silence before using my torch again. The place was getting plushier as I descended.

There was the door I wanted, slightly back from the landing; a big, pale pine door, innocuous yet solid. I knew where some of the bedrooms were, most facing the mews, but the unknown ones were the danger.

There was a slight tremor in my fingers as I fiddled with my keys but it was anticipation rather than jitters. Before trying the keys I ran my torch beam round the door frame looking for an alarm. It is a fact that so many places are heavily alarmed on external doors and windows but that roofs and interior doors are so often neglected. Even so it was more than conceivable that Mr Li Tshien did not trust

77

his colleagues. Nor did I ignore the possibility of infra-red alarms being fixed to the inside frames.

Kneeling down I tried the keys; they *had* to work for I would never get away with a jemmy here, on the landing. Almost immediately I got response and the click was as heavy as firing an empty Colt in a cone of silence. The sweat was rolling again, and it was no longer exertion. My hackles were up and this warning I never ignore. For some time I remained crouched on one knee in front of the door. When I did turn the handle the door would not budge. I wiped the sweat off my forehead with the back of one of the socks. A bloody double mortice.

I got control of my breathing and turned back to the keyhole with the strange sensation that I was being studied by dozens of Oriental eyes, all watching my technique and merely waiting for me to finish. I could almost feel their hot breath through the gloom. But it had to be done.

The lock proved awkward which it was designed to be unless I had the proper key. With prolonged hold-ups in exposed positions there is always the impression that the whole place is waking up and that daylight is near. I kept at it until I heard the heavy click. Rising, I relieved my cramp and softly turned the handle. Pushing the door I explored the empty space with my hand, entered quickly, then closed the door behind me. It was total darkness, so black that there were no shadows of any kind. I raised my torch.

The pencil beam shot out like a groping searchlight. But the bright beam was exaggerated by the complete darkness. I would need more light than this. Finding a wall switch I flicked it and a small central chandelier came on. I was carrying three folded handerchiefs; stretching two of them out I pressed them under the bottom of the door to prevent the light from escaping. With my back to the door I took stock.

The windows were heavily shuttered and I knew there to be grids between shutters and glass and an alarm fastened to the window. The office was not for a junior executive. It conveyed the position of its owner. There was a solid-fronted desk; a beauty. Carpet pale green, not lush but adequate; a small, carved side table with a blue and white vase that could have been Ming, with a flower arrangement. On one wall was spread a huge, immensely intricate lacquered fan, almost as good as Japanese.

The remaining space was taken up with dark wooden

filing cabinets to match the other furniture, contemporary chairs out of place, a delightfully painted waste-paper basket, a long, low table with a lamp and magazines including a well-thumbed edition of the little red book. A few silk prints hung on the walls. The red leather-topped desk held a table lamp, blotter and inkstand set, and a small pile of official-looking books on one corner. I was willing to bet that all the desk drawers would be locked but it made no odds. Opposite the desk, against the wall facing me, was the safe resting on a solid plinth of concrete partly inset into the wall. It formed a jarring note as if it had been deliberately raised on an ugly pedestal so that at no time would it be overlooked. Perhaps Ti Tshien did not like stooping. Before moving a step I ran my gaze slowly from wall to ceiling and wall to wall. A solid wooden screen with dragon motif formed a secret place in the corner to the right of the safe.

I was still standing against the wall, working it out. What alarms were there? My instinct was that it could not be this easy. There was the safe as Fairfax had said it would be. A key safe but solid and far too heavy to remove without tackle. What lay between it and me? I scanned those walls more thoroughly than I had ever done. There was an inconsistency in the way the silk prints were hung; two opposite each other were near the base wall, the others more scattered. I would have to get nearer.

While my mind was ranging over interior dangers my hearing, as usual, was detached to a point beyond the room boundaries. Years of practice which I had still exercised in jail; a built-in audio warning system. It did not let me down now. I'm not sure whether some unknown sense made me freeze before I heard, or instantaneously with it. What I was certain of was that I was suddenly rigid in mid-stride half-way to the desk, my muscles bunched in tight knots.

My ears had served me well. The soft pad on the stairs was so quiet that I wonder I heard it at all. The tension brake released and I doubt that I had ever moved so quickly. Light off, handkerchiefs ripped away and a quick silent slither under the kneehole of the desk. There was a brief shuffle on the landing then I heard the key in the lock. It rattled two or three times without the door opening and I detected impatience then reluctance as the key was withdrawn. I started to sweat as I realised what was happening. Chummy outside could not understand why the door was unlocked. The Li Tshiens of this world don't forget things like locking important doors. And now he was being as cagey as me. I did not hear the door open but a slight draught warned me. It was not easy to remain tightly crouched under the desk but I managed it. The light came on as I tried to bury myself in the wood.

8

He must have been doing what I had done except that the door was left open because I could still feel the air flow; he was just standing there examining the room. It was not difficult to imagine his thoughts. He was telling himself that he never forgot to lock the door at the same time arguing that no one could have entered. Had one of his staff asked for the key? Had he himself forgotten just this once? He didn't believe it but he could understand it. The room would appear exactly as he had left it and that would fox him. Obviously undecided he still left the door open as he padded across the room. I heard him move the screen so he was still suspicious. There was only one other place for him to look and that would depend on whether or not he was beginning to see himself in a foolish light.

Straining my hearing to locate his whereabouts I thought I heard him moving about near the screen. I emerged on hands and knees, was about to turn towards the direction of the screen when I heard his very soft tread across the room. Changing direction, I very carefully eased my head round the side of the desk nearest the open door. I nearly drew back quickly when I saw Chummy, but training prevented me and anyway he was not looking my way.

He was short and stocky with steel-rimmed spectacles, the usual "People's jacket, high collared and buttoned up to the neck; loose trousers over soft sandals. From my angle he appeared balloon-faced and innocuous, but I could not see his eyes and nobody with a right in this room was innocent. I remember thinking that he worked strange hours, but so did I and I daresay his occupation was more peculiar than mine.

When he moved one of the two prints that faced one another I knew that my caution had not deteriorated over the years. This was one that Fairfax had not told me about

81

and I would never know now whether I would have found it in time. He switched off the infra-red alarm that sent a wall to wall beam straight across the front of the safe then moved to the safe itself but out of my line of vision. I dare not push my luck too far by edging round the side of the desk.

The safe key turned and I realised that this *must* be Li Tshien. Clearly he now accepted that the room was empty and was probably checking his safe contents as a final reassurance that no one had been here. I crept back into my bolthole. If he came round to sit at his desk he could not miss me and I was not in the best of positions for action. I played it cool and let my eyes do the work. The safe door opened, he ferreted about then padded back to the desk, placing on it something metallic. Another key turned, much smaller, and my brain begain to cloud at what I must do.

The safe was open. Li Tshien stood at the closed front of the desk. I had never clobbered anyone on a job in my life. Yet now I had to. Here was an opportunity to save time, save the noise of explosion, possibly save being surprised again. My mouth was dry. But there was too much at stake to be squeamish. What would happen if *he* caught *me*? It was enough to get me crawling round the side of the desk. I came round on my side using my right elbow as a paddle and keeping flat against the wood. The size of the desk helped me for it must affect his angle of sight. Reaching the front I stopped, unsure of which way he faced and reluctant to poke my head forward; when I did my face was brushing the carpet.

He was standing close to the desk, and the only thing that saved me was that he was holding in front of his eyes a piece of white paper or a photographic print. Slowly I drew back my head, rose to my knees, and then very carefully to a crouch.

I stepped round the desk and swung at him in almost one movement. Underestimating the length of desk I bodged it. The print went flying and his glasses slewed, hanging from one ear as he half turned towards me. Instead of putting him down I had only dazed him. His chrysoberyl eyes were straining to break the haze obscuring their vision. Going after him, he fell back on his heels, dazed but not so much that his reflexes did not respond. One small amber hand groped about the desk and I suddenly saw the button. Grabbing at his jacket I yanked him away as his eyes began to clear to a murderous hardness. I saw the pinpoints of his pupils focus on me. His struggle had actually begun as I swung him round and thumped him at the base of his skull.

There was no finesse in the blow but he fell like a log, cracking his head on the edge of the desk as he went. Dashing round the desk I quickly closed the door then went back to examine him. I did not like the way he lay. The pulse was just about audible. Turning him over did nothing to reassure me; his forehead was oozing blood from a ragged gash of several inches already blue and swollen round its edges. His face was pale ochre. His soft cupid lips were open in an unconscious effort to seek air and his eyes had closed to crevices. Like that, he looked nothing, certainly not formidable, but I wasn't forgetting how he had looked on the point of recovery before I hit him the second time. As I stood he did not seem at all in good shape. Picking up his shattered glasses from the carpet I put them on the desk. This was not how it was supposed to have gone. The safe was gaping open. I glanced at my watch; ahead of schedule now that I had no safe to blow. Another speculative look at Chummy convinced me that I had nothing to fear from him for some time. Stepping over him I went to the safe. There was money, dollar notes and sterling; there were papers, sealed envelope, two small sealed cardboard boxes. There was no tin box.

When things start to go wrong they usually snowball. Hell, what now? Another search merely padded out time. If the documents had been removed from the box then which ones out of this lot were they? Looking back at Chummy I began to feel less sorry for him. What had he done with the box? And now I could see. It was on the desk where he had put it. Somehow I was nervous of that.

Going over I saw a negative partly hidden by a folded piece of paper. Remembering the print I searched behind the desk where it had flown. Even before I looked at it some terrible force urged me not to and I had trouble bringing it into vision as if someone was clinging desperately to my arm. I looked, and could feel the blood draining from my face. I remember steadying myself on the desk. For some minutes my system seized up except for a sense of dread. Unexplained fear swept through me until I was paralysed. The blood had rushed back to my brain, swamping it of reason yet something was struggling to get through.

When the first droplet of thought seeped out it explained my state of shock. I knew that I had been trapped

83

and that there was no escape. The gradual, grinding functioning of my mind threw out disjointed fragments of explanation. Fairfax had fixed me, the bastard, as surely as if he had turned the key himself.

My hand came up with the print once more as if by staring fixedly at it I was willing it to rise. And it was reluctant for it was trembling. I found myself walking to the strongest point of light under the chandelier, subconsciously hoping, no doubt, that I had made a terrible mistake. When I looked again there was no error. It was not the position of the man with the youth that had shocked me; it was the fact that I could not fail to recognise the man. It was not pretty. The Rt. Hon. Norman Corrie, M.P., the British Foreign Secretary, had been caught in a moment of abject weakness. Little wonder that Fairfax had handled this personally. I had to sit down on Li Tshien's chair. There was a nerve pain across my chest and I prayed that my scraps of thought would correlate and come up with some sane answers. Without understanding why at that precise moment I knew that I had been betrayed. I reflected that Norman Corrie was married with kids, I wasn't sure how many. There was no whisper of him being queer but I suppose that would make it worse if the news suddenly burst on a startled proletariat. The Chinese were holding a trump card if they wanted to put pressure to bear.

With more calm, I reached for the tin box and took out the folded piece of paper. It was a letter to the Governor of Wormwood Scrubs from the Home Secretary on Home Office notepaper. The letter was two years old and authorised the release from prison of Oliver Mervin Page and was signed by Norman Corrie. I quickly thought back. I was not well up in politics but I had reason to remember, as I was in prison at the time, that, two years ago, Corrie was Home Secretary. It did not take much to realise that Oliver Mervin Page was the youth in the photograph. Corrie had already been blackmailed. Christ, I had to get out of here quick. I had a vague recollection of staring dazedly round the room feeling a snarl in my throat as if I was at bay. And I was. Following numbness, too many confusing thoughts assailed me. It was all too much. Burglary and its many dangers I understood but this was political blackmail. I was a criminal yet a veritable saint compared to those in this deadly game. I could not reason it all out and stopped trying. Right now I had to hinge on those things with meaning, the old reliables like the buzz of warning in my guts to get out fast. When I concentrated on that I found it was not so easy.

One of Fairfax's men was waiting for me. He had probably positioned himself so that he would see me come down the pipe to the first roof. If I came down too soon he would be alerted; the external explosion had yet to go off and I could not go before then; there was still three-quarters of an hour to go. Three-quarters of an hour to stay in this place with Chummy still lying on the floor to remind me of my first act of criminal violence. His saffron face had dirtied to a greyish tinge as if it needed laundering and the shallowness of his breathing unnerved me.

Suddenly I realised that the light would be showing beneath the door. It might be common custom for Li Tshien to work through the night but it might also encourage another late nighter to call on him. I stuffed back the handkerchiefs and locked the door from the inside with Chummy's own key.

I returned to the desk, sat down and gave my thought processes some unaccustomed exercise. The Chinese were not going to permit burglary and assault at their Legation without raising hell, and I should have considered it before. They would seize on every bit of propagandist opportunity and ensure that the Press got it nicely blown up. They would probably place the blame on British Security and demand blood. Fairfax had lied to me when he had said that I had nothing to fear from the police. As I saw it now the Chinese would howl so loud that the police would have to move and Fairfax would craftily point the way. I was now convinced that he had already done it.

It was the fact that I had so carelessly overlooked Chinese reaction that made me certain that I had been betrayed. Had I considered for one moment earlier I would have realised that these people would not keep quiet—they would lash out hard. Fairfax would want to hush it up as quickly as possible and the easiest way was to hand me over on a plate.

This was what I had missed when I felt something was wrong. But I have not the devious mind of a politician. Only now, with the shock of what I had seen, the letter much more than the photograph, had sense struck me. I should have reasoned it before—I had not, having been carefully fobbed off.

It all began to make horrifying sense. Fairfax would have

reasoned it out long ago. Once in possession of the box, he had to supply someone for the drop-out. A nice idiot of a creeper with an habitual record of crime and a recorded admission that I gained excitement by it and had often announced that I had an ambition to break into Buckingham Palace. Furthermore, I had been to Grendon so was clearly a nutter.

While I reasoned this I realised that from the moment I handed over the box I was doomed. I would be picked up that night. The work would have my trademark; I would have been seen near the Legation or stealing the car, or both. They would have it all neatly wrapped up. The way long sentences were handed out these days, they would make an example of me to pacify the Chinese. I would be old before I came out. The Chinese would know it to be rubbish but it would save face.

Hatred began to well in me. Hatred of Fairfax, of the Rt. Hon. Norman Corrie, of the Chinese and of my inadequacies. Why me? But I knew why. What could I believe that Fairfax had told me? He had fixed it for Dick and he had got Bulman off my back. The former was my reward, the only pay-off, and I was glad of that. The latter was necessary to free me from police vigilance in order to do the job. There was nothing else I could believe. The money was a hoax for even if it was there I would not be around to use it.

Feeling sick to the depths of my stomach, listlessly I went over to the safe. In minutes life had become empty of hope and hopelessness was the great destroyer. I had no intention of rotting like a cabbage in prison. I gazed at the money in the safe and had intended to leave it there. Now I corrupted myself further and took the dollars and sterling and stuffed them about me. Fairfax had sown this seed too —he had hoped I would take the money to make it look my type of crime. I felt choked at what I was doing. But I would need money and dare not go to my bank nor my friends. From now on I had no friends. Not even Maggie. There was something else I could nick; I put the print, the negative and the letter in my inside breast pocket.

I slumped into the chair, staring at nothing. I could not help but compare myself, the tiniest of pawns, with the public image of the Foreign Secretary; my hatred of him was so intense. The bastard was probably sleeping, dreaming that Fairfax would present him with the necessary good news in the morning, while I carried the can. I sank so far into the depths of despair that I lost track of time. The explosion nearly blew me out of the chair. I listened to the rumble then heard another explosion somewhere outside and the professional in me agreed that the sound would have covered the noise of the Polo Ajax. Well, whatever Fairfax had staged, it made no difference now. I still had to sweat it out for the noise was so loud that it would have woken most people in the street. I had to wait for a while. From time to time I examined Chummy but he seemed neither worse nor better and showed no sign of coming round which worried me. If he snuffed it I might just as well stay where I was and take what they had to offer.

Time to go. The excitement must by now be over. A last look round changed nothing for me. I left the safe and the tin box exactly as they were, gave Chummy a whispered farewell and a sincere wish for his recovery for my sake, retrieved my handkerchiefs then put out the light and unlocked the door. I made no further move until my sight was adjusted to the darkness. Opening the door I peered out then stepped swiftly on to a seemingly empty shrouded landing.

The sensation to run was not new and I had it well under control; up the stairs with no less caution than on the descent. The light was still burning in the radio room and I could hear the pips of Morse. I half hoped that someone would emerge to put me out of my misery. The door handle moved and I froze. The door opened a fraction and I clearly heard voices speaking rapid Chinese and I thought this was it. The radio pipped away while the door opened wider and I could see the back of a white-shirted man. Suddenly I took a chance and dashed past to the storeroom door.

Once in the storeroom I did not waste time. I knew it to be futile, that I had no chance, but I went through the motions because that's the way it is.

Up on the stack of files, a quick clamber through the ceiling hole and out on to the roof where I crouched to brush off the plaster. On hands and knees I reached the front parapet facing Portland Place and cautiously peered over. To my left, well away from the corner, a car had crashed into one of the island parking meters. The tank had burst because I could smell the aftermath of a petrol fire and see a small scrabble of dying flame around the burnt-out hulk. What the second explosion had been I could not see but a spare can in the boot would have had a good effect. A police traffic car with its blue flasher going snuggled into the kerb while a couple of coppers stood by to warn passing motorists until the breakdown van came to collect the write-off. All nice and innocent-looking like everything Fairfax touched.

It was handy too, for one of the fuzz was almost certainly the beat copper neatly tucked round the wrong corner. I supposed the traffic car had put out the flames with its own equipment for I had not heard a fire tender. Well, that was that. I packed my gear into the umbrella and fastened the nylon to it. For the sake of Fairfax's man I still had to go through the motions. Creeping up to the Weymouth Street parapet I peered over, taking my time, sweeping my gaze into every shadowy corner as far as my vision could penetrate. Fairfax only employed the best, I reflected bitterly. Someone was down there but I could not see him.

Slipping the umbrella down on the rope to the lower roof I retained its end, for dropping it might send it snaking over the side of the lower building. It was awkward climbing over the parapet and locating the pipe and for a moment I thought I was not going to make it. I almost let go and what really made the cold sweat break out was the realisation that I had almost done it deliberately. I hoped I had more guts than to give up without some sort of a fight. Evidently I had for I found myself climbing down with my old precision. Just the same I was shaken.

As soon as I was on the low roof I ducked out of sight. I was certain that Fairfax's man must have seen me but would also expect me to take extra precaution in lowering myself into Weymouth Street, so he would expect some short delay. He was going to get one. I hated facing that solitary mews exit like the end of a short tunnel. It was against all normal rules to place myself in a hazardous position and the police were somewhere near the other corner.

Suddenly I was doing everything wrong. I ran silently up the mews without taking due caution but Fairfax's man would not wait for ever and then the heat would be on. Reaching the end I backed against the right-hand wall and sidled forward until I could see towards Portland Place. The police car must be just round the corner because I could see the blue reflection of its revolving light in the gloss of a solitary parked Daimler. So I turned in the opposite direction.

The umbrella was now a nuisance. I hung it on the nearest railings after stuffing the gear down my waistband, accepting that the only way I could survive was by crime. When I thought it safe I started to run, changing route, not really heading anywhere but getting distance between myself and the Legation. By now Fairfax's man would be biting his nails and the wheels would be turning.

I headed roughly south. On seeing the dull lights of the Charing Cross all-night Post Office I began to veer away, had second thoughts and headed towards them. It was now about 4 a.m., completely dark apart from street lamps and empty apart from the odd copper and prowl car which I had no difficulty in dodging. They weren't searching yet. Fairfax would assess the situation before moving and with what I carried he would have to move through the Special Branch. Once the Chinese squawked he would have no option and a good deal depended on how soon Li Tshien was discovered. But where could I go? All my contacts would be checked as a matter of routine; boarding houses, hotels, clubs would all come under the blanket.

Outside the Post Office I wondered if I was being really stupid. There was nowhere to go, nowhere to hide. I checked that I had sufficient change then went inside. Unbelievably there was a customer who looked a bit the worse for wear, having a mild altercation with a weary official. They glanced briefly my way. It was strange to see so large a place empty, like a derelict ship lost at sea, strange rustles and echoes. I tucked myself into the nearest phone booth. It wasn't the wisest of moves but wisdom had little part to play in what I did at the moment. The odds were so long that I kept getting little bursts of wanting to give myself up. I was tired, of course, but most of all disillusioned. I had offered loyalty and had been rewarded with treachery. So I'm simple. But it hurt.

Ringing Maggie was merely a desperate act to soften the blow for her and to give her a final goodbye. After tonight I did not doubt that her line would be tapped amongst others. Whilst I wasn't surprised at the length of time she took to answer, I found the waiting an eternity. It took me all my time not to keep looking through the glass at the two at the counter.

"Hell! Who is there?" Maggie, sleepy and irritated.

"Maggie, it's Willie, love." My heart was in my mouth. How was I going to explain?

"Willie! Is there something wrong?" Relief, happiness, sudden fear. It was all there. Blokes like me don't ring up at this hour with a confession of love. When I stumbled over my reply her voice became more urgent. "Willie, what's happened? Are you all right?"

"I'm all right, sweetie. I was just wondering how best to explain. It's not easy. Look . . ."

"Are you in trouble?" she cut in, sleep finally leaving her. Her anguish went through me like a burnt sword. I felt rotten. "Up to my neck. but don't worry. I'll be O.K."

"Oh God." It was a half cry, half moan. "Don't worry. Just like that. You ring me in the middle of the night to say you are in trouble but I'm not to worry. Oh Willie, how could you?"

"Maggie, listen." Could a man feel more wretched than this. "If I didn't think the world of you I wouldn't have rung. It may be a very long time before I can contact you again. I just wanted to explain, that's all, so that you won't get the wrong idea."

"But you haven't explained a thing." I had a quick vision of her by the phone, long-fingered hand running over sagging face as the nightmare began to catch up on her. In a broken, listless whisper she accused me: "You've done a job, haven't you?"

"Yes, but there's a difference. Listen to me. Tomorrow or the next day you'll read it in the papers. Just remember that it wasn't as it will seem. I didn't go in for money. Just remember that. The world won't believe me but it's important that you do, Maggie."

"Oh, Willie, Willie . . ." Her voice diminished to a strained whisper.

"I had to ring you, Maggie. I knew it would choke you, but I had to say goodbye, warn you not to believe all you read. Just tighten up those lips and kick me right out of your system." I even managed a short laugh. "You'll find it much easier to do than you think."

I heard her sighing very quietly. Then she said, "You'll need—some money."

How do you explain that you didn't break in for money but that it's stacked about you just the same. "I'll manage."

"Why can't you come here?" She was about to go round in circles, looking for alleys only to find each one blocked. Anyone in a trap did the same. I had. But I'd that much more time to face up to it.

"You know why. It's the first place they will look." This couldn't go on for it would deteriorate into a hopeless emotional mess. Feeling the biggest bastard on earth I said evenly, "Goodbye, Maggie. God bless you, sweetheart." Before I hung up I heard her try to force words but I never knew whether she finally got them out for the phone was on the hook.

Leaning against the side of the booth it was some moments before I realised where I was. Parting from Maggie was not new but there had never been one like this. Something had happened to me this time and it shook me to realise just how emotionally charged I was. There would never be anyone like her.

Self preservation tugged at me after a bit. I didn't much care about it just then but something kept prodding me to stir. I rang a few of the boys and got a mixed bag of replies. It's educational how cautiously a villain answers the phone in the middle of the night. Once they knew it was me I usually ended up the wrong side of a flow of invective but that was only because I had made them nervous and had awakened them at a lousy hour. It was taken for granted that I was in trouble. With only two exceptions they offered me shelter. Balls Up Balfour said I could come round right away and Bluie suggested I should spend the rest of the night with him. It wasn't what I wanted for I would be picked up at once. I needed a bolthole the fuzz didn't know about. I thanked them and gave up.

Well, that was that. I could not spend the whole night in the phone booth. I had no one else to ask. Nowhere to go for even the park benches would be searched. The official at the counter had dealt with his customer but I dare not even pass the time of day with him in case he remembered me. I was back in the isolation cell. As I stepped once more into the bleak, dark night I realised that I was carrying my prison around with me and that I had been ostracised from both visitors and cons. At last I knew what real loneliness meant.

9

The friendliness of a London night deserted me as if it too knew my fate. The streets suddenly were not just empty but desolate. Farther away lorries trundled down the Strand to Covent Garden, so I veered towards Leicester Square, not wanting to become involved in the activity of the fruit and vegetable market.

I stopped in a cinema doorway. The square in solitude expanded from the contraction of its daytime bustle; the little green park in the middle seemed to be breathing the crisp air, bright under the crystal drops of dew. There was one more person to try. A faint chance but curiosity might prompt him. Standing back while a prowl car went slowly past I slipped out and joined the shadows back to the Post Office. Now a few people were bunched inside and from the ready quips I assumed that they were from the market.

Checking the directory I rang Ray Lynch. The number buzzed for so long that I was on the point of giving up when he came on the line.

"Hello." Curiosity and anger mixed.

"Ray?"

"Yes. Who's that?" Undisguised annoyance. In the background I heard a woman's voice call plaintively, "For God's sake, who's calling at this time? Hang up, honey."

"It's me, Spider. Spider Scott."

"For Christ's sake, boyo, why the hell are you ringing up at this hour. I was fast asleep."

"I'm in trouble, Ray. I thought you might put me up for a day."

"You've done a job, have you? Listen, boyo, you must be mad to expect me to be an accessory. I daren't, Spider. I've a wife . . . what have you done?" Gradual weakfulness was producing the reporter as I had hoped it would.

"The Chinese Legation." He was going to know soon anyway.

"The *what*? You're kidding. Let me get some sleep."

I did not answer, banking on his deepening curiosity.

"Are you serious?" No trace of irritation or sleep now. The woman called out again and Ray's voice faded as he turned from the mouthpiece to tell her to shut up.

"Do you think I'd ring you at this time for a joke?"

"Look, you'd better come round straight away."

"You'll have to fetch me. I don't dare call a cab even if I could find one and it's too far to walk." He had a flat in Fulham.

"Christ! To hell with that, boyo." I heard him muttering with his hand partly over the mouthpiece and the woman shouted something I could not catch. Then he spoke to me again. "If I'm sticking my neck out this far I shall want a bloody good story, man."

"O.K.," I said. "But so far you've risked nothing. Officially there is no announcement that I've done a job."

He ignored this. "Where are you?"

I told him, heard him mumbling in annoyance, then he hung up without another word. It would have been easy for me to nick a car and drive to Ray Lynch's but that meant ditching the car near by and the police would be particularly interested in any stolen cars in the area tonight.

After a while I strolled down to Trafalgar Square; even the pigeons had not yet started fluttering. It was like a small concrete oasis with the still waters so dark that there was a completely false impression of their depth. Instead of a myriad of palms surrounding the pools they had concentrated into one vast symbol with Nelson at its head. What would it be like when they were all searching for me if I had nowhere to go? Hearing a distant car I began to head back to the Post Office, nervous, knowing that things could break at any moment. When they did, the place would crawl with cars and I could not understand the delay.

The car I had heard was not Ray's but he showed up soon after in an old grey Ford Consul, too light and noticeable for my liking. It came round the square all on its own and it was difficult to envisage the snarl up that would follow in just a few hours.

I kept out of sight until he coasted in past the Westminster Bank and the putty blob of his face peered out. I ran across the road as he began to brake and had the nearside door open before he had stopped. The sudden interior warmth made me shiver violently and I had not realised just how deeply the chill had bitten into me.

Ray looked across at me as he accelerated and I could see that his straggling hair was as he had left his bed. He wore an old overcoat with the collar turned up, the dull glow from the instrument panel added to his dissipated appearance. I could smell whisky and supposed that he had fortified himself against the unexpected night journey with a couple of stiff shots. "I must be mad," he said and gazed back at the road.

A little traffic was creeping about although it was only 5:30. For some time neither of us spoke but I was thinking furiously and so would he be. He fumbled for a cigarette and I helped him light it. At last he said, "You going to tell me about it, boyo?"

"Can't it wait till we get inside? I'm frozen." I wanted time to think.

And he suspected it. "Now don't play around with me, Spider, or it's out on your ear you go. I'm not sticking my neck out for nothing. A story or the street, boyo, as much as I love you." His cigarette played the puppet on his lower lip as he spoke and ash cascaded down his coat. His stubby fingers gripped the steering wheel firmly, the only real sign of his tension.

Treading warily I said, "You had better explain where your flat is and drop me off before we reach it."

He shot me a suspicious glance, always looking for the catch. "Why?"

"I want to case the area; know where I am if I have to make a break. And it's not fair to you if we arrive together. You can at least claim that you didn't bring me here."

He nodded grudgingly, not quite liking it but seeing the loophole for himself. "We live in a modern block," he said, giving me the address.

"Who is on the same floor? And are there animals?"

Another look, curious and still suspicious. "What difference can it make?"

"A lot when you're on the run. You know who to expect to bump into, who to avoid and when."

"Look, boyo, you're staying put in my flat until we sort it out. You're not budging." We were nearing Cromwell Road, passing an airline bus before he added, "Animals aren't allowed in the flats. There are only two others on our landing; an old girl opposite and a middle-aged couple farther down the corridor."

It was hellish risky but I decided that it would have to be the old girl.

"How long will you be?" he asked as an afterthought.

"Half an hour or so. It can save me grief later. You go straight in. Wait for me to give a sharp double rap on the door." Watching him closely I added, "Don't worry, if I'm a bit late."

He gave a disgruntled snort. "Don't worry about me worrying, boyo. The first sign of danger to me or mine and you're on your own." His restless eyes swept me briefly without compassion before he added, "We haven't known each other long enough to be understanding friends. Each wants something of the other and provided we have that we'll not upset each other. O.K.?"

"O.K." I had not expected him to fall over himself hiding me. I knew the risks better than he did. And I would have to give him some sort of story as near to the truth as possible. But first I must ditch the stuff I was carrying in my breast pocket.

He suddenly pulled up so sharply that I had to brace myself against the dashboard. I thought he must have changed his mind but instead he was making it up. As he leaned back, bouncing his fingers thoughtfully on the steering wheel, I noticed his pyjamas creeping out beneath his trousers.

"Round the corner is Ranelagh Gardens. It's the second block of flats along, the smaller lot. First floor." As I opened the door he added, "and don't forget, Spider boy, I want a good one."

I watched him drive off, foot on the clutch, a cloud of fumes hanging like a whirling apparition on the night air. It was still not six o'clock but a lot of people rose about this time. There were already lighted windows and there would soon be more. I had little time; perhaps not enough. Already I could hear more than one pair of footsteps as I hurried after the car. I found it badly parked outside the flats filling a gap in a long chain of cars, few covered, the remainder frosted over and glittered like diamanté.

My only hesitation was in making sure that the main lobby was clear, then I went up the wide carpeted stairs two at a time. Ray could not do too badly for the place was not a dump. Approaching the first floor landing I slowed, stopped and peered round the corner, Ray's flat was to my left, a plain door with a perpendicular letter box and the number above it. Further down the corridor was the second door. The door opposite Ray's was out of sight until I stepped forward.

Pressing my ear to the door I could hear nothing and was relieved to see that I needed only mica for entry unless it was bolted inside. Some flat dwellers feel secure because there are others around them. It's a mistake. I pressed the lock back as quietly as I could, hoping that she was a late riser. If Ray opened his door now I was done.

The catch gave and the door opened. The hall night light was insufficient so I had to risk my torch to avoid knocking anything over. Nipping in I put the lock on its catch and pushed the door shut. I stood listening, as usual aware that my own breathing was too heavy and tense. I hated working quickly and against all common sense like this. At this hour people are not so deeply asleep and it might not take much to wake her. I didn't want her screaming her head off then dying of a heart attack. Nor did I want Ray Lynch going through my things when I was asleep.

When I had controlled my own breathing I could hear the old girl snoring and in dismay realised that she slept with her bedroom door open. There is no reckoning with women; so many thought this was safer too. But at least I had located her; the door facing me to my right in the tiny hall. Immediately opposite was the only other door visible. Opening it I went in, quietly closing it behind me; the living room as I thought. I imagined a dinette and kitchen beyond it but I had no need to go farther. The close carpeting in the hall had reassured me and sure enough it was extended here.

I remember skirting a settee and was aware of the diaphanous glow of white net curtains over picture windows and of going behind an armchair for what I wanted. In one corner I knelt down, produced my jemmy and began to lift up the tacks. It did not take long to raise a flap of carpet and no time at all to slip the negative sandwiched between the letter and the print under the felt. I had only to tap the tacks back when I heard the old girl moving about and heard a switch depress. I could not see a suspicion of light anywhere; was she in the bathroom?

My frayed nerves were taking a beating for one night. I was rooted, wondering what best to do when a door opened and the light went on. It was becoming a habit and I prayed to God I would not have to clobber her—I didn't think I could. My mouth was desert dry, my neck wringing.

She must have been wearing carpet slippers for I could barely hear her. The armchair was covering me of course, and I would not be seen unless she actually came over to look. But I could not get out until she went and I had to tap the tacks back. The longer I took the more concerned Ray Lynch would become and the last thing I wanted was his ferreting about. All I could do was to stay still on my knees, head bent forward below the chair back, as if awaiting decapitation. The radio came on softly. Pop music. Then I could hear nothing more and risked a quick look round the chair. She had gone but a door was open at an angle to the windows and she had left the lights on, which meant she was coming back. Now or never. Hitting the tacks was now out of the question so I had to lean heavily on each one with the end of the jemmy hoping they would hold and not show. When I had finished I was not happy about it; a trained eye would see that the carpet had been raised.

How long would she be? The radio drowned any noise I made but it also drowned hers. I thought I heard a tap running. One second was just as risky as another. Standing up, I ran my foot round the lowered flap of carpet, trying to bed it down. Now I was playing in extra time and knew it. Skirting the armchair I took long strides towards the door. Light from the bedroom now streamed out into the hall. Taking the catch off slowly I allowed the lock to spring out against my fingers. On the landing I pulled the door behind me until the lock touched the metal inset. When I closed the door it would make a noise. Would she hear it and come chasing to the door?

By this time Ray would be wondering; there was no time left. Leaning across the corridor I rapped sharply twice on Ray's door and shut the old lady's at the same time. The click was unmistakable to me. If she had heard it I only hoped that Ray would respond first. He did and I pushed him into his own hall and quickly closed his door.

"What's the matter?" he asked, puzzled.

"You know what's the matter. I just don't want to hang around." The layout, I quickly saw, was the same as the old lady's. We went into the lounge. Ray now wore a thick woollen dressing gown over his pyjamas, a little frayed at the cuffs and one tassel missing; there was also a cigarette burn on the breast pocket. The furniture was good contemporary stuff. The air was thick with tobacco smoke and he was smoking now. So was the woman who appeared at the kitchen door. She eyed me at first with hostility then her expression became wooden as she leaned against the door jamb.

"Er—this is Spider Scott, Sal. You know I told you about him. This is my wife, Sally." They had been arguing about me; it was in the air and on their faces. Maybe I wasn't what she expected; she tried a smile and didn't quite make it. She too wore a dressing gown, blue nylon draped over a short nightdress by the way one lower leg peeped through. She touched her red hair subconsciously as if sorry now that she had not made more of it before appearing. She wore no make-up and although her skin was heavy she had once been very pretty. She was still attractive but had coarsened, her full lips downturned in a perpetual petulance of sulk. There were lines under eyes that were disconcertingly blue and, at the moment, hard and non-committal.

"Sal, we'd better talk, Spider and I. Do you think you . . ." She ignored him, still blatantly eyeing me and I was finding it difficult. "You look as if you need a hot drink."

"Sal . . ." But Ray's protest was cut short.

"Look at him. He's frozen stiff. I'll get you some coffee." She turned back before I could thank her. Ray gave me a shrug of apology but it was for himself; I needed the coffee.

"We can't talk in front of her. Wait till she's dressing."

It suited me. I was in no hurry but I felt a little better now that I had ditched the stuff. Ray lit a cigarette from the stub of the old one but his fingers were strangely free of nicotine and I noticed how carefully he held his cigarette. Was there a remnant of good habit in a man who years ago had been so neat and fastidious? Why had he let himself go? When I looked around more closely I noticed the same untidiness as Ray himself; scattered papers, an unwashed cup, badly arranged cushions suggesting that his wife was as bad as he.

Nodding to a chair opposite his own he sat eyeing me speculatively, impatient to question me but unwilling to do so with the kitchen door open. By his elbow was a half bottle of Scotch and a used glass; he poured some now half heartedly offering me one. I shook my head. At 7 a.m.? I couldn't make him out. Unshaven, in his shabby dressing gown and not too clean pyjamas, scruffy hair, pouched eyes, drinking whisky in quantity, he appeared almost derelict. Yet through his active eyes I could see his brain working at speed, undulled by the spirit, furtively anticipating the sort of story I might provide. He was a newspaper man, quick to scent; yet it struck me that there was more to his zeal than that; in the way he licked his lips and the tightness with which he held the glass there was a quiet desperation.

Sally entered holding a mug in one hand and a small sugar basin in the other. I noticed that she had applied a quick lick of make-up and that Ray had seen it too; he did not look too pleased. Feeling myself treading on eggshells it wasn't that easy to avert my gaze as she bent in front of me to put down the coffe while the front of her dressing gown flapped open. Ray was watching me, fingers on glass and cigarette momentarily frozen. Give me a cleverly alarmed window any day to this complication. With an effort of will I smiled at Ray, ignoring her until she straightened. "The cream's in," she said. "Help yourself to sugar." I said I would and thanked her. She went out and closed the door.

It would be silly to have ignored her existence, so I observed casually, "Pretty wife you have, Ray. The coffee is very welcome."

"Good. Now what about it, boyo. Why the Chinese Legation?" He seemed relieved that his wife had gone but maybe it was because he was anxious for his story. I stood up. "Er—will she be back for a bit?"

He shook his head confidently. "No. She'll get ready. You know how long they take."

"It was a tip-off," I said. To impress him and keep him quiet for a while, I took out my tools; jemmy, saws, Polo Ajax and detonators, plasticine and so on and laid them out on the settee. This removal made little difference to my appearance because my jacket was loose, but he must see that my pockets were bulging.

"Christ, boyo," he exclaimed, rising slowly. "Is that explosive?"

"Don't worry, it's quite safe."

He took a gulp at his drink, interested but not sidetracked and said, "Right. That's the how. Now what about the why?"

I grinned and winked and it took a lot out of me. "The usual reason." I started emptying my crammed pockets until they formed an impressive bundle on the settee.

"You mean to say you bust in for money?" He was disappointed, shaken.

"Is there a better reason?"

"The *Chinese Legation*? With the sort of precautions they take?" I tapped the pile of money. "How many private safes carry this sort of cash? Getting in was easy enough in spite of the alarms."

Ray was getting angry because he felt he had been cheated, this was not what he had expected. Draining his drink he poured another, his gaze darting around the implements, the money, and finally falling uncertainly on me. To give himself time he asked, "How much is there then?"

"I haven't counted it." I started to riffle through the notes wondering whether I had blocked him or whether he would come back at me. He went back to his chair, sipping his whisky and staring thoughtfully at me; he was too astute to accept it entirely.

"Four thousand dollars in hundreds, and twelve hundred pounds in fivers. All well used."

Ray did a quick calculation. "Say two thousand eight hundred pounds."

"Not bad for one night's work."

"With that sort of risk? You're kidding, boyo. Where does Sir Stuart Halliman come in?"

Why didn't I just tell him? Who was it had said that I had misplaced loyalties? Wasn't it Fairfax himself; so why should I bloody well protect *him*? I told myself that I was not; that in some odd way I was obeying an impulse to protect myself. I should never have come here.

"Sir Stuart Halliman?"

"You know who I mean."

"Of course I do, but I don't . . . Oh! Crikey, you're barmy. You mean he might have tried to use me? Me—a common creeper."

"Who better?" Ray was eyeing me suspiciously, then shrewdly as he thought of something. "Tell me, boyo. What possessed you to ring *me* for a billet?"

"Because they would immediately do the rounds of the boys I know. This is the only safe place."

"But you're talking as if they already know that it is *you* who did the job."

I had seen it coming. "I think they do. At least they will when they do a description check. My luck ran out when a car crashed into a parking meter in Portland Place.

The place crawled with coppers. I was out when I was seen but they won't forget me when news of this break-in comes from the Chinese."

"I see." He glared at the hand holding his drink, putting it under hypnosis, for it completely steadied. He was very still indeed, then he looked up bird-like, unhappy yet still with underlying persistence. "So you want me to be an accessory to an ordinary burglary?"

"I never pretended it was anything else."

"By implication you did when you mentioned the Chinese Legation."

"I'm sorry you took it that way. Look, you're right, Ray. I've no right to drag you in. I knew I'd been seen and I got windy." Finishing my coffee I rose. "I'll slip out."

"No you don't, boyo." A finger unwound from the glass and pointed at me.

"You stay here until I've made a few inquiries. If what you say is true they'll pick you up in no time." I knew then that he did not believe me. Rightly, he assumed that there was another factor and he was not willing to let it go easily. He also knew that had I anywhere else to go I would not be here. He went to the kitchen and returned with a transistor radio. I was shocked to see that it was almost eight o'clock. He switched on a moment before the news. It was the second item. "Last night, thieves broke into the Chinese Legation in Portland Place . . . one of the senior secretaries has been seriously injured and a spokesman for the Legation states that he is still unconscious. Large sums of money were stolen, together with secret documents which the spokesman said can only inflame the Chinese people and hamper those working for the true cause of peace. He went on to say that there are clear signs that British Intelligence forces are directly responsible for the break-in and that it is a disgraceful violation of diplomatic immunity and an act of war on the soil of the Chinese People's Republic. So far no one at the Foreign Office has been available for comment. By coincidence, there was an accident outside the Legation in which . . ."

Ray was staring blankly at me as the voice went on and then he cut it off in mid-sentence as he flipped the switch. In quiet anger he said, "You're quite an accomplished liar, Spider, I give you that. Secret documents and grievous bodily harm. Well, well. You forgot to tell me you nearly croaked someone." He was tense and worried. Suddenly he was sticking his neck out too far but his persistent curiosity came out on top. Accusing me was not kicking me out.

"You ought to know better," I chided. "Of course they are going to say that. Secret documents; I bet if I'd taken a Chinese newspaper they'd have said the same. Look, they've been caught napping, they're going to stir it up, aren't they?"

"Maybe." There was a strange brightness in his eyes, almost fanatical. "I've given you shelter and you're holding out. What else did you get?"

"Look, do you want to search me?"

"Yes," he said. "I do."

I stood up with arms raised in mock anger. "Then you had better get on with it."

Making no apology he searched me inexpertly but thoroughly. I smelled the whisky breath and watched his reddened eyes. When he stood back he gazed at me sullenly and said, "Now I know why you wanted me to go on ahead. Where have you ditched the stuff?"

"You must be raving mad. In the first place, the only stuff I should have ditched are my tools." I pointed vaguely to the settee. "Secondly, if I've nicked something for Sir Stuart Halliman what the hell would I have come here for? Why hide it?"

It was a good argument but he came back swiftly, giving something of himself away. "Holding out for more money, perhaps, boyo?"

I looked at him in disgust. "You know better than that. Is that the Ray Lynch who wrote an article about me when I last went to nick? What was it you wrote; 'A curiously honest man in almost every way except a strange weakness for crime.' I cherished those words."

Something flitted over his bloated face, a memory, a brief introspection. He sat down wearily, confused, frustrated and basically angry. Just as my instinct warns me on a job, so did his. He knew that there was something hidden and that he would have to go beyond me to find it.

"Look," I suggested again. "It would be better if I take my chances." But he waved his hand carelessly and ash flew off yet another cigarette.

"Forget it," he said. "You must expect me to look for a story. There's a lot that doesn't make sense, Spider. But leave it, for now. Anyway, I must get ready for the office." Finishing his drink he appeared none the worse for wear when he rose. He smiled a little, not very convincingly.

"When Sal and I have gone, cook yourself a breakfast. Stay here until we come back this evening."

"And then?"

"We'll have to see. Don't expect too much of me. The story you've told isn't much. Anyway you'll be safe for the day." He went off, leaving the door open. I sat there; but I wasn't wondering about Ray, I was remembering Li Tshien and how he had looked when I had left and the B.B.C. announcement that he was still unconscious. Oddly enough the Chinese had put out the complete truth as I knew it; it was an occasion where truth was infinitely better than the usual propaganda. I only hoped that Chummy would not die. If that happened God knows what I would do. Ray would have to hand me over for certain, story or no. Either way my prospects were so grim that I began to wonder why I had troubled to come.

They came into the room together. Shaved and dressed Ray appeared little tidier than before; his trousers needed pressing and there was a stain on the lapel of his jacket. His tie looked as if it had been tied without a mirror and his shoes needed polish. Sally was very different. Under the short fur coat she wore a beige suit with a skirt too short for her thirty or so years. Even though her legs were good still, it looked wrong. Her eyes were too heavily made up, lids vivid blue. But she was smart and cared for her clothes. They were an ill-assorted pair and I could see now that he was too short for her. She still gazed impassively at me but there was something there, perhaps in the way she held herself that was meant to reach me. I remained dead pan as they told me to make myself at home but not to answer the phone; they would be back about six unless anything special cropped up for Ray.

When they had gone I made myself some more coffee and explored the flat. One double bedroom, bed left unmade, large kitchen-cum-dining-room and bathroom. Nothing extraordinary but tidied up it would have been attractive. I stretched out on the settee, wondering, worrying, knowing that I could not last like this, that Ray would boot me out when he reached a dead end. Periodically I turned on the news.

As the morning wore on the Legation robbery adapted a different slant. The Foreign Office denied all knowledge and were appalled by the violation of the guaranteed sanctity of a Foreign Power in London. To back up their claim that they were not involved the police had now issued a description of a man they wanted to interview and it was a fair description of me.

So I had been absolutely right. I was the sap to appease the Chinese; they might not believe but they would have to be satisfied and the public would believe because most of them would not have the time or the interest to explore beyond the newspaper print. My brain was getting unaccustomed exercise; I was not used to delving into espionage and I don't think I was doing too well at it. Survival was the main thing. I had what Fairfax and the Chinese wanted; it was my only weapon and I must decide how best to use it if it could be used at all.

The next news mentioned that the condition of Li Tshien had worsened and that there was cause for concern. That got me off the sofa like I was catapulted. I was dead tired, but I could not sleep with this on my mind. I kept seeing his head hit the desk and hearing the crack. Suddenly the outside door opened and I leapt behind the lounge door, my heart thumping. It could not be Sally or Ray because it was only twelve-thirty. Yet I heard the front door quietly close and saw the lounge door open towards me. It was far too late to do anything about my tools which I had bundled on to the floor with the nylon tied round them. The door was pushed right back until one of my feet stopped it and whoever was there stood suddenly still in the doorway, obviously feeling the resistance.

10

Should I hit him or not? It was a measure of my condition that the thought flashed at random. Panic. Then I had a faint whiff of perfume and my legs weakened in relief.

"Come on, Spider," she said, as if I hid from her every day. Then she walked into the room. I could have killed her had I the strength. Her fur coat was on her arm and she draped it over an armchair as she went past, making no attempt to look back but knowing that I was watching her. I closed the door.

"You should have warned me you were coming back earlier. I might have hit you."

She looked back over her shoulder, smiling, her eyes challenging. "Ray would have been madly jealous had he known I intended to come home."

I sat in the empty armchair. "Why? He has nothing to fear from me."

Sally sank on to the settee, slipped off her jacket, revealing a thin, tight, fawn sleeveless jumper. She took time provocatively fluffing out her hair with calculated movement and crossed her legs, ensuring I got good value from them. "It's not you he's worried about, darling. It's me." The endearment was a tossaway as if she had once been in theatricals. Later I learned that she had.

"I don't understand." I understood only too well.

She eyed me brazenly. Now that Ray was absent she made it clear that she had made up her mind about me. I could not understand why she was so cheap, so disloyal to Ray.

"He's not exactly a find, is he?"

I did not answer, knowing that I would be implicated if I did. I wondered why she had married him and saw part of the reason when she suddenly got up, went to the sideboard and returned with a half bottle of gin, two glasses

105

and tonic water. Before sitting down, she produced two folded newspapers, tossing them over to me. I had made the headlines in both *The Standard* and *The News* lunch time editions. It was alarming to see it in banner headlines.

She went past me again to sit down, every move feline, designed, carefully enacted. She poured two drinks and passed one over. I put mine on the floor.

"Cheers." She relished a half glassful before focusing her very blue eyes on me once more. "You know why I came back?" She indicated the newspapers. "With that hanging over you I thought you might like some light relief."

"What do you mean by that?"

She stared, amused. "What do you think I mean by it. Don't be so bloody innocent, life's too short."

"I have a few basic rules which I find help me get along. One is I don't sleep with married women. It may be naïve but it keeps me free of complications."

Her glass stopped half way to her pursed lips. "Get *you.*" Then she laughed, throwing her head back and showing a good neckline. What was it that made both she and Ray so verging on the decadent. Did they do it to each other?

"Married?" Sally laughed again incredulously. "To him? Old tired Tim?"

"You didn't contradict him . . ."

"Oh no," she cut in, still smiling wickedly. "We must protect our image, mustn't we?" She gave me a long insolent look, half disbelieving what I had said. "Feel happier about it now?"

"My second rule," I observed coolly, "is never to do it on my own doorstep. Whatever he is to you he's giving me shelter. And whatever I am I can't abuse it. Perhaps some other time."

For a moment I thought she would throw the glass at me. She was unused to rebuff. "You bloody little crook," she said. "You sit there moralising while the whole blasted police force is searching for you. When you're inside with the long nights ahead of you you'll be sorry that you didn't take your chances."

She found solace in another gin, curled her legs under her and eventually gave me a broad wink. "Well, it'll be better for the waiting. Don't worry about Ray."

"Why do you two go on together?"

She sighed. "It's like a bad habit, difficult to break. There are times when we need each other."

106

I took a chance. "What happened to him? He used to be so different a few years ago."

She swung round to face me, careless how she did it. "Oh, he used to be quite the boy. He saw himself as a second Chapman Pincher. He was a good reporter; really good. But he suddenly got swollen headed and developed the notion that he could do it from bed with the bottle." Sally's expression softened as she reminisced, as though things might have been different. "When he was sent out reporting on projects, say some Goverment scheme or new enterprise, he would phone through a sentence or two of the official handout and prop up the bar with some of the others while the really ambitious ones went round with the officials learning something of what they were seeing. He thought he was lording it over them. Damned idiot didn't realise until it was too late."

"There's nothing wrong in being a reporter," I prompted.

"No. But he lost his big chance to someone else. There's a lot of difference between what he earns and what he would have got as a second Chapman Pincher. Those sort of chances don't come round too often. He started to drink. Then his wife left him. So he drank more. I guess he just lacked guts."

She turned to me almost viciously. "If you gave him that bloody story it could make all the difference, get him back on the tracks."

She was probably right, but there was a snag. "The story he wants from me is unprintable. A responsible news editor would not print it without checking and when he did they would clamp down, issue a 'D' notice or whatever they call it, and it would be completely unprovable. Ray would be even more frustrated."

"So there *is* something then."

I grinned at her. "I said the sort of story *he* wants. The one he thinks is there. 'Spider Scott—Master Spy'. Why did you join him?"

"Because I was a bloody failure and I needed a man," she said frankly. "At that time he had not yet sterilised himself with drink. We were good for each other. We could prop up a bar and talk of our failures like other people discuss their successes, until the tears dripped into our booze. Then we would go to bed and wake up realising that we were fit for no one but each other."

Her third large gin was making her morbid, but like Ray she was so besotted with the stuff there was little

107

visible effect. Suddenly she said, "If you don't make an afternoon of it I'll make it bloody impossible for you here."

"You already have," I said, rising. "I've decided to leave."

"Oh God, no," she cried, scrambling to her feet. "Look, you've got it all wrong. You owe Ray nothing. He's not doing it for you, don't you see. He's doing it for himself. If he finds nothing in it you're out, darling, right into the arms of the police." I knew it, but at least he had been honest about it.

"Oh, for God's sake sit down," she said desperately, pushing me back on to the settee. "If you're gone when he returns he'll blame me, anyway, and half kill me."

I had at least forced a shaky truce. I had to go for I knew that she would come back at me or in a fit of pique suggest to Ray that I had tried to molest her. But I wanted to hear what he had to say first. Taking me by surprise she leaned over and kissed me quickly. "Don't go. Not yet," she said hurriedly and I wondered what else I had unearthed between these two.

She prepared a lunch of eggs on toast and the taste of food raised my hunger. Afterwards she talked a little of her own life on the stage, how she had never quite made it. She had had the looks but not the talent. Reading between the lines she had probably spent most of her time on the casting couch, but a night in bed is no return for diminishing audiences and producers had seen the light. She could have done better than Ray but as she had pointed out, their combined weaknesses at least gave them the uncertain strength of the fusion of need.

Ray came in late and sullen. He greeted nobody but tossed the late editions of the evenings over to me before going straight to the whisky bottle with his coat still on. Something had gone wrong. As he poured, he glared at me as if I had personally arranged his downfall. Half his drink went in a gulp, then he tossed his topcoat on to the chair that had recently supported Sally's.

I scanned the papers. Now I had really made it. My full face photograph stared back at me with my name underneath. It was a police photograph; I appeared surly, awkward, but it could not be mistaken for anyone else. It was suggested that I might be dangerous. As it was designed to do, the police announcement that I might help them in their enquiries tamped down the ravings of the

Chinese. The British police were on the ball, already the suggestion that British Intelligence was involved was being overshadowed. The country was searching for the villain. I briefly wondered what the boys would make of it; probably think that I had blown my top. But it was a reflex thought, an escape for I was largely numbed.

The fact that I had been expecting it did not soften the blow. Whatever happened thtere was a distinct limit to the time I could spend here. There would be tremendous pressure on the police to produce me. Fairfax would want to know whether I had obtained the photograph and the letter, and would want to get his hand on them at the earliest possible moment.

And here was Ray harbouring the villain himself, a potential scoop of a lifetime and looking very sour about it all. He sat on the arm of a chair and swirled his drink restlessly round the glass as if challenging it to spill; his unconscious respect for the spirit kept it within the rim, then he swallowed hard. "Well, boyo," he said, "they've slung out a D notice on all extraneous matter regarding yourself."

"What's that then?" I pointed to my photograph.

"Well we can't keep the Chinese quiet and the rest is official handout but any titbits, any inside stuff like a story out of you will be sat on."

"Are they so strict?"

Ray shrugged, finished his drink. "They are since the last blow up. The present trend is to co-operate with police and official sources."

"So I'm no good to you then?"

"You weren't anyway, boyo, were you? Not exactly forthcoming. If I told my news editor that you were here he would demand that I got some sort of story that he might be able to use later and then that I should hand you over to the authorities."

"Why haven't you?" I asked quietly.

"You know bloody well why. You're sitting on *the* story, boyo, and I want it. I could produce one now from informed sources but it's not what I want. Damn you, Spider!" He got up and poured another drink. Sally had retreated to the kitchen and I could hear the clatter of plates.

"Ray, you have the only story I know," I lied. "If another one crops up later I'll see that you get it."

"Oh thanks a million."

"Look, if you'll bear with me for another few hours, I'll slip out before midnight."

"Where will you go?" It was half curiosity, half concern.

"I don't know, but that's not your problem."

"Wait. It could be." Ray came back to the chair arm and gazed at the floor. I suspected that his mind was working less untidily than his general appearance suggested. He ran his stubby fingers through his receding hair, his eyes bright with concentration. Slowly his fingers tightened round his glass and his puffed face came up towards mine, his gaze shrewd.

"I may be able to put you in touch with some people who can help you."

I gazed back at him suspiciously and during the silence Sally appeared in the open kitchen doorway, an oven glove in her hands; she was as puzzled as I.

"Why?" I asked.

"For Chrissake!" Ray glared at me but beneath his aggression was tension. "I make an offer to help and all you can say is why?"

"You told me yourself you're helping me for what's in it for you."

He shrugged, not quite spilling his drink and disposing of half of it as he realised how close he had come. "Later I'll get a story out of it. It won't be wasted. I'm not that much of a bastard that I'll hand you over to the police now. I've left it too late, should have done it at the outset. Meanwhile it's possible that I may have contacts who can help you get away, no more than that."

"Don't listen to him, Spider." Sally moved farther into the room.

"Shut up, you silly bitch." Ray glared back at her then looked sharply at me as if the first glimmering of suspicion that there might be something between us had struck him. Not slow to notice, Sally tossed her shoulders and flounced back into the kitchen.

"Look," Ray spread his hands, his eyes screwed. "It's just the seed of an idea, that's all. There's a bloke I know who may be able to get you out."

"Out of the country?"

"Yep."

"He's not likely to do it for love."

"Oh, he'll want something for it. But you've got money."

"Those jobs don't come cheaply. Is he bent?"

"Not in your terms. There can be no harm in talking to him."

"I don't know. It sounds odd."

"What's the matter with you?" Ray stood up, glass at safety level. "What's your alternative, boyo? The police? A life stretch? What possible harm can you come to compared with that? And the Chinese you nobbled doesn't seem too fit."

He was right but still I didn't like it. I needed to know more but before I could speak Ray added, "I don't even know if he's interested. I would have to ask him. And if he is you would have to sort it out between you, one way or the other."

I must have given him an old-fashioned look for he exploded, "Look boyo, I don't want you on my conscience. There's nothing in it for me."

"Since when have you performed acts of charity?" I deliberately goaded. "You made your position clear at the outset, now you've changed it."

Instead of being angry, he shrugged resignedly. "Take it or leave it."

Sally had quietly returned to the door and was eyeing me intently but if there was a message I missed it. Nevertheless she had reminded me that I could not stay here. "I suppose it would do no harm to meet him. Do I know him, or of him?"

"It's unlikely. After dinner I'll nip out to try to raise him." He looked at me from under lowered brows. "You don't have to look so damned suspicious. We newspaper boys know a lot of peculiar people."

"Me, for instance."

It took a little tension and distrust away and he smiled whimsically, his expression transforming into something wholly pleasant.

With a little time to spare while Sally prepared the dinner, Ray and I sank back into our chairs in a moody silence. I thumbed through the newspapers wondering how I could raise a question without him becoming suspicious. To pass the time I mentioned one or two news items on which he briefly commented but his mind was clearly anchored beyond this room. Then I saw what I wanted in the middle pages of *The Standard*: the Foreign Secretary was off to some conference with the Americans and Russians which it was thought involved the position of China—

amongst other things. As casually as I could, paper held well up, I asked,

"What do you think of this Foreign Secretary bloke of ours. I see he's off again." I could not see Ray's face but there was no suspicion in his tone as he offhandedly flung back, almost begrudgingly, "One of the best we've had." And then qualified it. "As politicians go."

Dare I? It seemed the right time. "I heard he's a queer," I said, turning the page.

"Christ, boyo. We all know that."

He meant, of course, that Fleet Street knew it. Still he had gleaned nothing. He laughed cynically, adding, "If we printed what we know about a good many public figures it would turn the public's stomach—apart from the laws of libel."

I wondered if he would remain so detached if he knew that the present Foreign Secretary had released a man from prison with whom he had had an affair. I was guessing but not wildly. I knew what prison was like—the gossip, and in these circumstances the possibility of a big mouth and blackmail. I wondered what sort of a job the man had been given. If the country got to know about this one it was anyone's guess what would happen. The old country would stink a good deal more in the opinion of its enemies and would have miserably failed its friends. The Chinese had known only too well what they had been sitting on. As I realised the H-bomb I was straddling, I imagined I could feel Ray's gaze boring through the newspapers. He had informed me what I wanted to know, and I seemed to have got away with it.

Dinner turned out to be some sort of hash Sally had scraped up. There wasn't much of it for habitually heavy drinkers don't usually eat much and I was left feeling hungry. But I was not complaining: it was hot and I had a temporary roof, a refuge at a time I could hardly expect one. Both of them seemed somewhat detached during the meal, both were preoccupied with their own thoughts but Sally was apt to occasionally let hers show in a way I found alarming. Whatever occupied Ray fortunately did so sufficiently for him to miss some of the dangerous glances she cast my way. Maggie would not have taken to her.

After dinner Ray slipped on an old Abercrombie and a greasy trilby, gave me a last thoughtful look, then said he was off to see his contact, that I was not to worry. As there was a perfectly good phone in the flat which he was clearly reluctant to use I was already worried but there was nothing that I could do about it. Time here was running out fast and there would never be anywhere else quite so safe.

While Sally washed up I slumped in the lounge. I should have helped but had no intention of being too near that questing body. Picking up the papers again I felt sick at the thought of what Dick and Maggie would think about it. Perhaps it was worse for Dick because of his colleagues. There was nothing that I could explain to him, nothing that would not sound false; a phone call would embarrass him, and I did not want him facing the choice of whether or not to report it. I could only hope that he would stick it out. As I sat there staring moodily into space I saw how quickly my conception of people the other side of the fence had been shaken in just a few hours. Sally finished her chores and joined me to make life more difficult. She sat opposite and was deliberately careless with her skirt. She never gave up but there was a wariness about her, as if she was not sure when Ray would return. I told myself that I would have to be a particular type of bastard to take advantage while Ray was out rooting for me, whatever his reasons.

"He's up to something, you know," asserted Sally, unable to believe that she had been rejected. I could see that she was trying to place me; was I sexless?—had other outlets—a freak?

"Does it matter?" I asked. "The whole country is looking for me."

"You might come to harm." But it was speculation, not concern. I laughed. "As soon as I walk out of that door I can come to harm. How doesn't really make much difference to me the way I'm placed."

"I could persuade him to keep you here for a few days. It could be cosy, give you time to think something out."

"Cosy. For him? Anyway you couldn't persuade him; he's too much to lose of the little he has left."

She bridled, thinking I meant her and instinctively plucked at her skirt hem without being too successful, Reaching for the gin bottle she began her evening stint. "How could it hurt him? I don't intend to leave him."

"It would if he knew of your little capers."

She tossed her hair back. "And who's going to tell him?"

"Drop it," I said, tired of the subject. There's nothing like the threat of losing personal freedom to cramp the

113

thought of sex. I wanted to think of escape, not of the inviting sensuous body opposite me.

The door key turned in the middle of the ensuing silence and we both jumped. I moved behind the lounge door from precautionary habit. Ray came in rubbing his cold hands. He had been out almost two hours. Dishevelled, he turned to face me. "There's a black Humber waiting for you downstairs, boyo," he said; just like that.

I stiffened. "Whose?"

Ray tried a reassuring smile that turned sick. "It's all right. You don't have to worry. He's not a policeman. Just sort it out between the two of you."

Sally, who knew him better, suddenly knocked back her drink and reached for the bottle, her hand shaking slightly. What did she suspect? I found myself trying to read two people I hardly knew. Twenty-four hours ago I would have taken them at face value. However innocent that may sound, that was the way of it. On cue Ray went for his own bottle and as he poured he spilled some of his precious spirit. So what played on *his* conscience. The silence was the fatal goodbye; the lowering of the coffin into the grave. And we all felt it.

"Does he have to go?" But Sally's appeal carried no conviction; we all knew the answer.

I began to pack my gear about me, my mind numb, unable to reach a conclusion. I had to walk out of the door, that I understood. I knew that outside the police and their allies were searching the country for me; at railway stations, ports and airports; in clubs, streets and the homes of any known contacts. Already they would have questioned Maggie and Dick, Balls Up, Bluie and others. But what else was there? What was Ray holding back? What was it that made him have difficulty in looking me in the eye?

Yet what could I do about it? It was the sort of chance I had to take for I had no alternative other than roaming the dangerous streets.

"Thanks, both," I said. "I think you know I won't mention your names if I'm caught."

Sally rose like someone out of a Greek tragedy, glass of poison held before her. I thought she was going to weep.

As I cautiously opened the door Ray called out, "Mind how you go, boyo. Good luck." Looking back I nodded. As I reached the stairs my stomach churned.

11

I went down the stairs quickly, hugging the sides from habit. It was nearly 11 p.m. The broad stretch of lighted foyer opened up below but I did not slacken. Hearing voices, I blew my nose as I crossed the hall and there is no better disguise for the few seconds I needed to gain the doors.

Outside it was crisp and wet. The rain had stopped but lights lanterned across the shiny road surfaces creeping into shelter. The Humber crouched immediately outside. My pace slackened considerably and I went down the stone steps to the street very slowly indeed. As yet I could see no one inside but as I approached, the front nearside door opened and I saw a hand quickly withdraw.

At the car I bent to see who was inside. A white blob under a trilby, white hands on steering wheel, the rest just shapeless shadow. "Jump in, Spider." An American; not too pronounced but unmistakable. I hesitated, wondering. There was a slight chuckle. "It's your choice, brother. No one is gonna make you." A good, cool, friendly voice, assured—and assurance was something I needed then. I climbed in and closed the door. The engine started at once and the car drew smoothly away.

I tried to get a better look at the driver but his hat was well pulled down and all I could see was a hooked nose; even the chin line was lost by an upturned collar. He drove with easy concentration. "Don't worry," he said. "You'll see me soon enough. The hat and collar routine is to hide me from any other guys who might know me." I could see him grinning. "After all, we're pulling a fast one. The British cops wouldn't appreciate it."

I nodded, then jumped as a voice from behind me asked, "Cigarette?"

Turning quickly I noticed this one was hatless and fair

haired but he had kept himself well out of sight. Now he was leaning on the seat back, square chin resting on forearm, hand loosely holding a packet of cigarettes towards me, one or two extended.

"No thanks."

He nodded and withdrew the packet, smiling politely then disappearing into the shadows. I could not help thinking that the cigarette offer had been made to let me know he was there, so that it was also a warning.

'My name is Joe and that's Hank in the back. You may as well have a handle for us."

The names were common enough to be worthless but as he said, it was something to call them by. "I'm Spider," I said facetiously. They laughed. Hank said, "I guess all England knows that by now. You're a very hot potato." His accent was much richer than Joe's, a Southern drawl. They obviously wanted to be friendly but like Ray, they were not doing it out of friendship. And they did not sound the gangster type.

All the time we weaved through the traffic, stopped at lights, caught up behind a bus or taxi I kept half an eye on where we went; the direction seemed to be north towards Highbury, Islington area. I could gain no impression about these two; they were not coppers, I was certain of that, but there was a suspicion of officialdom about them. If they were bent then I had not met two like them. So who and what were they?

Twice I saw a small Austin cruising on our tail, but being hunted sharpens perception and perhaps distorts it. Nearer to Highbury it disappeared. Joe showed no sign of having seen it. Lights flashed past. Occasionally I saw a copper or patrol car. Newspaper posters were on the subject. I was news, big news, seemingly the sole topic on the posters. It did not make me feel any better. Without taking his eyes off the road Joe said. "You've been seen in several places. Even Scotland." He chuckled. "It'll keep the cops busy." I was too numb to reply. So much for Fairfax and his straight-backed airs. I hoped he was worried sick.

The car drew off from Highbury Grove, taking one of the streets beside the green. Much quieter here and Joe pulled smoothly into the kerb outside a row of early Victorian terraced houses. We all waited by mutual consent until a young couple huddled past, then climbed out and mounted the steps to the front door. Joe in front, Hank behind me. Prisoner and escort. It made no difference.

Joe opened the door and, single file, we went in. The hall had a forty-watt bulb but it was enough to see the usual old style house; shabbily carpeted stairs leading straight up and a couple of brown-painted doors leading off the ground floor. It was the stairs for us, still Indian file, no word being spoken. We went up two flights then Joe produced his keys again and we entered a very large room. There was no shabbiness here but it was not my taste either. Very modern black leather armless settees and armchairs; white rugs, abstract paintings on salmon walls; large stereogram, television, an abundance of uniform occasional tables and a shiny cocktail cabinet which Joe promptly opened.

I gave my usual negative reply to the usual drinks question and as no one had asked me and to show just how independent I still was, I sat down, noticing that the blond stocky Hank had positioned himself by the door. He wore an American-styled English tweed two piece. His eyes were non-committal but his lips over his strong jaw line were toying with a smile—just to reassure me. His face was craggy, heavily-lined about the eyes, strong yet not un-friendly and he did his best to cover the door as if it was his favourite standing position.

Joe, on the other hand, was dark-haired and thin, fea-tures like untanned hide, hard and narrow and sharp. Now I could see that he was round-shouldered, held him-self badly in a slight stoop and had the habit of running the back of his bony hand under his chin as though one of them itched.

Suddenly I stood up, resigned to this meeting under semicaptivity. "Do you mind if I make myself com-fortable?" I started ditching the stuff from my waistband. As I dumped it I heard a click, which meant locks to me and turned to see Hank walking away from the door. So he had locked it. I didn't think it would be long before I found out why. Still, for the record I did not dump all my gear. Sitting down again, Hank now joined me, eyeing me through screwed-up lids with undisguised interest; he was powerful this one.

"Go ahead," said Joe belatedly; then over his shoulder, "You *sure* you won't have a drink, Spider?" All friendly American Christian name stuff. All together for a cosy chat. About what? I shook my head and Joe brought across what might have been well-iced bourbons. He sat opposite me, Hank to one side. I knew a technique when I saw one;

I'd suffered it enough at interrogation. And although I was convinced that these men were not the law I guessed another interrogation was opening up.

Unlike Ray, they did not need their drinks, they were merely props, something with which to divert attention if they needed to. Joe crossed his long legs and relaxed against the black leather, looking like a Red Indian, ill clad in a striped blue suit. I wondered at his ancestry and his very piercing dark eyes. His free hand was rubbing the stubble of his chin. "Cheers," he said, trying to be English as he raised his glass to comfort one and all.

I nodded. And waited. And spotted Hank watching me. Joe would do the talking, Hank would do the prodding.

"Now," observed Joe, trying the first difficult hurdle, unsure as yet of what made me tick. "The heat's on for you, right? Your only chance is to get out of the country?"

I nodded unwillingly. England was my home. Yet whichever way I viewed it I knew that he was right.

"Well then," he smiled, looking even more like a Red Indian in a gaunt, proud way. "We should have no difficulty in coming to terms. How much do you think what you took from the Chinese Legation is worth?"

Ever since we had entered the room I had been expecting it. I had a slight advantage; I was beginning to place them and mentally cursed Ray Lynch. But they could only know what Ray had told them. So I played it simple. "About three thousand pounds."

They exchanged glances and the silent Hank gave a faint nod.

"Three thousand," mused Joe, still rubbing chin on hand. "That's a lot of money, Spider."

"In dollars and sterling," I said.

"We'd have to see the goods," said Joe. "They may be worthless."

"The Chinese don't seem to think so," I suggested.

"No. True. On the other hand they might have bleated for the hell of it. Got it on you?"

"Of course," I said as I rose and took the money I had stolen and handed it over.

Joe thumbed through the notes then stared piercingly at me.

"What's the idea?"

"What do you mean?"

"This is all money. Where's the other stuff?"

"Of course it is. What did you expect"

"You're pulling our leg, Spider." It was a dangerous growl from Hank.

I turned. "What are you on about? Ray told me that you could get me out of the country; that it would cost me."

"So you hand it all over, just like that." Joe flapped the wad in the air and I could see a slow anger simmering as he hunched forward. Suddenly they were not friendly any more.

"Be your age," I said. "I'm in your manor, wanted, and there are two of you. You can take me any time you want, take all I have. By being open with you I hoped that you would be half-way to being reasonable. I'm expecting most of that back!"

Joe decided to give me the benefit of the doubt and the back of his hand came speculatively into action again; I wondered if he ever rubbed it sore. "Money was not what we had in mind, Spider. What else did you take?"

"What's Ray been telling you? Look," I exploded, "I'm just a bloody burglar. What do you think I took?"

Hank got up and produced a fistful of papers, dailies, evenings. My face stared like a zombie from the evenings, and to my dismay there was a photo of Maggie. Joe pointed to them. "In each of these the Chinese accuse you of stealing documents, right?"

"Not that again. First Ray, now you. You can't believe them, can you? You're Americans, you must know that. I'm a creeper and that's my haul. I didn't know it would blow up like this."

"We are not going entirely on what the Chinese say. We have other sources of information."

Fairfax would hardly tell them. And I was the only other one who knew. "Balls," I said.

The silence was like a current, flowing, sharp and petrifying. I had never seen two men go so still.

Then Joe gradually unlocked. He tossed the notes on to a chair and put down his glass. As he rubbed his long chin he eyed me balefully. "So you're gonna play the innocent." In restrained anger his accent was thicker. "You know that we can toss you straight into the can?"

"Anyone could. Anyone with the opportunity."

"Then what gives with you? Why play the sucker? Look," he said, both hands coming up pleadingly. "Let's not cross wires, huh? Maybe we started badly." He licked his lips and his bright gaze faltered and I realised that he had not expected snags. "We can get you out, right? But

119

it's not money we want. We have a shrewd idea of what you hoisted and we're willing to pay for it." He quickly looked at Hank for backing. "We are willing *to pay you*. Now do you understand?"

"Of course. And believe me I wish I had something to sell. But this is all twaddle about secret documents." While I spoke I wondered at my own motive for maintaining loyalty to a man who had betrayed me.

"We don't think so." Joe stood up. He might be thin but he would know a trick or two. "Undress, Spider."

I saw the chunky Hank rise. "Get stuffed," I said. Joe spread his hands. "Now look, feller, be reasonable. You said yourself that we can take you. Well, that's what we'll have to do if you're intent on being stupid."

I got ready to kick his shin if he came nearer then gave up the idea as Hank joined him with a snub-nosed .38 in his beefy hand. And Hank wasn't trying to smile any more. Their charm had been replaced with cold-blooded zeal. They did not like being made fools of.

Joe gave it one more throw. "Look, Spider, on security matters your government and ours play it very close together. This time they seem to be holding out on us. We're just curious, that's all. We've no intention of using it against them."

"How much is it worth?"

I could almost see him sigh his relief. A quick glance at Hank, then, "Not less than eight thousand dollars, not more than twelve, depending on what it is."

"That's a lot to pay for curiosity," I said, rising. Before his anger could move I started to strip.

They went through my clothes like the experts they were, using a powerful light on the hems of underwear and shirt. Nor did they forget my shoes and socks. Then I was treated to further indignities and I was examined as if I was secreting drugs in nick. They even combed my hair with a flea comb. They knew their onions but weren't too pleased at the end of it.

I dressed and sat down again. So did they. Joe actually reached for his drink and sipped at it; the prop had become medicinal. And they stared at me hostilely yet thoughtfully, as if by this alone they could penetrate my secret. I certainly wasn't telling two Americans the secret indiscretions of our Foreign Secretary, who by now was doing a bit of sweating himself, I suspected. Good. I had to suffer. And it would be *my* jail sentence. I was bound to finish there.

"May I have a drink now?" I suggested.

They did not answer, still giving me the silent stare. Then Joe made one of his observations. "The fact that you are holding out makes it the more interesting. You'll talk eventually, Spider."

"Torture? I didn't think you people went in for that."

"Listen," snarled Hank, and because he spoke so seldom it was more effective. "You're a two-bit hood the police would give their eyes for right now. You've embarrassed your own country. No one will shed tears if you're roughed up a little before we hand you over." Which was probably true, so I shut up. Then I went over to the drinks cabinet and poured myself a bourbon because there was no Scotch. I did not like bourbon but I needed the warmth and temporary strength it could give me. They made no attempt to interfere for they were mulling over the problem. Joe obviously made the decisions and his face had the ascetic quality of sharp intelligence, even so it seemed that he required the physical strength and automatic backing of Hank to finalise. Right now he probably wanted to talk it over with Hank but would not do so in front of me nor did he want to leave me.

"Would you like me to wait outside?" I asked facetiously. They glared woodenly. Let's face it, they had a problem; they could either beat it out of me or try to trick me. It depended on how important it was to them.

But while I was putting on the face, doing my own private bit of flag waving, I did not feel so cocky myself. Where was all this leading? Fairfax had sold me out. Ray wouldn't have handed me over for nothing. Could I survive from night to night like this? I knew that I could not. Everyone wanted a return. Soon I would be on my own, on the streets; watching shadows and running from those that moved. And it would not be long after that before I was running from those that did not move. I could not survive, not in winter because I could not even take the refuge the tramps took.

I sat down and looked at the two Americans who were now giving the matter due thought. More sanely, I suggested, "I have the money. Why not make the best of it? You say you can get me out—well I'll pay. That was always my idea." And what would I do when I was out? But I refused to dwell on it.

"We don't need your money." I could now see a red weal on the back of Joe's hand. He needed a shave. "Spider, we might up the price, appreciably. But we must have some inkling of what you took from the Chinese. God dammit, we know you haven't it on you so why are you worried?"

"Well, I'll tell you. I can't read Chinese so I put it all back. In the safe. I probably got their papers mixed up so they squawked."

"All right, have it the hard way." They both stood up.

"Look," I said hastily. "Why don't you talk it over in the next room?"

"We don't need to. And I don't think our lock will hold you. Right?"

"You can't tell. Some of these locks . . ." But Joe cut me short.

"And if the lock did hold you, why you're a pro, Spider. You'd simply hack out the door frame. Right?"

I did not reply. They had made up their minds. I rose rapidly.

"I'm sorry, feller, but you've only yourself to blame. If there was some other wa . . ." They began to close in and I let Hank have my bourbon straight in the eyes. It was a mistake. He came in like a tank with its visor down. Blindness did not stop him. He was on beam and gave me a swipe which I half rode but which nearly took my head off. I fell sideways over an armchair, dazed and in pain. I kept rolling from sheer instinct. Wobbling to my knees I saw a pair of blue clad legs and swayed as one of them drew back.

Trying to collect my senses I rolled again and swung my legs out to catch Joe off balance. I shakily reached my feet as I heard him crash. The room was swimming as if I was in a fish bowl being moved about. In the middle of the wavering bowl I saw Hank wiping the spirit from his eyes and trying to peer round for me at the same time. I was still too dazed to take advantage of Joe's position and he was up on his feet before I could move towards him.

His head was clear but his pride was hurt. He came at me like a scythe, a fast chopping movement that thumped my shoulder and momentarily paralysed my left arm. My knees began to go but I conjured that little extra and kneed him in the crotch as he grabbed me to make the final cut. As he jack-knifed I thumped him hard on the jaw, almost breaking my knuckles. Grabbing him as he began to fall

I thanked God he was skin and bone for I could see Hank advancing with his .38 drawn, and deadweight even Joe took some holding.

But I did hold him and kept him close to me as a shield from red-eyed angry Hank. Making a supreme effort I managed Joe with one hand and groped under his jacket with the other. Finding the harness I reached the butt and pulled it out. By slipping my gun hand under Joe's armpit I was able to increase my support of him at the same time aiming at Hank.

"Drop it, Hank." I sounded like one of them, but he got the message, realising that he would hit Joe if he fired. Yet he hesitated.

"I've nothing to lose, Hank. Everyone's after me and I face a life sentence. It wouldn't be any extra for snuffing you." He worked it out, saw logic and dropped his gun.

"Move back from it."

He wanted to get his bare hands on me but he moved. While he was still backing I dropped Joe in a heap and quickly scooped up the other gun, not moving my gaze from Hank's blazing sore eyes.

"Unlock the door, Hank, and leave the key in the lock." Hank wasn't arguing any more. His training was against him; he was far more certain than I was that I would fire. He unlocked the door and moved aside when I waved the gun. Backing on to the door I slipped out the key.

I made him move over to the far wall, then went to pick up my money from where Joe had tossed it. I also picked up one or two of my tools, leaving the nylon behind.

"Now I'm going out, Hank, and I'm locking the door behind me. If you rush the door while I'm still the other side of it I'll empty this gun at you."

He did not say anything. Backing to the door I opened it, slipped through, and quickly locked it. I ran down the stairs and was out on the porch in seconds. For some moments I stood there in shadow. They had not handled me too well; their blatant offer of money for a sell-out had been made without real knowledge of me. I was certainly no saint but I was not a traitor either; the old country still meant something to me, although I couldn't tell you why.

From under the portico I took in the wet, bleak scene; it was drizzling again and the lines of parked cars huddled for protection. I was back on the streets with nowhere to go and was reluctant to move. The weight of the gun in my hand made me realise that I was still holding it. In the

123

shadow I opened the cylinder and dropped the bullets then did the same with the other gun which I had stuffed in my pocket. Firearms had no part in my life of crime so I stepped forward and dropped both guns into the basement.

There was no one to turn to this time, so I took the steps to the street slowly. I suppose part of me was on the look-out but right then I did not care too much. I could try breaking into a church; might snatch a few hours' sleep if I could bear the cold. And then what about the next night—and the next?

With a full day's dark growth on my chin I must look a thug. I was grateful then for the indifferent street lighting. Turning up my collar against the rain, pushing my hands into my trouser pockets for a little warmth, I hugged the shadows and strolled slowly north. I was feeling sorry for myself but I reckoned I had good cause. What worried me most was the desperation I was feeling; I would have to eat and drink and that meant more stealing for I dare not show my face.

Hearing the suction of tyres on a wet road behind me, I pulled in as far as I could. Was it seeking parking space? Turning round, I could see its approaching black shape beyond the line of parked cars. There was no police light on top but it might be a Q car. When it passed a parking space I began to run for I knew that I had been seen. Behind me I heard the car accelerate slowly. As I lengthened my stride someone stepped from the shadow and put out a foot. I went flying, hitting the wet pavement and skidding along it on my face. The pain in my knees was worst, but someone saw to it that I did not suffer and tapped the back of my head with a blunt instrument.

Oblivion solved my problems for some time. During the black period I did not dream at all and in a way was robbed of its comfort for I knew nothing. It was when the darkness began to recede, light vacillating through my heavy, fluttering lids that my problems began. Hearing my own moans bore oral confirmation that the pain had returned; my knees, hands, face—and my head—were broken, by brain swelling through the cracks in agony. And I felt sick.

I had learned another language for I heard myself talking without understanding, then realised that there was another voice. But the realisation was thin, unconsciousness still almost complete. Recovery was something I tried to fight off with the return of feeling. Oblivion was what I needed but the will to discover was too strong. I struggled back feeling very sick indeed, vaguely wondering why I bothered.

I tried to feel my head but my arms would not move. This more than anything made me strive for consciousness. Anything that smacks of retardment or shackling immediately reminds me of nick and how I loathed it. So I fought back, trying to concentrate through the great agonising thump in my head. Before I finally came round I knew that my arms were tied behind me.

They had me in a basement. The rough brickwork came swinging into vision before all else. Then I smelled damp and eventually could see it staining the walls in dark undulating patches as I finally focused. A single bare bulb dangled on a dusty flex.

Two men loomed into sight. Always two of them, I thought. But not the same two.

12

I was weary, sick, and in great pain. Being bound to a chair in the middle of a filthy cellar did not raise my morale either. I was tired of being a tennis ball, passed from player to player especially when the players kept changing identity. And I was utterly tired of being used.

They approached slowly and with prison cunning I did not reveal that I had come fully to and let my head droop sideways. The way I felt it wasn't too difficult. I was catching on hourly to the fantastic situation I had landed myself in. These two looked the Russian equivalent of Joe and Hank.

There were differences; they were older for a start; late forties or early fifties; they appeared more experienced and had certainly fixed me from the outset. And there were similarities; the pudding-faced, thick-set one had not Hank's pleasant looks and needed only a cloth cap to appear the typical revolutionary, but he had the same bleak determination, and in the hard brown creviced eyes was utter ruthlessness; this man was harder than Hank, much harder, and he was not restricted by any reluctance to strike an Englishman. He had a way of quietly staring as if I was a specimen object and not a human being; he emptied me of hope. This man would respond only to his own impulses or an order from a superior.

The other man was obviously a higher official; well groomed, in a beautifully cut suit. But for his handsome, high-cheekboned Slavic face, he might have come up from his country estate. He was a grey man; clothes, thick waving hair, eyes like hard glazed early Chinese porcelain. Even his fine brows were grey and his tie which should have contained more contrast. But he was a gentleman to his manicured fingernails, if the definition is accepted as breeding and poise. Tall and elegant, a quiet hypnotic charm exuding as he neared me, a reserved smile playing with firm lips, eyes crinkled to reassure but the porcelain brightness untouched by its props.

I prickled, unable to take my eyes off him; he had a demanding presence and held his holdered cigarette in the Western fashion. Something about him chilled me through. Evil? That's how it reached me, veiled behind a compelling urbanity.

Whether it was accident or design I don't know, but already he had used a psychological weapon against me. To an old lag the space of the cellar represented possible freedom for I was planted right in the middle, but my pinioned arms and legs meant I would have to pay for it. This boy knew his stuff. I sat there, feeling trapped, frustrated and a bloody fool on exhibit.

Matey approached nearer and I was left with no illusions that he would have fitted in with the court of St. Petersburg at least as well as with his present masters. Cold efficiency would be his metier, his sources of direction immaterial.

"Good morning, Mr. Scott." A marked accent but complete fluency. "Let me apologise for your discomfort. I would rather untie you, especially a man who has suffered so much confinement, but your rather rugged treatment of the two unfortunate C.I.A. men led me to take reluctant precautions. Under any other circumstances I would naturally take your word that you would not attempt to escape." He smiled with complete conviction and this was his strength. Women would go for it if his interests leaned that way.

You polished bastard, I thought. Still simulating half awareness I wondered how he and Fairfax would react to one another. It would be interesting for their approach work was quite different. My mind must have wandered a bit for I suddenly heard words I did not catch, then I received a tremendous flat hander round the ear and crashed sideways with the chair on to the rough stone floor.

My ears had a high-pitched whine in them and my body was a series of private battles. I could not move even if I had the will, but someone, Pudding Face for his Highness would not spoil his manicure, roughly righted the chair with me slumped heavily in it. I don't know which of them had hit me, it had been so fast and unexpected.

"I trust that cleared your head?"

I gave up acting asleep.

"A useful remedy, the hard slap. Doctors will tell you. The delivery was purely medicinal and I can see that it has already worked. Good. Can you hear me clearly now?"

I nodded and glared balefully at him. That had settled it; they would get nothing out of me. Russian gits. I was angry but knew little about them or I would not have been so confident.

Matey smiled at me. "You look as if you would like to kill me, but you shouldn't, y'know. I want to help you and believe me, you are nothing without help; quite doomed."

I tried to loosen my wrists but gave up.

"Li Tshien is dying. You remember him? I am told that you smashed his head against the desk. There is also a complication, although it will make no difference ultimately to the poor man; it will, however, harden a judge's and a jury's heart against you—some of his smashed spectacles are embedded in his eyes. So he is blind, too."

I thought back desperately. I remembered the smashed glasses. My stomach heaved and I wanted to be sick. I had not smashed his head against the desk, but I would not get far denying it.

"There is nothing in the papers about that," but my voice did not sound my own.

"You mean the English papers? I can assure you that it is in all European newspapers, and the Chinese and our own. It does not read very well and the stigma on British Intelligence has never been worse."

"What have they got to do with it?"

"Oh, my dear fellow. Really. Sir Stuart Halliman must be exceedingly disturbed. But why did you do it? Did you belatedly realise that he would betray you? If you did you were right. We all know the crass hypocrisy of the English gentleman."

He was trying to trap me of course, hoping I would burst out in some kind of defence and thereby betray myself. It was clear that nobody but Fairfax and the Chinese knew for certain what had been in the box. The inclination was strong in me to retaliate but I held back with difficulty.

Matey was watching me intently behind his smile. "*We* would not betray you. We look after our people. Always. And they are well rewarded. Do you believe that?"

"Yes," I said, truthfully.

"Why do you believe it?"

"I can read."

"You are thinking of Blake and others? They are only

the obvious ones, Mr. Scott. Our success is based on complete honesty to those who help us. It is the only pattern for success. If I say that we will smuggle you out you can accept without question that that is precisely what we will do. We are very good at it." He raised his brows modestly but was not boasting. "You will be well looked after."

"I'm not a communist."

"That does not matter. We will find a good use for you. You have talent and attributes which we can use. We may not pay as much as the Americans but you would be safer. In any event, you would not want for anything."

"You are offering this for free?"

"If you help us."

"What am I supposed to do?"

This was the crunch. Very carefully he removed the stub of his cigarette, dropped it and ground it out with a precise movement. He blew carefully into the holder, wiped it and with a handkerchief inserted it into his breast pocket. I am certain that his mind was working in the same calculating way. His smile had gone and it made a chilling difference to his gaze. I was afraid when I stared back at him, but pride would not allow me to drop my gaze.

"I think you know well enough," he answered coldly. Now that the crisis had arisen he showed no pretence. "Let me have the documents you stole from the Chinese and I promise that you will have no further worries."

He was better at it than Joe and twice as deadly. His offer was probably genuine. I believed that they had kept their promises for the reasons he had given. Word gets around. It was tempting. Politics meant nothing to me; politicians had the gift of the gab, skins like rhinos and as much real ability. They were greedy, vain and useless. So what did it matter whether I was operating under the Russians or the British. I needed security. But was I the type ever to get it? I wanted to know more, and there was only one way of seeing how many faces Boris had.

"Everybody seems to think I stole documents because it was the Chinese Legation. You've searched me; you know what I stole. I wouldn't have the first idea of what documents to steal."

"If you were sent in for them you would have been briefed."

"Who the hell would send me in with a record like mine?"

"Mr. Scott, I have no time to argue, particularly with a

129

man who seems determined to secure his own downfall. Let us consider your position. The whole British police force is searching for you. Without our help they must find you. The Chinese have made such a fuss that you will get maximum penalty and soon the additional charge of murder will be made. Do you want our help or don't you?"

"Of course I want it."

"Then where are the documents? They are the price of your freedom."

"There aren't any. Not that I took, that is."

He looked much as Joe had done but in a more frightening way. When his charming smile left him it was like gazing at a death mask. Pudding Face stood by in a completely subservient position but I would hate to see him given his head. Boris was not staring at me to determine whether or not I spoke the truth. His mind would not have dwelt on it, he was accepting that I was lying because he decided a long time ago that everyone did under interrogation. What he was now deciding was what would most effectively make me change my mind.

"I was hoping," he said, "that you would be helpful without undue pressure. Voluntary co-operation is more valuable than the screaming confession of a tortured man. There are more refined ways of making you talk but they take time and of that we have precious little. However I have protected you so far from something you will now have to know."

Turning to Pudding Face (he called him Fyodor) he rattled off some Russian and the hatchet man ran out on the double. Matey walked up and down in front of me with his hands behind his back, not giving me a glance as if he was very sure of what he was doing and had no doubt at all of the outcome.

But the interlude offered me no hope. I began to see my earlier resolve as plain wishful thinking, and I was sick to the stomach at thought of Li Tshien. I could not remember about his eyes but I remembered well enough his deathly pallor.

Fyodor returned with an open cardboard box and gave it to Boris who promptly held it out for me to see. Inside were two .38 pistols which had a vaguely familiar look. He knew how to excite my nervous system all right. The guns were all too ominous.

"Do you recognise them, Mr. Scott?"

I began to sweat. He took a pencil from his pocket and

lifted one of the guns out by the trigger guard, dangling it under my nose. "Can you smell cordite? You should, they've been recently fired."

I could smell it all right and that wasn't all that smelled. You bloody bastards. I thought.

"We had been watching the house for some time. The C.I.A. can be very careless. It can be proved that you were there. Mr. Lynch of the *Daily Express* called earlier. Then our American friends left with him and returned with you. I don't think that Mr. Lynch would hold out for long under police pressure, do you?"

It was strange how he became more English as he neared his objective; his accent was now barely audible; his gestures more casual.

"What are you getting at?" I did not feel so good.

"The opportunity was too good to miss. We saw you discard the guns in the basement and drop the ammunition. It was a foolish thing to do in any circumstances. So we collected them ourselves. We found eight of the twelve rounds but they were more than adequate."

I had suddenly stepped into an icebox. I cannot recall a spasm of cold so intense as this one. I tried to stop the shudder but he could not have missed it for it hit me like a shock. And then he made me wait knowing that at last he had me on a piece of string. Dread addled my brain. It was all leading to a point where I had no choice left. Closing my eyes shut out his face but brought the horror of reality nearer and bloodied figures with hollowed eyes loomed up behind my lids. The pain I had felt before had gone, dramatically anaesthetised by a gripping fear. Before I had at least had a bizarre hope, now I had none.

Opening my eyes again, he was smiling, at last genuinely with a touch of sadistic pleasure. Fyodor still wore no expression at all. Matey stood with one hand holding the box and the other dangling the gun. He was rocking on his heels, well satisfied.

"It must be unusual," he taunted, "for the spider to be caught in his own web. You are quick to perceive. I give you full marks."

I held my tongue because only the ripest blasphemy entered my mind and it would be wasted on an atheist like him.

"You realise why I hold the gun like this?"

I realised but said nothing. He would keep it up now, pushing me all the way.

"Your fingerprints are all over it. And the other one, of course." He turned to Fyodor with a smile and I saw a flash of gold teeth.

"How would you like me to return these guns to the room where the two dead Americans still lie?"

"You cold-blooded Russian bastard," I yelled. "Why did you kill them?"

"But didn't I explain? An opportunity to blame someone else is all too rare. They were of no great importance, those two, not even to the Americans; they were of the lower order of the C.I.A. and they bungled the handling of you which I won't do, I can assure you. They did not really warrant killing but the chance to do it without taking blame was too tempting. You are an ugly killer. You blind people before they die and you shoot people dead. There is not a person in the world who will not believe these things once you are captured. Even the charming Miss Parsons will believe, because the weight of evidence will be so strong. Regardless of what it does to you it will certainly break her heart. It cannot be easy for a decent-minded girl to eradicate from her mind that she has been made love to by a triple killer. Imagine what that will do to her."

I did. I began to wonder how he knew about Maggie then remembered that a couple of newspapers had tried to interview her and had taken her photograph. I fervently hoped that she would do nothing silly. Boris, here, knew how to turn the knife in the wound all right. I rubbed my wrists raw struggling with those bonds. All I wanted to do was to get my hands round his neck and squeeze the life out of him. I struggled so hard that I crashed over on my side and only then did the real frustration taunt me. Tears of rage pricked my eyes because I could not get at them and they just watched impassively, doing nothing to help me up.

My temper began to abate as they knew it would and I could feel blood trickling on to my hands where I had seared my wrists with the rope.

"You're a very emotional man. I always understood the British to be level headed."

"You murdering bastard," I snarled.

He laughed unpleasantly. "You have it wrong. *You* are the murderer—you must learn to accept the idea. After all we have only anticipated the inevitable on the one hand and applied a little backing on the other."

As I began to cool off I felt drained. My spirit was at its

lowest. I was already in a bad enough fix before this bastard got hold of me. My pains returned slowly as if under the direct control of Boris. There were new ones in my arm and shoulder as I lay. "Can you get Fido to help me up?" A last sling of bravado.

"Is that how you see him? A dog? I don't think it will disturb him. You can stay there until I have some sense from you."

He looked taller from ground level and I could see how brightly polished his shoes were. At last I detected colour in him; he wore red socks. Well, that figured.

"What's the deal now?" I groaned.

"Once I have the documents I will dispose of these guns."

It was damned difficult eyeing him on my side so I stopped trying and spoke to the far damp patch on a level with my gaze. "What about getting me out?"

"That still stands. We will see that you will be beyond British justice."

There were two ways of taking that and in my present morbid state I did not like the sound of it.

"Are you going to kill me afterwards?"

He hesitated and obviously had not expected the direct question; I made the effort to gaze at his face but it did not help me.

"You deserve it. You have behaved idiotically. But no, you won't be killed if for no other reason than that bodies are not easily disposed of and I don't like hasty plans. If you were found dead other governments would then know that we or someone now held the documents."

"These documents aren't what you think."

"We will judge that. If the Chinese had them they should be interesting enough. But I see that you at last have the sense to admit their existence."

I stayed silent for a bit. It was the first time that I had admitted it to anyone, and I felt wretched. They had sprung the trap so tight that I was left no alternative. Also, Maggie had enough on her mind and I couldn't see Dick remaining in the force as the brother of a triple murderer. I had no illusions that Boris could and would make it stick. He was a professional, a hackneyed word these days, but he was one, every fibre of him. It was the only thing in him that I appreciated.

He spoke in Russian and Fido got me straightened without too much strain. I was glad to be upright but they had no intention of my getting too used to the idea.

"Where are they?"

I had a pang of resistance followed by hopelessness. They would get it from me in the end. "I hid them in someone's flat."

"Where?"

"Look," I said. "You can't go barging in on some old lady. It will frighten her to death and it won't do your image any good. I'll have to get them myself."

"Exactly where are they?"

Again I toyed briefly with the idea of lying to him, then I saw the gun box and realised it was useless; there was another reason—I was convinced that Boris never missed a lie. Like I sensed danger he had his own highly sensitive lie detector. He might miss the truth on occasion but never the lie. So I told him, hating myself and listening to my own voice with great humility. I did not want to know myself.

He listened carefully then mulled it over after passing the gun box back to Fido, who trotted off.

"I think you are right," he said finally. "You are a trained burglar, a good one to break in on the Chinese like that, so I accept that you get them back. While you are in her flat, however, we will not have our eye on you. That worries me."

I shivered as he fixed me with a special laser beam stare that went through me so that I felt it. "I'm only going because of the guns and what they can do to me and my friends. You'll still have those, so what are you worried about?"

"You've shown yourself to have misplaced loyalties."

"So I've been told. They won't help me now."

"No. But I intend to ensure that you are in no position to act foolishly. I'm going to see that you are robbed of some of your energy and strength. You must be slowed down. You're not a good risk."

I did not take too much heed of this. He was being ultra cautious. Fido came back and Boris gave him a quiet instruction to unfasten the bands holding me to the chair. My hands were still tied but I was now able shakily to stand up.

I stood swaying a bit, then I stretched to ease my limbs, breathing deeply. Fido hit me in the guts in the middle of my intake. My breath burst like a blow-out and I doubled in an agony that left me helpless and sagging on my knees.

The pain had all my concentration, my lungs were rasping, then a white hot carving knife went through them as he struck me with incredible force between the shoulder blades. The hatchet man was getting a reward for being a good dog.

Sprawled now on my face I was trying to retch, breathe and ease the pain at the same time. There was no retaliation I could give for it was taking everything I had not to flake out. If I had had any sense I would have let myself go, but I was cursed with a stubbornness that had got me into more trouble than not. That silly little Union Jack shot out of my head because I was not going to let a bloody Russian see me as chicken. For the same reason I would not cry out though God knows I wanted to as his boot nearly stove in my ribs.

Christ, I thought as the pain engulfed me so that I curled up like a hedgehog, if it goes on I won't be able to do the job. But the dog had to have his bone and I was punched and booted around that floor until the sheer agony of it made me wish I was dead. When I vomited I nearly choked myself and the excruciating pain in my straining guts made me throw up again. There was no way I could wipe my mouth and I wanted to beg them to unblock my nose and windpipe. But I said nothing, biting down a fantastic swelling hatred. In a few minutes I was sure I would lose consciousness.

Half choking I took what he had to give me only because I could avoid none of it. Not once did he touch my legs, arms or face. Pain beccame my sole sensation. Death, I thought blindly, would bring relief. Save my friends. Always my friends. I would be out of their way; no further embarrassment to them. Do them all a favour. Die. You're nearly there. Just let yourself slip. The pain will stop and they'll have to do their own burglary and might bodge it and get caught.

Then into my wondering mind came a floating vision of the old lady I had not even seen. If she got in the way they would kill her and it would be my fault. And if I died the bloody sadist who was kicking me to death would live to kill again. By Christ I'd fix him some day. Hold on, Spider. Hate him with everything you have. Concentrate on it. Hold that thread and you'll eventually get him.

Voices. Somewhere, but on a limbo. In Hell; it couldn't be the other place, not for Spider. A command. It must have been, it was sharp, cutting through space. Silence.

Void. The earth spinning, as I rolled away from it towards the sun, feeling its increasing heat all over me. Put the brakes on quick. Can't stop. Heat overwhelming. I'm on fire. I rolled and rolled, trying to back away from the tremendous heat until I realised that it was part of me. I *was* the sun. It was me. Red hot, holding the earth to my magnetism. The blue planet. But it wasn't. It was changing colour, yellow. Stationary. Strange shape. And glaring, glaring until it blinded me.

I opened my eyes more carefully. Still the glare but not so bad. It was nearer. No cloud. Dust layers and I could see the bright glow of the earth's centre glowing hot from this distance. I looked again. Very, very carefully, for even moving my lids sent spasms through me. God. The light bulb.

Had the kicking stopped? He had left me with a body of inflamed nerves, and grossly bruised muscles. On top of everything I had tremendous cramp in my arms and slowly realised that I was lying on top of them. Rolling sideways I was sick again. So sick that I did not want to move ever again. Convulsions ran through me. I wanted to stop them because each bore more pain. But I had no strength and was on my last ebb of resistance. They had timed it to the last vicious kick. Experts; professionals; bastards.

I heard a choking rasp and realised that I was gasping for air. Suddenly I was being lifted as if a crane had hooked me through the arm. When I realised that my arms were free I nearly wept with relief, would have done, but although I could not see them I knew they were there.

Someone was still holding my arms, then they let go and I crashed to the floor. I was left there, but I could use my hands now and after a while began to push myself up, first on to my knees where I stayed for some time, and finally, very shakily, on to my feet.

I stood swaying like a drunk, the coarse brick walls moving through mist. I was not sure whether I would not be better on the deck. The agony would be about the same. Deciding to stay where I was did not help me put a foot forward so I stood rooted, weaving like a reed in a wind, holding my guts with both hands.

Then came the voice; sharp, authoritative, loathsome.

"Come, dear fellow, you are not hurt that badly. Pull yourself together."

The stupid fool. He had let Fido go too far. I had no strength to answer.

"Walk."

He might have shouted, "By the right, quick march."

Taking a step I felt myself going, gasped in agony, righted myself, and took another as if I was in a bog. I tried opening my eyes wider. Things steadied a little. My breath was still rasping and belatedly I realised that I could now reach for a handkerchief so I wiped my nose and mouth and it did me good.

They were standing in front of me. Fido did not even look as if he had enjoyed himself. Maybe he was one of these freaks who got no satisfaction until the victim is screaming for mercy; maybe it made no difference anyway.

They were near but were not exactly risking life and limb. Had I reached out for them I would have fallen. I had not the strength of a baby. So this was slowing me down? I took another tottering pace like a child learning to walk with my arms raised for balance.

"We must hurry. We have not all night."

I focused on Boris and tried some words through gluey lips and a swollen tongue. "You think I can manage like this? You're mad. I couldn't rob a money-box."

"Walk round the room. Come now."

I suppose it was less painful than having the sadist at me again, but only marginally. I set out round the walls like a doubled up tortoise. I wanted to vomit again but there was nothing left and my empty stomach heaved against ruptured muscle until I had to lean against the wall. There was no question of playing against time. I knew that the job had to be done in darkness and I wanted it over. If it was left to the following night Boris might take it into his head to slow me down again. Anyway I wanted an end to the whole business; I wanted out and away from these shores where I could sit and lick my wounds. So for my own sake I set off round the cellar again, trying to make progress. I think Boris realised it for he kept quiet. One thing was for sure; I would not be able to break into a run and that was all he was worried about. Just the same, when I stared over at him I caught a quick speculative expression as he wondered whether for once he had miscalculated. At least he was concerned enough to explain:

"Your head, your legs and your arms are untouched. So you should be able to think and use your limbs. I'm sorry that it was necessary to beat you, but I'm prepared to take no risks. Drugs would have affected your whole body and I want your fingers and wits alive. Now we must hurry."

Have you ever tried using your limbs when your body is roughed up? Every step hits at the stomach, every arm movement tightens the pectoral and back muscles. Breathing was difficult. I gave it three more slow marches round the exercise yard, finding myself a very special isolation prisoner guarded by two screws who could teach our screws a thing or two. They would have the Mountbatten Committee on these boys in no time.

I was half dead but ready. Giving Boris a nod of acquiescence produced a black scarf from Fido and for a terrible moment I thought he was going to strangle me as he approached. Backing off, Boris called out to me that he would merely blindfold me and my relief made me realise that I no longer wanted to die. The regular masochist, that's me.

Between them they helped me up some worn stone steps, one on each arm. Although I could not see a thing through the thick scarf my sensitive feet detected the wear. Not that it helped at all. It was hard going up those steps and I gave the odd groan to remind Boris that he had overdone it. Certainly they were not rough in their handling of me now. They needed me.

We stopped on level ground; a key rattled in a lock; double mortice. But it was instinctive appreciation of a situation. I had no one to tell these little gems of wisdom and they would merely clutter my brain with a lot of other useless information. Still, it kept me in trim and told me that my mind was functioning again. . . .

Cold air suddenly blasted in, grasping my overheated body with icy tendrils that sent shudders through me. More steps, open on one side I detected, and leading to street level I guessed. Iron gate swinging back. Silence. Making sure the street was empty? Then I was bundled forward and gasped with pain as I was forced to bend to get into a car. Once in it was not too bad but I was cold and could not stop shivering. Car doors banged, someone got in beside me: nothing was said. No wasted words with these boys.

We moved off. During the first few minutes we took so many corners too fast that I was flung around until I howled at them to cut it out. I knew that they were trying to fox my directional sense but they did not have to be so stupid about it. Then the car slowed, my bandage was whipped off and I was not surprised to find myself sitting next to Fyodor.

138

It was all right for me to look now so I did not much bother. We were in suburban London and the streets were still empty and wet. I looked at my watch; almost three-thirty. I had left Joe's place I suppose about midnight. In three and a half hours flat these boys were well on the way to getting what they wanted.

Boris issued instructions from the driver's seat without looking round. "When you have the documents, return with Fyodor to the car. We will then keep to our part of the bargain. Oh, and I have arranged for some of my men to be strategically placed round the block of flats."

That was not what worried me for I would have expected it of him. Boris would write his own name down daily in case he caught himself lying. "What's this about Fido? I don't want him with me. I go into that flat alone."

"Oh no. Fyodor goes in with you."

13

This threw me. It was going to be bad enough without such a complication. "I'm not working with him breathing down my neck. The old girl sleeps with her bedroom door open; you're pushing your luck."

Boris was undisturbed. "Fyodor will silence her if she wakes. He can help, you see."

My body was not hot any more. The cold was like sudden camp. To my dismay when I looked out we were nearly there.

"I'm not doing a job worrying whether Fido here is going to croak the old girl and then pin yet another one on me. I'm not *that* much a bloody fool. I never work with anyone; take it or leave it."

I was not feeling brave; I was worried sick. Boris was quiet for a while and his preoccupation was apparent from the way he drove round the block of flats three times before gliding into a side street not too far away. The manoeuvre was partly observation of course but I knew that I had thrown him a bit. Slipping into a parking spot he pulled up and switched off his lights and engine. We sat there silent in the darkness while he made up his mind.

"All right," he said. "You go into the flat alone. Fyodor will wait outside the flat door."

I still did not like it but knew that was as far as he would go. "O.K." Getting out of the car was no more painful than getting in and my breath caught me like a skewer in the lungs. From Boris's standpoint the beating made good sense for they could have overtaken me with no trouble at all had I tried to run; the thought never crossed my mind for it took me all my time to cross the road. Fyodor padded along beside me and I suddenly realised that I had not heard him speak.

Not quite four o'clock; about the quietest hour of night

when sleep is at its deepest. Sleep? What was that? I had not had any time for two nights, though strangely I was far from it at this time. It was a simple enough job I had to do but underrating it could be disastrous; one good penetrating scream is more effective than a burglar alarm.

I did the blowing my nose routine as we crossed the lobby and Fyodor sported a well-pulled-down trilby making him more thug-like than ever. The porter was either making his tea or having a quiet doze somewhere, for my searching eyes couldn't find him. The stairs brought my stomach muscles into play and I suffered. The pain slowed me down and twice I had to stop. Now that his master was not in sight Fido's gaze showed that he regretted not doing a proper job on me. We reached the first floor and stopped.

Getting my breath I relaxed so that the worst pains ceased and took note of the two doors. I wondered if Sally and Ray slept with their respective bottles by their bed. Because of my condition Fyodor had carried my gear under his jacket and I now held my hand out for it. I only needed the jemmy, torch and the mica. He handed them over with reluctance and I briefly considered thumping his head with the jemmy. But apart from the fact that it would probably ruin the tool I've no doubt that he would use some fancy grip that would send me through the wall. When he tried to follow me to the old lady's door, though, I risked putting my hand on his chest to stop him. It was like trying to push a barrel of lead.

"One more step from you and I'll go back and tell Boris." He did not understand a whispered word but he got the message. For a few seconds I looked into the empty depths of his eyes then felt his pressure relax against me. He was not so dumb that he had not weighed it up. Frankly it made me nervous that he was there at all, he was too exposed.

Creeping to the old lady's door I opened it, heard her heavy breathing, then looked back at Fido. He was standing by the head of the stairs watching me. Resisting the temptation to give him the soldier's salute I went in softly, closing the door behind me.

Regular breathing came from the bedroom and I was glad that so far she had been spared the drama going on around her. With luck she would never know and it was better that she did not. A quick beam showed the lounge door closed so I crossed to open it. To block off sound I closed it behind me. Now I could use the torch more freely, provided I focused on the corner I needed. Behind the arm-chair I found the carpet as I had left it so I raised the half-bedded tacks with no trouble and flapped back the carpet.

There they were, the cause of all the trouble. The letter, the print and the negative. It was like finding them for the first time. The same fears hit me. My hand trembled; the print glistened animatedly in the torchlight. I was weak and in pain but that was not the cause of my tremor. How could I be any more certain that the Russians would keep their word than I had been of Fairfax when faced with these same documents.

My uncertainty was real. Boris did not trust me but he might consider it necessary to get me out as he had promised. Yet why should I trust any of them? They were all treacherous liars behind suave manners.

Finally it was not my fears that persuaded me. I stick to that to this day. It was the photograph of Britain's Foreign Secretary caught in a moment of weakness that obliterated all other facets of his character; that and the letter which must have caused an agony of mind for him to succumb to blackmail. Maybe I gave him too much credit. Perhaps I felt it as a national shame when in fact it might have meant little or nothing to him except now when he was again under threat but this time by people more ruthless than himself. Why the hell should I cover for him?

Kneeling in that corner, my fading torch lighting up the glossy print as if it were an obscene play being spotlighted on stage, my thoughts and fears were confused. Only of one thing was I increasingly certain. I could not let a bloody Russian see this—and then use it against my country, even though I represented nothing but its criminal element. To allow a Russian to see it was letting the lot of us down. I could not do it.

So what should I do? Burn them now? Fix the lot of them—myself included? No imagination was needed to guess at the sweet revenge Boris would mete out.

Automatically I gently tapped back the tacks then slipped the photos and letter in my inside pocket. Carefully, with the aid of the chair, I straightened, barely resisting a groan. I was not fit enough for profound thought but I had to make up my mind quickly with Russians outside and Fido keeping the keyhole warm. And where the hell was it all going to get me? Each step I took landed me deeper in it. For the first time since becoming involved with intelligence agents I began to think like them. Propping myself against the wall I allowed my mind to wander up the devious paths that Fairfax, Joe and Boris had followed. It was hard work for me for I was not used to conniving but the only way I might beat them would be by using their own methods. They were well practised and I was a beginner at this sort of conflict but I could try. I'd had enough of being their punch bag and had little more to lose. Each one I had encountered had pushed me further in the mire; as sweet a bunch of sadistic hypocrites as you could meet.

To get back to realities. I wondered whether Boris had men outside or was he bluffing. How could I get out without Fido knowing?

Carefully picking my way to the net curtains I pulled them aside to note French doors leading to the small balcony outside. I opened the doors, stepped on to the balcony, made sure the curtains were as I had found them, then closed the doors. The chill air got me again and I huddled back. The humps of other blocks and buildings reared up like a kid's brick game. The isolated early riser had switched on the odd light. Above me a baby bawled. But the streets were silent as yet. Where was Boris down there? And his men? Was Fido worrying yet?

Looking right and left I noticed that the nearest drain pipe was out of reach and the balconies were too far apart to cross from one to another. Remembering another dark night in another town when the police had almost got me, I glanced up to the balcony of the flat above forming a canopy over my head. With the body Fido had left me I was in no condition to try what I had in mind. Yet I had to if I was to survive. If my strength went or if I could not bear the agony then the drop to the pavement was enough to fix me for good.

I took some deep breaths to test the pain factor. Even that I had to do carefully. I would never make it. I considered Boris then the photograph and decided I would have to discover my weaknesses the hard way. So I went to the edge of the balcony to look down into the damp street, and its rugged line of wet car tops.

The easiest way would be near the wall so I stepped back, suctioned the wall with the flat of my hand and raised my knee to the top of the balcony rail. Had I been fit I would have put my foot on it but as it was the spasms gripped me. The only way I continued was by telling myself that I would get used to it, not notice the pain so much, as I forced on. In the sense that as I pulled myself on to my feet on top of the rail I nearly passed out, I suppose I was right. I toppled forward, overhanging the street at a dangerous angle, but my reflexes saved me and both hands now held desperately to the wall. Releasing one hand I reached up and with relief obtained purchase on the base of the upper balcony. Before the beating I would have pulled myself up with ease; now I had to find the least agonising position.

By now I had both feet on the top of the balcony rail and both hands gripped the balcony above me. I was stretched to the limit and not too comfortable The test would be when I pulled up and my back and stomach took the strain. Fido was probaby getting nervous and it was a good incentive although I dreaded moving. I braced myself. Get it over quickly.

I heaved with the full power of arms and shoulders and my feet left the balcony. The movement was quick, the agony acute, but I slung up one hand and got a grip on the top rail of the upper balcony. It had to be done in one movement, for I knew that I could not survive a second attempt. My arms did well. It was when I crooked one leg to obtain foot purchase that my body started to resist. Suddenly I was saturated with sweat and I began to tremble. I clung on with hands that were fast losing feeling. The back of my eyes began to burn as the blood pounded in my head and I thought I was blacking out.

Part of me went out for I don't remember too much except the sheer pulsing torture of it. Most of my actions must have been the instinct of survival, or plain cussedness. Whatever it was it worked. While I was unaware of working at all. Luck too came into it. My balance was right and I must have got my foot lodged first time. Conscious thought returned when I found myself doubled over the upper balcony, my feet outside, my dangling hands touching the floor. From there I literally dragged myself over while the moist salt blocked my eyes and trickled into my mouth.

For some time I lay on the concrete balcony in a huddle, listening to my breathing and unable to move. Victory is a good tonic; I had made it. Laughing a little light-heartedly I recalled in a sort of daze that the last time I had done this I had managed all the way to the roof. I got up and staggered. I had left the jemmy on the lower balcony because I could not carry it and cope. If the old lady had no more problem than wondering how it got there then she would survive. I doubted that Fido would try to break in; he probably would not know how without an axe. Finding the French doors latched I slipped through the mica and lifted the catch. Inside I gave it a couple of minutes. No sound. Shone the torch. All doors closed. I negotiated the furniture, noted the odd but explicit combination of a pipe and a pair of crumpled nylons on a low coffee table then passed into the hall and listened. Whoever was in the bedroom had been claimed by sleep or exhaustion for there was no sound. Leaving the flat I went wearily to the stairs and started to climb them. I was exhausted but the stairs were like an escalator compared with the balcony climb. At each landing I had to rest but I was also looking for something. I did not find it until the fifth floor and by this time I was in slow motion. There they were, the burglar's invitation cards; two bottles of milk and one newspaper.

Whoever lived there had been away only this day or was expected back this day; it was a bit late for the latter so I took a chance and let myself in. Stale air informed me that all windows were closed. No sound of breathing. One by one I silently tried the doors and with a discreet use of the torch established that the flat was empty. There was a chain on the front door so I put it on, knowing that I would have a little warning if someone came.

Searching the flat produced a few pointers. Articles in drawers, cosmetics on dressing table indicated a man and woman association; a letter revealed that they had gone away for two days to visit mother who was not expected to last. They were tidy people; the flat was spotless, too clean to expect a char. I help myself to cold meat and cheese from the fridge, some wholemeal bread and milk. I did not worry about leaving fingerprints for I did not think it mattered any more.

After that I relaxed on one of the two single beds to sort things out. I did not intend to sleep. I went out like a light.

I awoke cold, aching and in daylight. Sitting up quickly, pain shot through me and I slowed down. Shivering, I think it was the cold that woke me with the drop of metabolism. My head was pounding and I shakily went to the bathroom, found some aspirin and took three with water. I felt terrible yet I had slept for nine hours. It had been a stupid thing to do. Someone may have called, the occupiers might have returned. My original idea was to snitch a blanket and sleep on the roof.

The central heating had been switched off but I stopped the shivers by having a cold water wash and a painful shave with some kit my unknowing host had left behind. I did not remove my moustache. The time was now 2 p.m. Not wanting to leave in daylight I pushed my luck and decided to stay a little longer. I made some tea and never was a hot drink more welcome. Afterwards I washed up and put things back as I found them, tried on a couple of suits in the wardrobe, but found them much too small. I was still in a bad way but at least I was beginning to feel human.

By early evening I was becoming a little nervous knowing that I was pushing my luck by staying. It could not last. At six o'clock I was restless to go but wanted to contact Maggie and she would just about be home. I gave it a few more uneasy minutes expecting someone to come to the door at any minute. Back in the comfortable lounge I rang Maggie and waited breathlessly. The sense of guilt in my simple act was tremendous; my mouth went dry.

She answered, weariness and dejection seeping out in the offering of her number.

"Which number did you say?" I tried to keep the tremor from my voice not wanting anything to mar recognition. Her immediate hesitation told me enough. She made the mistake of sharply drawing her breath then she slowly repeated the number. I could feel the tension from where I stood. If someone was listening, would they detect it?

"I'm sorry," I said. "I've got the wrong number," and put the phone down.

Would she remember? It was an old prearranged distress call I had used on her many years ago. Was it fair to expect her to? It was a chance I was prepared to take. I listened at the front door before opening it and slipped through on to the empty landing. On my slow way down the stairs I wondered if Boris was still around with his merry men or whether he had given up the ghost. I reasoned two ways; that as I had disappeared so completely he would expect that I had fled; two that if I had not fled I would hardly be stupid enough to use the front door. I decided to be stupid.

My handkerchief act across the hall got me through the doors and out on to a fairly crowded street. My only disguise was a two-day growth on my lip; it wasn't much.

It was a long hike from Fulham to Maggie's drum and I had no intention of making it. Boris had put back most of my belongings except the two thousand eight hundred I had taken from the Chinese but I was in no condition to be angry about it.

It was a strange unnerving experience walking the streets with so many people on them, almost all of them having seen my face in a newspaper or on television. So I kept to the inside pavement, dabbing at my nose with my handkerchief when I thought it prudent. Eventually I called a taxi, giving the address behind the same prop and getting into the cab out of his sight almost immediately. Boldness sometimes pays but taxi drivers are not idiots and most of them keen observers. I sat directly behind him so that he would have to screw his head off to see me.

Before we reached Notting Hill I assessed the fare, added to it, told him to pull up and passed his money through the opened glass panel behind the seat. While he was counting it I was out and away, the crowds much thicker here. Walking to the nearest cinema I paid, handkerchief still up while I had a fit of coughing, and went in. I sat through three hours of films without really seeing a thing. If the taxi driver had recognised me and the fuzz had expected me at Maggie's then they would have expected me some time ago. It was hard on Maggie but I was hoping that she would understand.

I came out just before the crowd. The streets had thinned considerably. I trod more warily now as I neared Maggie's place. Sticking my head into this noose could not be worse than those I had so far survived. Back to shadow hugging, crossing when I spotted a copper, changing direction at the approach of a prowl car. There was an outside chance that they may have finished with Maggie, that they would not expect me to leave it so late to go to her. There was also a matter of routine precautions. Coppers are not fools and Dartmoor is full enough to prove it.

The nearer to Maggie's the more I used the back doubles. Fortunately the block was stuck off the main road but that gave the law a better chance for observation. Entering the long street which contained the flats farther down I had the unmistakable warning of coppers.

The street was not well lit but I was not the invisible man either. There were two entrances and the fire escapes were round the back but if one was watched they all would be. Difficult. Over each entrance was a nice big light so that residents would not trip over the steps. Stepping back in shadow my radar told me not to go farther.

It was late but not sufficiently late for the streets to be empty. A good half of the flat lights were still on. A patrol car turned a corner and started cruising along nice and slowly so I took to the nearest portico. After it had passed I ventured out to see it stop on the opposite side to the flats. A man was leaning over talking to the driver's mate from the pavement. So they were still at it. My word, Fairfax wanted me badly. Yet I could not let Maggie down now and there was another reason.

I had to get in. Climbing would not help me this time even had I been fit enough. And the place was obviously crawling with coppers. Maggie's flat was on the third floor in a side street so I could not tell whether or not she was up. I should have put a bit more thought into it while in the cinema. What would Fairfax do? Boris? I walked slowly away from the flats and down the usual line of parked cars. I had to walk some way and it took two cars to provide me. And I had to be very, very careful with the torch.

A Morris 1100 is an easy car to open. Slip a piece of mica or a penknife down the straight side of the louvre and you'll knock down the catch. With the louvre open slip your hand through and open the door. I nicked an umbrella, a hat, a raincoat and a seat cushion. By this time I was some distance from the flats. In a doorway I loosened my jacket and stuffed the cushion down my back. Trying on the raincoat almost split it but by leaving it unbuttoned, a necessity because I could not make it meet across my chest, it was at least bearable in spite of tightness under the armpits. Having a normal sized head I was luckier with the hat.

With furled umbrella I set off. A stoop took away my height and the cushion made me a semi-hunchback. The hat hid my hair and shadowed my features. The umbrella was a prop but it was well furled and gave dignity—and a weapon if I needed one. The raincoat fitted badly but it was a good one and I hoped the whole effect would be rather eccentric.

Eccentrics do not hurry, at least that was how I saw it. That was the hardest part, toddling along, tapping my umbrella like a blind man for I could not swing it with my stoop. When the flats loomed up again I needed all my nerve. I had evaded the fuzz often enough but I had been fit and fast and I had been going away from them. Never had I tried to dodge them by walking straight at them. The police car had gone.

The greatest difficulty was in keeping my pace regular, to resist the almost overwhelming urge to run. When I had my copper on beam I crossed the road unhurriedly, knowing that I was now under surveillance by at least one pair of eyes. The block loomed up but I had my head down as part of my stoop. Strangely enough my position eased my stomach pain.

Reaching the block I plodded on. There were probably two of them this side and as the street was at the moment empty, they would be watching me with interest. The first entrance came in sight and I hoped I had sufficient bottle to go through with it. Deliberately I went past the first entrance and it took all the nerve I had. I was not proving something to myself or being stupid; I merely saw it as insurance. If they were not already on to me my action would help to throw them.

But the space between the two entrances was the longest walk of my life. The hair on the nape of my neck prickled all the way as if someone was aiming at my back with a rifle. At the second entrance I turned without change of pace and plodded past the strip of lawn to the open doors at the head of the stone steps. My mind was so much on the eyes boring into me from across the road that I tripped over one of the steps. I did not fall, but it shook me, reminding me of every muscle. Turning round slowly I tapped the step with my umbrella, upbraiding it as an eccentric might. Then I passed into the hall, under the glare of lights.

I should have taken the lift; it would be the natural thing to do. Yet I had a great fear that someone else might get in from the first or second floors and my feeble disguise would not stand close scrutiny. So I took to the stairs. An eccentric might well have done but it was unikely that someone as seemingly handicapped as I was would do so. I knew it; I made my decision.

Stairs were becoming part of my life and I had learned to take them slowly. There had been at least two people in the hall as I crossed it but they had been shapes on the fringe of my vision and I had not turned to look. Reaching the third floor without incident, I rested for a while against the wall; I wanted to be breathing normally when I rang Maggie's bell. Now I was here I had different fears; afraid

149

of her and what I had done to her. Had I the right to take for granted that she would want to see me? I was dead nervous when I rang the bell.

She opened the door almost immediately. We stood staring at each other for several seconds and I felt the biggest bastard on earth when I saw the lines of anxiety etched on her face in only two days. We clasped each other tight and silently and I knew that it was still the same between us. Taking my hand, Maggie closed the door.

A little life had returned to her face but she still looked drained; there were no tears and I was left with the impression that she had already cried herself dry.

"You're still dressed," I said, as we sat clasping each other as though expecting to be torn apart at any moment and that was the size of it.

"Of course. When you telephoned I knew that you would come."

Dear Maggie. I told her exactly what had happened, leaving out the violence. It was important that she knew and I did it to sustain her. There was little time. "I have some clothes here, Maggie. These I am wearing have been too well described."

She went to the bedroom and came back with fresh slacks, a sports coat, underwear, socks and a shirt.

"Take your shoes off, Willie. I'll clean them while you change. Would you like a bath?"

"Wouldn't I half but it's too risky. I mustn't be caught with my pants down."

I was already stripping fast, not thinking, so that when she cried out, "Oh God, look at you," it startled me. "Look at your body," she cried in anguish.

I had not seen it myself. Looking down, it shook me a bit, but my thoughtlessness needed quick covering. I grinned. "I'd be all right in a multi-racial society."

Maggie picked up my shoes and hurried from the room, not trusting herself to speak. While I finished changing I thought about the police. Maggie had already checked a few times with the light out and had seen no sign of extra cars and men arriving. They would have been here by now had they recognised me. She had told me about their constant visits and the tremendous harassing she had suffered from all sorts of people, some of whom sounded like Fairfax's men.

She returned with the shoes and I slipped into them. We had not yet faced reality but I could see it coming when she sat opposite me. When she adopted her probing pose I was always uneasy.

"What happens next?" Maggie was good at ferreting my lies so I had to be careful. Since I had decided to think like those other conniving so-and-so's I took a bit of practice and talked round it.

"I have some sort of plan," I replied. "If I go on as I am it's only a matter of time before I'm picked up. I know I can't last, Maggie, but please believe in me for a little longer. How's Dick taking it?"

"Not very well. He feels—let down. He's talking of resigning. He worshipped you, you know that."

The past tense did not escape me. I felt rotten yet reminded myself that a good part of the reason for the fix I was in was due to trying to help my brother. When the chips are down people can be bloody self-centred. Except Maggie. Her loyalty and love had not changed, but I had expected Dick to have more faith.

"Don't worry about it, Willie. He'll come round." Her hand squeezed mine and it made up for a lot.

"Whatever happens don't let him resign," I pleaded. "Don't tell him we've met. Don't compromise him, but try to persuade him to hold out a little longer. I know how it must be, the side glances from his mates, but try to stop him resigning."

"I already have." She rose and looked sadly down at me, "I suppose you're off again? Did you come—just for the clothes?"

I nodded. "But more important for Balfour's address. I can't remember it and I know it's not under that name in the telephone book." It was difficult to explain without hurting her. "You know I wouldn't call to see you, Maggie, I wouldn't put you in that sort of danger if it could be avoided. There is just a very very faint ray of hope but to exploit it I must be mobile and that means different clothes."

"Your moustache looks terrible," she said, trying to remain composed. "They said on television you might try to grow one."

"Oh, hell."

"Hold on, I've something that might help you." While Maggie was gone I transferred the photo and letter to my clean jacket. She had not seen them nor had I explained the details of the cause of all the trouble; she had enough on her mind without national secrets.

When Maggie came back into the room she was blonde. It took me by surprise. The transformation was so marked that at first I thought another girl had sprung out on me. She whipped it off and I was left floundering at the remarkable change.

"Try it on," she said.

"Wear a girl's wig? Me?" Taking it from her I must have stared at it in horror for she laughed briefly and it was good. God, if only things were different.

The cut of the hair was what I call chopped; a razor cut I think they call it, but still clearly for a woman. She read my thoughts.

"I can trim it. Put it on."

It was a strange feeling for me. There were them and there were us. Suddenly I was becoming one of them and I did not like it much—even though long hair was the rage with the boys. It did not fit.

"Come here." Maggie fiddled about with it on my head and finally taking it off carefully, snipped up the back. "Try it again, but pull it on carefully or it might split up the cut."

It went on nice and tightly. I looked at myself in a mirror. Blimey. I never thought I'd see the day. But it was good, if damned effeminate. When I turned round Maggie had produced a dummy head which she fitted the wig over and went to work with the scissors. "I'll make it look more like a man," she explained. "Put these on." She handed me a pair of large-framed spectacles. Putting them on I felt one side give as the hinge went but it did not fall away. "I've broken them."

She looked up. "Never mind, they'll hold for as long as you need them. Can you see all right?"

"A bit fuzzed but they'll do."

When she had finished the wig I was no more comfortable about it but I certainly accepted its possibilities. I shaved off my moustache, because of its contrasting darkness, with the kit I kept at Maggie's.

"You look quite different," she said with obvious satisfaction. "Nothing like your photograph or description."

We were in a state of semi-elation when the door was knocked and wiped the excitement straight off our faces, freezing us solid. The silence was so complete that the clock sounded like a metronome. Then another discreet knock that puzzled me. I signalled Maggie.

She went to the door. "Who is it?" she called.

"Tell Mr. Scott that if he does not act sensibly I will inform the police that he is here. Within seconds the building will be surrounded."

Boris. I had underestimated the bastard. I stared at Maggie in despair.

14

There was little time to think. Boris would not break in; it was too risky; too much adverse publicity in the offing. But he would anonymously call the police out of sheer vindictiveness if he did not get what he wanted. I mimed instructions to Maggie.

"Mr. Scott has not been here for days. If you don't go away I'll call the police, whoever you are." Maggie was still close to the door.

I could imagine Boris's expression of disbelief. "Miss Parsons, don't waste time. I followed him here, I congratulate you, Mr. Scott, on your impromptu disguise. Ingenious. Unfortunately I saw you adopt it."

He was speaking close to the wood in order not to arouse others.

"What shall we do?" Maggie silently mouthed at me. Personally, I was for letting him in and clobbering him. Then what would we do with him? It would not be fair to Maggie. I really needed time to talk it over with her, to discover the alternatives. Boris knew it too; did any man know more completely the machinations of a desperate human mind when faced with one of his ultimatums.

"You have sixty seconds from now, Mr. Scott. Hardly time to leave the building, I think. And you cannot move too fast, can you?"

I shrugged helplessly at Maggie. "I'm coming out, Boris," I called. "You'll have to extend your time limit, I'm only half dressed."

"Fifty-two seconds."

Giving Maggie a sudden savage kiss, I pulled open the door before she could protest. Boris was smiling quietly in triumph as he stood leaning casually against the wall. His assurance faltered when he saw the change in me. Fyodor stood like a statue on a plinth mislaid halfway down the corridor.

Boris raised his grey homburg at Maggie and turned on his plastic charm. "Good evening, miss. I am sorry to disturb you at this hour but Mr. Scott and I entered into an agreement."

Stepping out into the corridor I turned to speak to Maggie but she had rushed back into the room. Meanwhile Fyodor came up behind me and we dropped into the prisoner and escort routine again. Then Maggie was back in the doorway, her face deathly white. "The police are here," she announced almost inaudibly. Boris frowned and I was, startled. We all stood there in silence, then Boris snapped; "You mean police reinforcements?"

Maggie pointed helplessly to the window behind her. "Car loads of them."

Both Boris and I dashed past her into the room to stand either side of the window. A common enemy had temporarily drawn us into reluctant liaison; it would be a great embarrassment to him if he was stopped or held by the police. Diplomatic privilege would protect him, but not against his superiors or if the Foreign Office requested his withdrawal.

"Maggie," I hooked my arm at her. "Stand in front of me here then pull the edge of the curtain back slowly."

Standing behind her as if to remain out of vision, I peered over her shoulder until my lips were touching her ear. Below us, several cars had pulled up. No flashers were beaming but the unmistakable exodus of uniformed police could not be missed. They were surrounding the entire building. A mouse would not escape. In my softest voice I whispered. "As we go down the stairs, thump Fido over the head with a mallet. He's the one outside." My arm was round her waist and she gripped it tightly. I had asked a lot of her but I did not think I was endangering her at this stage.

Boris said, "Why have they come? Had they seen you enter they would have been here long ago."

I was up against it anyway, impossibly so. It was good to see Boris concerned. "If D.I.5 had a man out there he might have recognised *you* and *Fido*. He added two and two."

"You appear so different that we will have to bluff it out."

"Do you think I would get by, Maggie?" I held her by

the arms for she was half dazed by the turn of events, and I was not happy myself. She looked back with glazed eyes. "Your clothes and hair are different. I think it might work, but only if they did not know you. I don't think it would fool someone like Sergeant Bulman."

In Boris I saw the slightly lesser of two evils; maybe I could fix them both. I turned to him.

"If I'm seen with you it will put the lid on it."

I could see that he knew it too, yet he dare not let me go. "We will go down the stairs together. I will then walk out alone while you stay with Fyodor. If I get through without incident you and Fyodor will follow. And don't try anything foolish again. Your only future is with us."

I shrugged an acquiescence, then he added, "It will be natural, I think, for us to take an interest in the police behaviour. To try to walk through them as if they are not there will be madness. It is a danger we cannot avoid."

Well, it would get him out of Maggie's hair and that was what I wanted. "Goodbye, Maggie, thanks for everything."

Boris tried to be the cavalier. "Do not worry, Miss Parsons." He smiled, raised his hat again. "Good day." He led the way out of the flat, I followed and Fido tagged on as we left the room.

To distract I asked Boris what he had done with my stolen money. Reaching the head of the stairs he did not look back, but told me over his shoulder that it would be returned to me once the deal was complete. Everything was so plausible with Boris; I was sure that he could convince anyone of the necessity of putting a bullet in them. We started down the stairs in single file and then there was a sickening crack behind that paralysed me into inaction.

I wanted to turn but was afraid to. Boris wasn't. He began to spin round and his movement triggered mine. With a snarl I smashed my foot in his back and he crashed down the stairs. Not waiting for him to stop I spun round to see Fido swaying on the top step, his flat gaze glassy, non-seeing as he gripped the rail to steady himself. Jumping the two stairs between us I hit him under the jaw so hard that I swear his feet left the carpet. Something cracked; judging by the pain it might have been my hand but later I discovered it was not. As he crumpled I helped him on his way with my left foot and he rolled like a hedgehog to join an unconscious Boris on the lower land-

the moon shedding its light into every corner. From below the iron platform I was on gave me good cover but an opening door might be seen. So I waited, cramped and anxious, expecting a sudden shout to go up. They were taking their time but they would make sure that all the gaps were closed before moving in. So what space did that leave me?

A chunk of cloud came up like a hand over a torch. Still crouched I turned the door handle, hoping that there were no bolts, and pushed. I was in on hands and knees, knocking the key on a rough mat and sniffing the smell of cooking. Closing the door in slow motion, I put back the key and turned it. If the flat was similar to Maggie's I would find my way round.

Beyond the far door was a short corridor, bedroom to the immediate right, lounge straight ahead. I did not use my torch which had little life left, but picked my way carefully. At the bedroom door I listened and could not hear a thing. The sudden dread that Shirley Ames might still be out and would walk in at any moment hit me like a thunderbolt. Her scream of fright went through my head. Then I pulled myself up by the chinstrap and entered the lounge. From there to the front door was no problem. There was no hall but a sort of recess that could be used as a mini study.

This was it; the moment of truth. Opening the door I stepped boldly out, straight into two coppers.

I don't know who was more surprised. Shoving my head back round the door I whispered loud enough for them to hear:

"Goodnight, Shirley. See you tomorrow, darling." And I turned round grinning at the two rosy young faces under the big helmets. 'What's going on?" I said, upping my accent to meet the demands of the flats.

"Your name, sir?"

I hastily recalled which visiting cards I was carrying in my wallet. "Certainly, but why? What's the fuss?"

"We're looking for someone. Your name, sir."

I could not believe what was happening. A change of hair, eyebrows, spectacles and not least of all clothes—incredible. But careful how you go, Spider. "James Cummings. What's he done?"

"Have you an identity on you?"

"Only a card." I dished it out, representative of the Marlon Group Limited.

He looked at it as if it meant something. "No driving licence, sir?"

"Not on me." I held out my hand for the card. He returned it. "I take it I can get out. I must catch a cab."

He nodded. "I'm afraid you might get stopped again, sir. The place is surrounded."

"Good Lord. Who are you after, Jack the Ripper?"

They gave me a grave nod in unison, very important looking, and I started down the stairs blessing young, inexperienced coppers. I reminded myself that some coppers would recognise anyone under any disguise—just a few who knew the small points about bone structure and so on. And they had a nose like mine in reverse. I'd have to try to stay away from them. Even so it had been a reasonable test.

That was how I felt before I reached the hall. When I took the turn of the stairs, my stomach dipped. The hall was flooded with them, plain-clothed and uniformed. How I kept my legs going I don't know but I dare not hesitate. Suddenly I felt an abject fool walking into their arms like this. So many pairs of eyes turned in my direction when they heard my footsteps that I damned nearly ran back up. My mouth was dry again and my legs had disappeared.

Two plain-clothed men detached themselves but to cut it short I went straight up to them. "It's all right, officers, I've just seen your men on the second floor."

"Really, sir? How do you know we are policemen?"

"Come now," I said in my best Oxford and gave them what I hoped was a sweet smile. "I gather you're looking for someone."

"About your height, sir. Dark hair, clothes. Seen him?" He whipped out my photograph and flashed it under my nose like a warrant card. I stared down at my own sullen face and how I refrained from making a break for it I'll never know. They must surely see the sweat and the fear in my eyes. Yet I heard this strange posh voice reply, "That's the man they showed on television. Is he here?" I could feel my voice quivering yet it *sounded* level. I was dazed. Coppers were turning to look at me then turning back to natter among themselves when they noted I was taken care of. In the back of my mind was the dread that Fairfax might enter and if I fooled him for ten seconds it would not be for longer. I had to get out of here before I gave myself away.

"I take it you haven't seen him, sir?"

Answer, you fool. Don't forget your accent. "Not here. I mean not in the flesh."

Christ, there was Alf Bulman in his inevitable raincoat on the far side of the hall talking to a uniformed man. They would have dragged him out by very virtue of the fact that he would never forget me. I was facing him straight on. I rubbed my nose and thought, well this is it, get ready to run. But how would I get through this lot? I had yet to realise how many were outside.

"Which flat have you just come from, sir?"

When would the idiot let me go. "Number 21."

"Do you live there, sir?"

I noticed that his colleague had a register in his hand and was looking down it. "No. I was visiting a friend." Bulman was nodding his head as if terminating a conversation.

"What is your friend's name, sir?"

How desperate did I have to get before I belted him one and fled. My nerve could not hold up under this, it was not my forte.

"Shirley Ames." The one with the register nodded; in the near distance Alf Bulman glanced casually over.

"Social call, sir?"

"Don't be impertinent. Use your imagination." My anger was not feigned, I was running out of bottle. Yet it had the right effect. He grinned sheepishly; man to man.

"All right, sir."

I took it that I could go. Try walking through a scattering of coppers who are all looking for you. *You* know that you're you and you're just waiting for *them* to realise it. Your legs are melting rubber and you reckon you begin to smell like it. Eyes watch you, casually, but shrewdly, and you walk slowly through stares like criss-crossing searchlights of variable strength; but you are the focus. You want to reduce height, hide your face, turn up your collar, run. Yet if you are to survive you will walk straight at full height, chin up, taking the interest in them that they would expect of you, then your nerve is good or you've been touched by madness.

My nerves were shattered and the blood was racing round my brain. At this stage I really had little conception of what I was doing. From the corner of my eye I saw Alf Bulman and as casually as I could, turned my head away. Surely they must be in Maggie's place by now? Would she have the nerve to delay them. They must have found Boris and Fyodor, and Fairfax's men would have some idea of what had happened. I was hoping that all Fairfax's D.I.5 men were upstairs. The presence of the two Russians would satisfy them of my own presence.

Just as I was nearing the big glass doors two pairs of footsteps broke out behind, hurrying towards me, but by now my legs could not have broken into a trot. They came up either side of me, but just as I was about to struggle they carried on past not even holding open one of the doors for me. I caught the door as it was swinging.

As I passed outside the roar from Alf Bulman remained in his throat or he simply had not recognised me. I was out into the air.

On the other side of the street, a row of uniformed men stretched out at intervals and between them and me were odd bods in plain clothes with a couple of higher-ranking uniformed types. No one approached me and I guessed that the fact that I had been allowed through was good enough for them. I stood on the steps looking about me because it would have been unrealistic to do otherwise. It was impossible to gauge the size of the cordon thrown round the building, but I reckoned that they must have run into three figures counting the detectives. Which made me a pretty desirable commodity.

I stepped on to the pavement as a taxi came sliding up. At first I thought nothing of it and as it began to pull up to disgorge a passenger I almost hailed it. I was stopped in my tracks by its registration number. It was Fairfax's special cab. Nipping smartly behind it as it came to a halt, I felt the warmth of its exhaust fumes on my leg as I crossed the street and started to walk in front of the spread-out line of the law, as if I was a general inspecting troops. I did not feel like a general. I felt like a crook on the diciest run of his life.

All those eyes bored into my back, but in fact at this stage I doubted if they took much notice of me at all. I kept walking until I rounded the corner, heading for the main streets. Afraid to look round I kept going, too tense for relief, still not believing that I had escaped the net.

I was not yet out of the woods. Once they realised that I had fooled them, they would recall the tall blond bloke with the tatty haircut and would scour the streets. Meanwhile, the wig still had its uses. I hailed a late cab and gave him an address near to Balls Up's place. If I could fox the police I knew that in the dark I did not have to worry too much about a cabbie. Later on he would remember so I gave him a point that would leave me a fair walk the other end, so that they would not connect my dropping-off place with Balls Up.

It left me with little time for the net would encompass any spots where I had been seen. As I sat back in the cold leather I reflected there was an outside chance that Maggie would convince them that I had not been there; she was not a good liar and if they thoroughly searched, they must find the other stuff. There was no danger of Boris telling them because he would deny all knowledge of an association. Right now, Boris would be faced with some of the problems I had just missed and this pleased me.

I dropped off in a dark area not too far from Wormwood Scrubs so I was quite at home. I did not expect to be followed but I made sure for my life depended on my next few moves and I only hoped that I was capable of seeing them through.

I walked for half an hour before I came to a shabby narrow street with hardly a lamp in it. Nineteenth-century London. The whole damned lot needed blowing up, scouring and rebuilding after a decent disinfection period. Right now it was just what I wanted. Coppers moved in pairs and were more easily seen and heard.

There was no name above the drab printing shop. Once there had been paint on the woodwork. An antiquated printing machine hid behind a dirty sheet glass window with rude words fingered out of the dust. The shop itself cringed back between a junk shop and a small tobacconist's, just a shade cleaner than the print shop. Yet Balls Up scratched a living, did a little better than that when the boys called on his artistry and not so well when he operated for the wrong people and finished up inside.

The door was locked, the whole area in darkness. Balls Up was too trusting for a villain; no bolt was on the door so I let myself in and started up the worn, bare-boarded stairs; he could afford carpets; he merely did not see the point in buying them. He probably kept his money under the floorboards. Passing the room where he so often had his all-night gambling sessions I opened the next door.

Stale air and sweat assailed me and the noise of erratic snoring. Only one person there. With my back to the door I switched on the light; no shade, low-wattage lamp, bare boards but for a couple of grubby Indian scatter rugs that had probably fallen off the back of a lorry. A ball of grey hair stuck up from a bright red counterpane like an un-washed mop. Then he shot up in bed, eyes wide, his right hand groping down the side of the bed searching for something to hit me with. I did not feel like grinning but I needed his confidence and his help so I managed one, then whipped off the wig and glasses.

"Christ! Spider! You bloody idiot, why'd you come in like that, mate?" Then, as sleep left him. "Why come 'ere at all? Old Bill* has been round 'ere, looking for you. You're in it, mate; right above your eyes. And they've put a price on your 'ead, fifteen thousand."

"And you're going to help get me out of it, Balls Up," I said, still grinning. He hadn't shaved for a week and looked an old, creased man.

"Oh no." He swung his legs out of bed; he had been sleeping in his underpants. "You can't stay 'ere, mate, they might pop up again any moment. They've put me through it, I can tell you. What did yer want to screw the Chinks for? Any other time, Spider. They say the Chink's dying, I can't risk it, mate."

I put him out of his misery. "I'm not staying, Balls Up. I wouldn't do it to you or any of my mates. I've got a job for you to do; dead urgent and you could do it on your head."

It was half past two when I left Balls Up and went searching forlornly for a cab. I was not exactly in the right area for finding one but I kept going, heading all the time towards Soho. In the end I had to nick a car and use my crocodile clip because time was running out. I left it in Shaftesbury Avenue before cutting up Dean Street into strip club land.

If there are going to be people about in London at the dead of night, then a good proportion of them will be in Soho. And the coppers and cars are not short there either. So I was in a highly nervous state. There was additional worry; my normal description was all over the country but should I now remove the wig? Was it going to be an aid, or my downfall? Did the police yet know about it? The other thing was Balls Up's mention of a price on my head. This was something new. Apparently some donor interested in Anglo-Chinese relations had put up the money as a measure of diplomatic goodwill. Fifteen thousand pounds. It was an amount with a familiar ring and I had no doubt that Fairfax was behind it.

*Police

It meant that I could not even trust the boys. Fifteen grand tax free was a sizeable sum and I might well have made a mistake by going to the inveterate speculator, Balls Up. He was a good bloke, basically, but like anyone else he could justify himself by saying I was doomed to capture anyway so that he might as well cash in. That's what they would all say. Ray Lynch must be hard at his bottle for not hanging on to me a little longer. If I was isolated before I was now in solitary and yet it was essential to communicate whatever the risk.

When I tried to break into the Gainboy Studios I cursed Bluie Palmer for bolting his door. There was no ground floor window that led to his place and I did not fancy using a jemmy on a street door even if I had one. Stepping back I looked up but his studio lights were out and the floor above that where I believed he lived was also in darkness. Hearing a policeman's tread I had to push off to return a few minutes later.

This time I rang the bell, leaning against the button and hoping like hell that it worked for I couldn't hear a thing. A man and a woman passed me, slightly drunk and very amorous; I heard the man ask her name so he wasn't doing too badly on short acquaintance. The trouble was that there would be plain-clothes men around here and I was pushing my luck.

Hearing a window open above me, I stepped back and saw a pale face leaning out staring down at me.

"For goodness sake, what do you want at this time of night, darling?"

His tone told me that he had not recognised me and his lack of interest suggested that he might have someone with him. It was a complication; I had half expected it.

"Bluie, let me in for God's sake. I must talk to you for just a minute." My loud whisper carried. Odd things happened in this area but recognition could be fatal.

"Oh dear!" His plaintive whine informed me that he had recognised my voice. "You really shouldn't have come here, Sp—"

"Let me in," I snarled, cutting across my name. "For one minute, that's all. I won't stay."

The window closed and I stood hopefully. I knew how he felt. I was not being fair by implicating him, yet that's what mates were for—to help out. When I heard his soft tread on the stairs I was relieved. The bolts shot back and I was in.

165

"You may be gorgeous, darling, but I'm taking a frightful risk for you."

I followed the green short, silk dressing gown, the bare legs and the strong perfume up the stairs. From the studio floor upwards was richly carpeted and when Bluie led me into his lounge I could see at a glance that he made a lot of money from his dubious photography. There were flowers and tassels and drapes and the whole room had the touch of a fussy woman; Bluie's own touch. But there was nothing wrong with his Scotch and for once I had one, large and neat.

"Keep your voice down, darling," he said as he motioned me to an old gold cushioned chair. "I have a friend staying with me." He smiled sweetly, looking me over appraisingly and I had to keep my feelings deep within me; I needed this man's help in a way I hoped would take his fancy, might even excite him; so I risked it and smiled back. Gradually I was learning the diplomatic game and began to disgust myself. Patience, too, I was learning as Bluie cooed. "The wig looks heavenly on you, ducky. It's definitely you. You know it's lucky for you that I don't need the money and that I'm fond of you; they're offering ever so much for you. What *have* you done, you naughty boy?"

The only way I knew how to handle Bluie was the old way but I had to swallow it. I dare not upset him by as much as one word. So I aroused his professionalism and when I did that his interest centred on what I was saying. Just the same, I had yet to meet a well-breeched man who would close his ears to the offer of another easy pile of bunce. Just how fond of me was he?

What do you do when there is a price on your head so that you dare not let even your friends see you and you are faced with several hours of darkness? It was cold and I was without an overcoat so even a quiet kip in a hidden doorway was out of the question. With what I had in mind I would have rung up Ray Lynch again but I reckoned that fifteen grand would be too tempting for him.

The first thing I did was to get out of Soho and that is not easy to do unobserved, day or night. After that I kept walking. Even this did not bring warmth for there had been a sudden drop in temperature. I was tempted to jump the railings of the National Gallery and prop myself behind one of the big Corinthian columns for a rest and

166

sleep but the cold kept me going. I was grateful then for the long sleep I had taken in the empty flat.

I could not walk and let my mind wander so my plight was with me all the time which meant that every second was like a minute and time dragged. I must have dived into a score of recesses, doorways, alleys, at the approach of foot coppers and patrol cars. Suddenly there were more of them and I wondered if the call had gone out and a new hunt was on.

There was nothing pleasant about London's dawn. A wet greyness crept over the buildings, giving them a shadowy drabness that matched my own mood. As the light increased I maintained my wig on the basis that although the police may know of it, the general public might not. With the increased light came more people, vehicles, danger. I kept walking.

The sun came out and with it some warmth. When the morning was really humming with crowds I dived into a news cinema and bought myself a couple of bars of chocolate. Sitting at the back I snatched a little sleep and stayed there for three shows. The chocolate made me thirsty but I could bear that. If only I could listen to the news I would know what to do about the wig unless the police were playing it crafty.

Back on the streets I played the police long range. The far sight or glint of a helmet was enough to send me another way. No one paid attention to me except some of the oldies who gave me the glare reserved for blond long hair-dos.

Two o'clock was the deadline. I had to hang around Charing Cross Post Office where there are usually police around. But it had to be somewhere near enough to Soho without being in it, and not too long a walk for Bluie. I spotted him crossing the road, green velvet jacket, red tie, tight check trousers, swaying his way with a large envelope under his arm. He went into the Post Office up to one of the writing counters and put down the envelope while he filled in a form. Sidling up next to him I started to fill in a form, changed my mind, screwed it up, threw it in the nearest bin, picked up the envelope and left.

On the run you are safer in crowds especially in London where you have to be beautiful or a freak to attract a second glance. The police weren't so indifferent and the number of coppers they had called out during the night was not for an exercise; their ears would be burning today, their eyes sharper. So I took the greatest care crossing over to St. James's Park.

In spite of winter, the park was not deserted. I buried myself as far from the Mall as I could and sat on a cold bench to study the contents of the envelope. They gave me a lot of food for thought. I considered Fairfax and the low trick he had pulled on me; of the C.I.A. and the K.G.B., of Li Tshien. Of them all Fairfax did not come out of it too well and in my hands I had the means to strike back at him. I decided to contact the Chinese.

15

They would watch the main stations, so it meant the hazard of crossing Trafalgar Square again to the Charing Cross Post Office. It seemed that I was beginning to live there. There were unhappy moments waiting for a phone booth to become vacant but a place like this is always busy. Eventually I was in.

Before phoning I searched my mind for another course and reluctantly decided that there was none. The ringing tone went on for so long that I thought they were not going to answer, then a clipped sing-song voice came on the line and I asked to speak to Li Tshein. There was silence, background voices, then a guarded "Who is speaking?"

"Tell him it's the man who took the letter and the photographs." This slayed him. The voices became so rapid that they sounded like a tape being played at too fast a speed. Then another voice, more authoritative, no less guarded.

"What do you want with us?"

"I want to do a deal, to return what I stole except the money."

"Then you come round at once. Straight away. We talk." I could imagine them doing their little tricks and me doing all the talking.

"Don't take me for stupid," I said. "Are you interested in talking or not?"

"Yes. We talk."

"Then meet me in half an hour on the wooden bridge in St. James's Park."

"Not possible, half hour. Two hours, maybe three."

"You won't find me there. The police will have me by then. And the stuff. Half an hour or not at all. One man on his own. If I see signs of others, I'll be off." They wanted time to discuss it of course and I did not intend to give them any.

169

More gabbling, high-pitched and argumentative—it was all Chinese to me. Eventually, "We come now."

I snapped, "I said *one*."

"Yes. One. We come now." There was one thing about the Chinese; I did not have to worry about them telling the police.

I stayed in the booth with the phone at my ear until someone else wanted it, then got out quick in case he started to study me.

I strayed back to the park with plenty of time in hand. The envelope contents were distributed about my body in various pockets. Reaching the wooden bridge, I leaned on it and watched the ducks and swans. An old lady close by was throwing pieces of bread to them.

Half an hour was a long time on the bridge with a cold breeze rippling the water. This was one of the times I would have preferred an overcoat but it's impossible to work in one and to run with one is to carry an anchor. I was not sorry when I saw a Chinese approach; a short, thick-set, Mongolian-faced man, pale in an English winter, muffled with a thick woollen scarf, heavy Crombie overcoat, thick gloves and a trilby hat. He wore steelframed spectacles and was altogether an image of too much reminiscence. He stopped on the bridge and looked about him, giving me barely a glance. Waiting for the old lady to finish fattening up the wild life I said, "Are you looking for Mr. Scott?"

He gave me the inscrutable look that pins men to walls and ignored me.

"I'm Spider Scott," I said. "I've changed my hair." He took more interest in me then, but was still highly suspicious.

"Would you like to hear me describe Li Tshien's room to you? Tell you where your radio room is?"

That helped. He came up beside me and we both leaned over the bridge, as unlikely a pair as you could meet.

"You have the things with you, Mr. Scott?"

"Some. I want two thousand eight hundred pounds for them."

"This is ridiculous. That is the amount you stole from us."

"And the Russians stole it from me. That's what I want and I want it today."

Surprisingly he pulled out a crumpled bag in which

170

were some broken biscuits; crumbling them he tossed them to the birds and a series of concentric pools broke out on the water. "How much did British Security pay you for stealing what is ours?"

"Everybody thinks that," I said. "If they paid me I would not be selling now. The C.I.A. offered me money and escape. The K.G.B. offered me escape and money. But I have a conscience about Li Tshien. I did not mean to hurt him. I'm willing to sell them back to you at the price of replacing the money I stole. Plus one other request which will cost you nothing."

"I must be sure that you have them to sell. Remember that they are ours—our property that you are demanding money for."

"Can it," I snapped. And in case he did not understand me, "Who did *you* steal them from? How much did *you* pay in the first place. If you took the photograph yourselves you certainly pinched the letter."

"I will speak to my superiors about the money. May I see what you have?"

"If you are not empowered to negotiate you are seeing nothing."

"All right. All you bourgeois think of is money. I will see that you have it."

"At half-past four o'clock. I'll ring you at half three to tell you where we'll meet."

"That is not enough time."

"Take it, or leave it. And while we're talking of money all you Communists think of is bloody blackmail. That is what you want them for, isn't it? I'd sooner be a thief."

He was biting his tongue to get back at me for I had cut a wound in his indoctrination. The cold murder left his almond eyes and he said, "Show me."

I produced the letter and handed it to him. On its own it was useless; only coupled with the photograph was it devastating evidence. He put it in his pocket and I made no attempt to stop him.

Then he gave me a very special look that was a complete examination, penetrating, as if he had managed to focus inside my head and knew how my mind was working. It made my flesh crawl. This fellow wasn't going to forgive me, ever. I struck back.

"Any tricks and I'll do one of two things; I'll send what I have to a news agency and start the biggest scandal of all time. We'll lose a good Foreign Secretary and maybe a government. But you will lose most. There won't be a paper in the Western world that won't publicise the slimy, degrading tactics of the representative of the Chinese People's Republic. Or I sell them to the C.I.A. or the K.G.B. As you hate them both, I leave you with the thought. What I'm asking is chicken feed."

He nodded almost imperceptibly but there was no fear in him, only unadulterated, undisguised, fanatical hatred. He shuffled off, looking miserable from the rear.

Taking the subway at Cockspur Street, I went into the Gents' and shut myself in a cubicle. It was claustrophobic, too much like solitary, but it was safe for a few minutes. So I had now been reduced to hiding in toilets. I gave it as long as I dare then it was back in the cold and over once more to the Post Office. I did not expect to find Fairfax's number and address in the phone book so I rang Ray Lynch at his office. He was out. I did not know where Sally worked so I took a chance and rang her at her flat. She was in and suffering from a cold. I was touched at her relief on hearing from me; one day hardly constitutes a friendship but she was sincere. I asked her how I could get in touch with Ray. She did not know where he was. Did she know Sir Stuart Halliman's address? She said she would look in Ray's special address book. She came back and gave me an address in Eaton Terrace, Belgravia, then she asked, "What are you going to do, Spider?" And "What happened to Ray's friends?"

"They weren't too friendly, but don't blame him." I was about to tell her to take a stiff drink and go to bed with her cold then realised that it would be fatuous advice. So I said, "Tell Ray I'll give him a scoop. I mean it. Tell him to get off the bottle and wean himself back on his job. I can make it for him." Hanging up, I reflected that Fairfax was going to pay for what he had done to me.

At four o'clock I rang the Chinese Legation. I was half an hour later than arranged but I wanted their resistance down. My cunning line of thought began to appal me. They would be thinking too and that more than worried me; they would put their heads together with one thought in mind; how to fix me for fixing them. I was expendable in all their eyes, even my own. So I was not too confident when I demanded that the same man was to meet me at the same spot as before.

This time I arrived late at the bridge and had developed eyes all around my head. If they were going to make a

172

move it would be now or after he had left. That's why I had made certain of daylight with the night not too far ahead. There was no bounce in me when I went to join him on the bridge. There were plenty of people in the Mall and a few on the park paths. There were also two policemen but a good distance away.

He raised his eyes to me, but not his hat. I still did not like what I saw. "You have the money?" He nodded. "You have the photograph?" I nodded back, then took another good look around the park, particularly at two parked cars on double yellow lines opposite the ugly lump of the Admiralty Citadel.

"How's Li Tshien?" I asked, dreading the answer.

"Do you not read the newspapers?"

"I'm not in a position to buy one. He's still alive?"

"Is that important to you?"

"Yes."

"Then I will not tell you one way or the other. You must sweat it out, Mr. Scott."

You bastard, I thought. Let's get it over. I passed him the positive face down, ashamed to look at it with him. On the other hand, he turned it over and gave it close scrutiny, finally slipping it inside his overcoat.

"The negative, please? "

"The last time we met I said that there was something else I wanted from you."

Those flat suspicious eyes warily roamed mine and I hoped I had the nerve to carry it through. I told him what I wanted. At the end of it, he gazed blankly at me and said, "I am pointing a gun at you. I can shoot you, take the negative and run to waiting friends or you can give it to me now." Then, "I promised you the money, nothing more. I have it here."

"Shoot me," I challenged. "You might be doing me a favour. But you won't, because you dare not risk the scandal; there are too many people about." He had a gun all right. I could see part of its shape through his overcoat pocket. "If you do as I ask I will guarantee the negative through your letter-box tomorrow morning."

"You are a thief. Why should I trust you?"

"You are a blackmailer, which is why I don't trust you. Look, Wong or whatever your name is, you have the letter and the print; enough to work on. I agree that the negative is proof that the positive is O.K. You think I can still do a deal with someone else with the negative. So I can. But they cannot do for me what you can do. I'm in your hands. Anyway, I wasn't stupid enough to bring the negative with me."

He nodded too quickly as if making up his mind halfway through what I was saying. "All right. We will then be back at the beginning minus a little cash. All right, Mr. Scott, I will have to trust you." He handed me a packet which I opened. I was not going to count it there but there appeared to be a very substantial amount. When I looked up he was already walking away in his unlikely gait. I reflected that it had all been *too* easy. I looked around and noticed the cars still there.

Time was back on my hands. If I could last out another twenty-four hours there was a little hope; if I was captured before morning there was no hope at all because everything depended on keeping the negative out of official hands until then. There was no certainty that the Chinese would do what I asked them. There was absolute certainty that if I was captured before they could move they would make no move at all and I would be landed with a life stretch.

I moved slowly through the park away from Trafalgar Square and towards Buckingham Palace. Turning suddenly I noticed that one of the cars was moving down the Mall at a snail's pace; the other had branched off at right angles, so that they could form a pincer movement at the end of the park.

Apart from being in bad nick I did not want to run for it would draw attention. Their chesslike minds would have figured that out. So I about-turned just to confuse them. The car in the Mall pulled up sharply and a cruising taxi driver almost rammed it. The two passengers in the back seat of the car shot forward on the seat and I caught a long-range glimpse of them.

They say all Chinese look alike but that's if you haven't clobbered one of them and have every reason to remember his face. Pain or not I risked a jog across the grass before they U-turned in the middle of the Mall and drew the biggest chorus of motor horns for the day. The car survived but if they tried that manoeuvre too often the cops would get them.

My sight of the passengers had not been all that good but my heart had thumped out. One of them had a strip of adhesive diagonally across his forehead and had looked remarkably like Li Tshien, glasses and all. The sight had startled me. The bastards. And if it was Li Tshien that

174

made Russian Boris a bigger bastard. Blinded and dying! The relief weakened me and I plumped down on a bench, my head between my hands. It had to be him.

The cars, of course, were there to follow me until such a time as their occupants could pounce. They knew that I had no shelter, that if I popped into a cinema I would have to pop out again. They knew that the only place I could hide would be in the darkest loneliest alley or derelict house so that all they had to do was to keep me in sight and wait for the streets to clear when they could safely scoop me up. If the Chinese got hold of me I would lose on every issue.

I got walking again and headed for the Strand, the one-way section that terminated at the traffic lights outside the white bulge of South Africa House. Their Chinese minds should have considered the one-way systems and unless they knew their London they would burst a gasket as they watched me walk against the traffic. Cutting down Villiers Street I turned under the arches and came back into Northumberland Avenue. They would cruise around, but provided I could lose them, my chances increased. What spurred me on was the thought that they wanted *me* as well as the negative; they would not want the police to question me, it might not help their image.

The office workers were beginning to pour out of blocks around the Strand and the traffic was thickening noticeably, buses spurting to avoid the rush-hour crowds. This was better for me; people were too intent on getting home to notice. Diving into the News Cinema in Grand Buildings at the end of the Strand I spent a couple of hours there mulling over my next step. I had to be sure that I had shaken off the Chinese because if they saw where I was going it would destroy everything.

When I left the cinema it was dark with a near December nip. Crossing Northumberland Avenue and Whitehall I headed down the wide stretch of the Mall with the park on my left; it was almost empty, just odd people taking a short cut.

I don't know why I turned; normal precaution, perhaps, but when I did I went dry.

A blue Ford Consul was idling just behind me. I recognised its number plate first. How had they got back on to me? I stood and turned; people walked past me giving me curious stares that I could have done without. There he

175

was, diverting across the park at my sudden stop. It had to be he, a well-muffled Chinese. I had been so clever in slipping the cars that I had overlooked the elementary risk of foot tails. He was in touch with the cars with a small transmitter like the police use.

I cursed myself for negligence and for being stupid enough to mention the Americans and the Russians to the Chinese. I had frightened them so they were staying with me. And they had me on an open, fairly isolated stretch. The nearer I got to the Palace the quieter it would become.

Again I retraced my steps. At the corner of Cockspur Street outside the Canadian Pacific building, I dived into the subway, sprinted along it and took refuge in a cubicle in the Gents'. I did not stay long enough for them to conclude that was where I was. After a couple of minutes I left and there, at the exit, two Chinese waited for me. They were both young, in dark overcoats and both ignored me as I came out.

I went up to the nearest one. "What do you want with me? I'll keep my word if you do what I ask."

He looked blankly at me but did it with such indifference that the message was clear. Then he gabbled in Chinese as if he hadn't understood, looked at his colleague and shrugged. My stomach turned; the way I translated the message gave me the impression that I would not translate many more. They were biding their time and that could only mean one thing.

There are four exits from Trafalgar Square subway. I could not see that it made any difference which one I took. So I took the Strand; that was where most people and most of the lights were. At a time I would prefer to keep away from lights I was being forced under them. I needed light to keep the Chinese at bay, darkness to dodge the police. I supposed that if I handed over the negative the Chinese would leave me alone but if I did that I might just as well cut my own throat.

Occasionally I saw the blue Consul, sometimes the other one, a green Mini. Once I saw both at the same time, one behind the other. Always behind me was at least one Chinese, no longer trying to hide the fact. I kept going; there was no one I could turn to and I did not delude myself that the Chinese wanted the reward money. They wanted to kill me and they only had to hang on to succeed.

Friendliness took a new dimension. Crossing the Strand

I entered the forecourt of Charing Cross Station, passed under the arch and bought myself a ticket to Clapham. It came as no surprise to find my oriental friends forming the short queue behind me. I heard one of them ask for a Brighton ticket, as I turned away; they were taking no chances.

At the departure board I idled about. It was an awkward time; too late for rush hour, too early for the theatre first houses to turn out. Quiet, yet with sufficient people around.

I made my move, not rushing, no sudden dive for a departing train. Through the barrier and into an empty compartment which was easy to find at the time. I sat in a corner away from the platform side so that my escorts would know that I had no intention of jumping back on it. They arrived just after me, seating themselves opposite one another on the platform side so that I was neatly sealed off.

It was strange how they ignored me, casting not even a glance. A patient pair awaiting a grim opportunity. They might even try it on this train but not in the station. They chattered away in a range of high-pitched pings, so animatedly that they might have been arguing about a football match. No one else got in our compartment which was probably carrying more than most.

A few whistles, a clatter and we were pulling away. Next stop Waterloo, just over the Thames. We reached the bridge and I had my door open and had jumped for the track in something like my pre-Boris speed. It was a dicey move dropping between electrified tracks but it was better than waiting to be killed. I took a tumble and rolled from the huge wheels gathering speed. Then I was up, shaken and hurt, but mobile.

Something, a pebble, shot through my hair and then something plucked my jacket and spun me round so that I almost fell into the passing train. They were shooting at me.

Bundling myself between the tracks I tried to make myself invisible as I saw the shape of someone leaning out of a lighted, disappearing window. A shot whined high over my head and another ricocheted off the granite chippings with a big exploding spark. God, they were desperate.

As the last coach trundled past I crossed the tracks, very careful to avoid the live ones, to the steel barrier that separated the railway from the footbridge the other side. The thought of my friends having a radio link with each other was enough to spur me. I was shaken as I awkwardly climbed the gridded barrier. They intended to make sure that no one got that negative.

On top of the barrier I waited until it was clear, then dropped to the footbridge. None of this did me much good but it was no time to complain. With two cars both ends of the bridge would be covered. Taking my chances I jog-trotted towards Waterloo. The motion half killed me but that was preferable to the real thing so I kept going. The lights of Festival Hall spilled across the Thames and farther up the river a ship's siren blasted a warning.

After a while I had to slow to a walk and was disgusted to find myself still unnerved. Being shot at was an unhealthy experience. That was another score to settle with Fairfax.

At the end of the bridge I stopped to view the huge court-yard of Festival Hall spreading to the river's edge. From the number of people there was obviously a concert on.

Slowly I descended, pushing the padding back into my jacket where the bullet had caught it.

They were waiting for me at the foot of the stairs, not the same two, but with the same look about them. They were hanging on grimly, knowing that eventually I would wear down and their turn would come so that they could finish me calmly and not panic as they had done on the train.

Taking a lesson from them I walked past as if I hadn't seen them. I had my pride, even if it took all my effort to show how much I didn't care. They tagged on. I stopped; they stopped. There was a lot of movement outside the Hall. I went to examine the posters. To this day I could not tell you what was on them. I waited; they waited, I used to be good at giving the police the slip but Fyodor had done too good a job on me.

I was afraid to leave the vicinity of the Hall. Behind it there were too many dark passages; in front was only the river and the bridge I had just crossed. One of my escorts was careless in the use of his transmitter and I saw him talking into it inside his overcoat. Whistling up the others I supposed so that there would always be someone on to me. It had not been funny from the outset; now it was nightmarish. Just then I could think of nothing more to do.

As if knowing it too, my escort looked over at me a

that precise moment. One even smiled slightly; not humorously; it was the reflex of victory; of his prey being irretrievably cornered. I couldn't manage a smile back. I tried a prayer.

16

Then things went crazy. Suddenly. Unexpectedly. Where the foyer had been practically empty, the doors leading to the stalls burst open and were held back as crowds of people emerged. Through the great glass doors I saw them coming, all seemingly talking at once and then they burst around and beyond me, pouring out in their hundreds. It was the end of the concert.

Feeling a brief pang of excitement I fought against them, bustling my way towards the stalls, murmuring apologies as I went. "I'm sorry, I've left something. I'm sorry, madam, pardon me, I've left my hat." Taller than most, I had no doubt that my Chinese shadows would initially visually follow my blond top, but once inside the auditorium I knew that I was out of sight.

The gangways were packed with orderly people shuffling towards the exits. I had to fight my way back, offering my inane apologies repeatedly until I deemed it time to dive into one of the now empty rows.

Dropping to my knees I poked around under the seats, out of sight of everybody. Tearing off my wig, I left it as a souvenir and put the glasses in my pocket. For a couple of minutes I watched the stream of passing legs then risked it and rose. Of all the chances I had taken I reckoned this one reasonable. I had to get back into the mob before they tailed off too much. There were other exits but I gambled on the way I had come in. I reckoned they would not expect me back the same way. Allowing my knees to sag a little my height was reduced by an inch or two and people were packed all around me; people who had just heard a thundering good concert and were still talking about it, thank God.

Out in the air, groups were breaking up, people making for the car park or the station. I immersed myself in the biggest stream towards the cars. I saw nothing of the Chinese largely because I was intent on keeping myself hidden; there might be more of them now though and I wondered how they were positioned.

I decided to nick another car. I could not do it with all these people about and I did not want to land in a traffic jam. So I tagged on to a group who seemed to be making for Waterloo station. It was nicely dark and my friends were probably still looking for a blond top. With luck they were going frantic.

The traffic streamed past for some time but the moment of danger arrived as it eventually thinned and the footsloggers had diminished around me. Then I saw a Consul strategically placed facing the oncoming crowd so I sidled inside a loose group of four, developed a limp and lost height.

Once past the car I risked a quick look back and all seemed well but they might be cagey with so many people about. Taking a chance, I dived into a darkened side road —in the hope of finding a car. One or two people had obviously parked here rather than near the hall for I could hear footsteps ahead and behind me.

Passing under a street light, dim in this old part of London but not dim enough, a light shone straight in my face, blinding me. Too late I smelled copper. How could I have missed him? Instinctively I kicked out at the lamp and the beam swung up like a searchlight as I caught his wrist. He swore and the lamp crashed to the ground, the beam pivoting like a demented lighthouse.

Still half blind I tore into him as he tried to draw his truncheon. It wasn't his fault that I caught him so easily. He probably had a fractured wrist where I had kicked him and how they can move at all in those bloody great overcoats has always baffled me; his truncheon was not halfway out of its special pocket before I thumped him on his jaw. I had a vague glimpse of his open mouth, then he was sagging to his knees. I didn't wait to help him down. There were shouts behind me and I was off.

Someone half-heartedly stepped in front of me. I could have swung past him but in that fraction of time I saw he had been opening his car. He wasn't too young but there was nothing I could do but belt him. I tried to pull my punch and went for his body. He doubled and gasped, falling back against the wall.

The car door was open. It was a Jag, and would have

181

the acceleration I wanted. As I jumped into the driver's seat I realised with a shock that a woman sat petrified in the passenger seat. She was young and white-faced, and stared at me in terror.

I switched on as the police whistle shrilled and there was a pounding of footsteps. The old boy was still doubled up holding his stomach. I felt bad about that, worse as the girl beside me suddenly unfroze and rained blows at my head, screaming that I had hurt her father. It wasn't my night. I rammed the automatic gear lever to Drive and did the tyres no good the way I pulled away from the kerb.

With one shoulder hunched and face half averted against her sudden attack I managed to pull out without hitting anything, then switched on the beams. My passenger had gone berserk, which wasn't helping my driving or my face so I chopped one of her arms hard side-handed and she fell back numbed and clutching it. Before she could move in on me again I said, "Try anything more and I'll strangle you."

She was frightened enough but the threat terrified her into defeat. She started to cry. "You've injured my father; he's an old man."

I kept my eyes on the road. She seemed a nice kid and I did not want to scare her.

"I only winded him. He'll be O.K."

"Please let me out. Let me go."

I risked a quick glance. She was pretty. Violence had suddenly entered her world. She had read about people like me. Now it was happening. "I can't stop now, love. They'll be after me." I was feeling the excitement of a good car under me. "As long as you sit there you'll be all right." Had I told her the truth it would have sounded ludicrous; that I did not want to ditch her in this area at this time of night on her own. It might have given her a good laugh.

I can never drive with my windows closed and it was no different now. That's how I heard the first police siren. I could see nothing. There was other traffic now but the sound was somewhere in front. The copper must have been active on his little radio; they were too popular, those damned things.

I had to get to Eaton Terrace as fast as I could. Having been so bent on initial escape I had gone for distance but now it was time quickly to collect my bearings. Hell, I was heading towards the Oval. Swinging into Kennington Lane I spotted the blue flasher cutting through the light traffic towards me and tried to brake to normal speed. As we passed each other I saw his brake lights come on in my mirror, right indicator on, then he was skidding in a U-turn to chase me. I watched my mirror like a hawk, let him come screaming up behind me, thumped the brake sharply and U-turned in a movement that made the girl scream and the traffic concertina to a stop.

I had judged it nicely to the fraction of a gap. The police car could not follow immediately. It braked again, but by then I had my foot down overtaking in a way that must have roused the mildest driver to a frenzy of invective. The girl was having a bad time of it too. She was crying quietly in a pathetic, resigned sort of way, hands up to her face.

I kept going, making enemies all the way, hearing the siren some distance behind me. Aiming at Vauxhall Bridge, I kept my foot down. The police radios must have been hot for another siren sounded ahead of me and the old blue bobble blinked away as a car drew out of an intersection making an effective road block straight across the road.

There was traffic in the facing lane, too much to try to ride against it. If I stopped I would have had it. The pavement was clear just there so I swung left past a lamp post, brushed it, pulled over as I mounted the kerb with a jerk that kept the girl busy with her fears and did nothing for mine, took the police car on the inside, just avoided going through a shop window then swung crazily back on the road.

We rocked a bit but she settled while the police tried to get after us from an awkward angle. We roared over the bridge like we were taking off, careered straight up Vauxhall Bridge Road, did a couple of left-hand squiggles and finished with a scream of tyres in Lupus Street, heading west.

My violent manoeuvring had finally subdued the girl into a terrified silence. I sensed more than saw that she sat rigid, clutching her bruised arm and waiting for the crash.

There was not so much traffic round here in Pimlico which was just as well, for I was not looking for No Entry or one-way traffic signs. I took the turns as I needed them and prayed that there would be nothing coming the other way.

In spite of my breakneck speed, the sirens were closer but they had the advantage with their hooters and flashers clearing the way; I had to rely on other motorists quickly spotting a madman and making the best they could of it.

We did a beautiful drift into Sutherland Street but still Eaton Place seemed at the end of the world.

The flashers were now in my mirror. Ahead of me another appeared coming my way and swinging over to cut me off. He had yet to get the tempo of the chase; keeling the other way we circled each other between the parked cars, passing each other on the wrong side of the street in a frenzy of movement that induced a motor-cyclist to jump off and pull his bike into a space by the kerb.

There were so many flashers behind now that they seemed to be playing musical chairs as they juggled for position. The sirens were baying like hounds closing in for the kill.

I had to give a touch of brake before crossing Buckingham Palace Road heading towards Ebury Street, beyond which lay Eaton Terrace. Almost there but more sirens were sounding.

It seemed to me that there was one sound in the world, the whining sirens wailing in agony; the engine noise was an integral part of me, without it I would feel deserted. The local residents must be having the time of their lives speculating on this massed police activity. The luck could not stay with me; a little earlier or later and the traffic would have been much more dense.

I entered Eaton Terrace in a wide skid and not knowing how the numbers ran. The howl was around me now and then the worst happened. Two prowl cars cut me off at the top. Braking too quickly my rear end swung but I kept the brake down hard while we swayed between the rows of parked cars. Bold figures showed themselves on one of the big pillars of a portico; they weren't the numbers I wanted but they were a guide.

My rear was sealed off as the chasers came roaring up and windows began to open and curtains were pulled back. The din was terrific. And then, the sirens were switched off one by one until they tailed into silence, with the blue lights blinking out each end of the street.

Car doors slammed, heavy footsteps approached as the coppers spread across the street in opposite approaching lines. We had stopped in the middle of the street but I wasn't worried about a ticket for parking.

"Cheerio, love. You'll be all right now." I opened the door and stood beside the car. Then I yelled out, "Stay there or I'll give it to the girl." They did not know whether

184

I was armed or not; they pulled up. Which way did the numbers run? It was a fifty-fifty chance.

Suddenly the girl broke loose from the car and fled to the nearest row of police, her footsteps at that moment the only sound. Police lamps shone down on me like floodlights on a stage. They must have seen that my hands were free. Without an instruction they came bearing down at me again. Once they had the girl they came much faster narrowing my space to move.

There was no time to work it out. I ran hard across the road heading beyond the boldly numbered house and towards the upper line of police. They must have thought that I was going to break their cordon for they slowed and hunched like a group of wrestlers. Behind me the second row came pounding up and I expected to be seized at any moment.

There could have been little space left when I veered towards one of the houses and raced up its steps just as someone's hands clutched at me. Wriggling away I kicked backwards, heard a grunt, then reached the top of the steps. There was no time for the door. As I climbed the railings the police momentarily halted, thinking I would either fall back or crash into the basement.

I did neither. Crouching on the railings I gave myself all the impetus I could muster and hurled myself like a ball straight at the plate glass window of the ground floor, arms round knees, head tucked in. I took the break somewhere across my shoulders. The sound of shattered glass triggered a vibrator alarm and as I crashed on to the floor I knocked something over.

It was one of those pulsating alarms, something like a siren with a sore throat. On top of that there was a hammering on the front door and somewhere inside the house a bell was ringing its head off. There was such a cacophony of sound that wealthy Belgravia would have a topic to shock sensitive minds for ever.

I had fallen heavily and I collected more bruises. As urgent as it was to get up I could only do it slowly, unwinding like an old man. Glass crunched under my feet then the light came on and there was Fairfax, straight-backed and expressionless, in a woollen dressing gown with some crest on its pocket and a .38 pointing nice and steadily at my middle. I must have looked a wreck standing there with the cold air sweeping around my back and the insistent cry of coppers yelling to be let in.

185

"I saw you coming," he said as if we were in the middle of a conversation. "Why couldn't you ring the bell, that window is going to freeze the room." It seemed that he could hear nothing of the frantic clamour particularly of the alarm shooting straight through my head.

"Look," I snarled at him, pointing to the broken window, "if you want your stuff delivered get that bloody pack of bloodhounds off my back."

He stared briefly, made up his mind, nodded and slipped the gun into a pocket. "Stay here."

As if I had a choice. He left the room and I could hear voices at the front door; some were raised angrily. I stepped out of the draught and was not surprised to find this a period room. On the way in I had knocked over a stone bust on a white marble plinth. The thick carpet had saved both them and me from serious injury. Glass lay scattered about but I was too weary to do anything about any of it. Suddenly the alarm switched off and the relief was enormous.

Fairfax returned, severe-faced and angry about the eyes. "I had to telephone the Police Chief to make them see reason. The Superintendent outside thinks it extremely odd that I don't hand you over immediately and I really cannot blame him. They insist on leaving men outside. Now let us get out of here to somewhere comfortable. Dammit, I'll never live this down."

He led me across the hall into a more spacious room hung with small gilt-framed oils and a collection of miniatures. Without a word I sank into a deep-seated armchair. He went to an old Tudor chest. "Don't go to sleep, there's time for that later." He poured two large brandies, handing me one. "Don't tell me you don't drink. You need it." He sat opposite, shrewd eyes puzzled. "Now what the devil did you run out on me for?"

He was right about the brandy; it was stoking my depleted central heating system.

"Because you sold me down the river, you bastard. You set me up as a scapegoat to pacify the Chinese. They would have banged me away for life."

"Oh, come now. We'd have had you out in two years."

I could only stare furiously at him; no denial, no suggestion of an apology for treachery. Blasphemous words stuck in my throat.

He blandly went on, "Well, where's the stuff?"

"The same bloody question from you all; C.I.A., K.G.B., the Chinese, and now you."

"I thought the others might have a go, it was too good an opportunity for them, that's why I was so concerned."

"Concerned for what I carried? Not for me?" He was getting under my skin again.

He permitted himself that brittle smile of his over his brandy goblet. "You are evidently well able to look after yourself, Spider. Well, where are they?"

"I've sold them back to the Chinese."

I had to hand it to him; there was a momentary stiffening of fingers on glass but otherwise no sign. Then his expression slowly changed and he gazed at me as if I was his closest friend and had let him down.

"Then I was wrong about you." His words came slowly as if his disappointment was at being wrong in his assessment, not that I had gained revenge.

"What did you expect me to do? Hand myself over for a lifer because you had stabbed me in the back?"

"I don't care for your analogy. The money is in Switzerland although you have clearly decided that it is not. Once the Chinese had received their face-saving gesture from us, after a couple of years you would have been free. As it is, you are still wanted and will have to take the full consequences. There is nothing that I am prepared to do for you."

I said, "Don't come the aggrieved stuff with me. You got yourself a tuppenny-ha'penny creeper and decided that I was expendable; I didn't matter; I was a villain with a record. You didn't mind using me provided you could get shift of me afterwards in the quickest possible time."

Fairfax sighed slowly and put down his glass. He rose, and for once he was not quite so straight-backed. Only then did I realise the strength of the blow I had given him. Going to a Georgian display cabinet he removed a beautiful figure, gazing at it with affection and pain. "The trouble with you, Spider, is that you have a chip. At no time have I regarded you as petty or small or a villain. I needed your integrity. It never occurred to me that you would discard it."

The old bastard had this way with him of always making me feel in the wrong. It was *he* who had ditched *me*, I kept reminding myself.

He held out the porcelain figure to me. Taking it I considered it a piece I would not have missed had I been out on a job.

"Know what it is?" he said.

"Meissen," I said. "I could get a fair price for this from a fence I know."

"I dare say," he rejoined drily. "I stole it during the war from a German museum in Cologne. That and others. Quite a few of us were at it."

Handing it back I did not know what to say. He had let me see something of his fallibility behind his rigid mask of self-respect. He had equated himself with me and he need not have done it. A bit slowly I climbed to my feet. "Can I use your phone?"

"A condemned man's last request? You may."

"I want this person to ring me back. You will want to know about it."

I moved over to an antique phone that the G.P.O. insisted they would not connect to their systems; again it revealed the position of this man.

He said, "You'll see a number embossed on the side. Tell them to dial it back. It's not the real number but it will be relayed here."

I got Ray Lynch out of bed; he was drowsy, half drunk and irritable. When I told him who was speaking he half sobered and became attentive. "I'm giving you a scoop, Ray. Listen carefully. Ring Li Tshien at the Chinese Legation. Tell him that you have spoken to me, that I am safe and not in police hands; and if they want me to stay out of them, this is their last chance to do it my way; that I'll call in the morning if he gives you the story. Then ring back here and report." I gave him the number.

Fairfax, re-seated, was watching me curiously but I wasn't ready for him yet. He was trying to weigh me up again as if acknowledging that he had made a mess of it first time.

"While I was with Boris and Fyodor they told me that they had killed two American agents called Hank and Joe who had a drum in Highbury. They had done it so that it would look like me."

"Boris? Tall, aristocratic with his chunky muscle man? Yes, it's typical of his style. There would be no point in killing the two Americans. The police might be fooled but other espionage agencies would not have been. The Russians are very good at blackmail."

"So the Americans are alive?"

"One dark, Indian appearance, the other a fair-haired, all-American boy?"

"That's them."

"They were alive this morning. They knew that the Highbury place was blown; in fact they left there today."

"That bastard Boris had me sweating over it."

"Colonel Kransouski. Impeccable manner. Very good at his job. I'm surprised that you did not sell out to him."

"I very nearly did, but I . . ." I suddenly realised my mistake.

"Go on."

What the hell. Taking a good look at Fairfax I saw that he had wilted in the short time we had been together. He considered he had insurmountable problems; might even lose his job with the certainty that the Foreign Secretary would lose his, with accumulative repercussions that would echo down Whitehall and up and down the country. I wished Ray would ring back. He did as I finished my brandy.

"Boyo," he howled down the phone, "you're a bloody marvel. I've been on to the newsroom, everything is set. Thanks, Spider, my old boyo. This one we'll celebrate. You can explain then."

I would have to contrive an acceptable story. When finally I put down the phone. I turned to Fairfax. I knew that I was grinning but my whole body was trembling and I could not stop it. Seeing my uncontrollable shakes, Fairfax brought me another brandy. Before sipping it I dived into my inside pocket and produced the print, the negative and the letter, throwing them down on the inlay of a Sheraton table.

One at a time he picked them up and I saw the tremor in his fingers. He looked at me with immense relief and for once I felt that the feeling was *for* me and not for what he held.

"I got two of the boys on the job," I explained. "One turned out the letter, the other fiddled the photo. He retook the positive, deleted the head on the negative, then reinserted it so that both the print and negative cannot stand expert scrutiny. It will look as if the head had been placed on someone else's body. The letter will also show up as a forgery if the chips are down. All the Foreign Secretary need do is call their bluff."

His relief was tinged with concern as the possibility of a new danger entered his head. I could read his mind on this one. "You needn't worry," I said, "you must know that the letter on its own is valueless. The bloke who faked the photo would see nothing wrong in it if you get me. Anyway he's not a blackmailer. Strange how villains had to straighten things out for you, isn't it?"

"Well, well," Fairfax muttered, clearly delighted but not willing to show too much. "I thought I could not be *that* wrong about you. What of the phone call?"

"Tomorrow's headlines in *The Express.* 'Li Tshien, Chinese diplomat who was brutally assaulted, has regained conciousness to emphatically deny that the person who attacked him is the person wanted by the police and displayed in newspapers and on television. Representatives of the Chinese People's Republic cannot stand by to see such injustice . . .' and so on. 'The person now described by Mr. Li Tshien is short, stocky, and fair-haired . . .' Have you got someone like that you can tuck away for a couple of years?"

Fairfax smiled; it was almost full-blooded. His features began visibly to relax as I watched him rub one eye. "Look here," he said, "you must ring Maggie to let her know that you are a free man. Then I suggest you go to her, bathe, change, and we can meet tomorrow evening for dinner." Then, in frank appraisal, "I was not wrong about you , Spider. You are the only one to come out of this creditably." He sat back, completely relaxed. "You know, I have a colleague who could use you. On a different basis, of course. Better than drifting back to crime, what?"

The old blighter had already put it all behind him. He mused over my name. "Spider Scott. You wouldn't do anything foolish like putting your initials on your issue briefcase, would you? Tell me, have you ever been to Japan?"

I couldn't leave him quite so self-satisfied. "By the way," I said. "I promised the two lads two thousand quid each for the forgeries. I knew that you wouldn't mind paying; cheaper than the reward—tax free, of course. And you can pay for a car hire to take me to the Chinese Legation to deliver Bluie's fake negative in the morning."

The cigar was choking me, but as Fairfax had given it to me at dinner I'd finish it if it killed me.

"This is the life," I sputtered to Maggie who sat right close to me on the settee in her flat. We both had our shoes off and our feet up on the bed stool in front of the fire. Maggie was gazing at the ceiling relaxed and happy, stil wondering about it all.

"Have some more lemonade," I suggested, reaching for the champagne bucket, another gift from Fairfax.

"No thanks." She squeezed my hand.

I didn't blame her. This high living is overrated. The back of my throat felt like an incinerator from the cigar and the champagne was dry and flavorless on my palate. If I'm going to drink I'd prefer beer. Still, it was free; I kept at it in the hope that I might get to like it. The dinner had been good, though; I could cultivate a taste for good restaurants without straining myself.

I was richer by seventeen and a half thousand pounds. Maggie knew that I was richer but not by how much. The story Fairfax and I had contrived very vaguely reduced me to the role of inadvertent decoy, the innocently involved bystander who had received a little handout by way of compensation. I was content.

Pulling Maggie closer I drew on the cigar again which resulted in a violent fit of coughing. When I recovered I leaned back again still wheezing. I eyed the cigar like an enemy but refused to discard it. "This is the life," I said again.

The
#**1**
Bestseller

AVON

$1.95

Open Marriage

A
New
Life
Style
for
Couples

Nena O'Neill and George O'Neill